UNDERSKIN

A NOVEL BY

ORIT ARFA

Route 60 Press
United States * Israel * Germany

www.oritarfa.net

Cover design: Diana Shimon
Cover photo: Yossi Zamir

ISBN: 978-0-9961-6203-6

For Lani and Anat

AUTHOR'S NOTE

Underskin is an adult novel containing graphic descriptions of sex. But, as literary, erotica it also contains "graphic ideas" meant to arouse your mind and soul.

All characters are products of the author's imagination set against the backdrop of modern historical events. Many sites, restaurants, bars, and cafés mentioned are actual places in both Tel Aviv and Berlin; as such, it provides a tour through these two vibrant, unofficial "sister" cities.

Gird your loins, and enjoy.

PART ONE

TEL AVIV

CHAPTER ONE

He hates me.

Okay, so I have no real basis to make this claim, but he must.

I could tell simply from the way he said, "Do you mind watching my stuff as I take a swim," that he's German, not that I've ever met an actual, live German.

I've never heard a German talk about "watching stuff" and going for a "swim." I've heard Germans talk about "killing Jews" and going for a "slaughter."

The only German I've ever really heard came from the Holocaust movies I've watched since sixth grade, maybe earlier. The language of Hitler. The language that killed six million. Not the language of a hot man—did I mention how hot he is?—whose stuff I'm now watching.

And, if I have any doubt he's German, all I have to do is watch him walk—no, saunter—to the shore, his back to me. That back. That broad, toned "Aryan" back with shoulder blades nestled in sheer muscle. Legs as sturdy as oak logs. Was Hitler actually accurate when he described Germans as the "Master Race?" Because this man is probably the most physically superior being I've ever beheld.

Even the way he dives into the ocean seems to come out of an Olympic diving routine. Germans were always good at sports, not like us Jews. I look at the men around me—the Israelis—unattractive by comparison. It seems like the buffness that my Israeli compatriots develop during army service turns into flab after they trade in their guns for steady-paying jobs as part of the life-long battle to make a living in this difficult country.

This German won't hate me because I'm Israeli. I don't think it's politically correct for Germans to hate Israelis, or at least admit it—maybe not even to themselves. I'm worse than a simple Israeli. I'm a "settler," born and raised in the "West Bank," as the Europeans call it. My hometown is a city named Ariel, the "capital of Samaria," as I like to call it.

This German's hatred for a Jewish settler like me would be instinctual: Jew-hatred is in their *kishkes*, bowels. You can't kill so many Jews without such hatred being passed on genetically. No wonder Germany voted in the European Union to require goods grown or manufactured in the Jewish communities of Judea and Samaria to be labeled with "product of the West Bank." This EU rule is simply an extension of Nazi laws that required Jewish businesses to be marked with "Jew."

But why should I worry that *he* hates *me*? He should worry that *I* hate *him*! He should be the one with something to prove, for what his grandparents did to mine.

I wonder if I should tell him where I was born, not that we'll ever speak again. I've been baking in the Tel Aviv sun for over two hours, and I'm tired. I have five digital pages left in a novel I'm reading about, what else—the Holocaust—and a Jewish woman's quest to unite her grandmother, a Holocaust survivor, with the long-lost lover from whom she was forced to separate during the war.

Shit. I can't leave, even if I wanted to. I told him I'd watch his stuff, which consists of a towel, sunglasses, and a paperback book with a German title, clearly not about the Holocaust. Maybe I should just go. Let some thief steal his stuff. *Serves his ancestors right!*

It's Shabbat, the Jewish "Day of Rest," and coming to the beach in the afternoon has been one of my favorite rituals since early spring when I broke off my engagement with my ex-fiancé, Alon. The warmth of the sun and breadth of the ocean soothed my lonely, single heart. Lately, though, I wish I had a man to share my beach blanket with.

Alon would have made me a "settler" of a different kind. Marrying him would have meant that I "settled" in love, mostly because I was never fully attracted to him. Slightly overweight and two inches taller than my 5'6", he made up for his looks with his support and love for me.

A freelance architect, he also graduated from Ariel University. We met on the job about a year and a half ago collaborating on a project. We talked about one day starting our own architecture firm—and family. We both grew up in a traditional Jewish home, the kind he wanted to create with me, in which we would keep Jewish rituals in spirit but not in Orthodox practice.

Yet, I'm sure had we married, my eyes would have wandered...to men who look like that German.

As the Aryan poster boy returns, I unfortunately get a full view of his chest. That chest, with just the right amount of hair nestled between protruding pecs that form a sturdy curtain over his hard abs and a nascent six-pack. I look around at my countrymen with their dark forests of hair, the kind that would tangle a collar, forming tassels over nascent pot-bellies.

I smile meekly as the German returns and leans over to grab his towel. His light blue, sturdy swim shorts are clearly of a high quality, probably designer.

"*Danke*," he says. I look at his eyes. No—they're not eyes, they're bulbs. Fluorescent blue, neon bulbs. A strand of wet, dirty blonde falls over a blue flare. "You know what that means, right?"

"'Thank you' in German," I say, with as much nonchalance as I can muster because I want to sneer when I say the word "German."

I try not to look at him as he wipes his chest and those athletic calf muscles coated with dirty blonde spires. When I do, I catch him checking out my body, too. I quickly cover my legs with my sarong so that he won't look at my "settler" body for a satisfaction he doesn't deserve. And because I didn't shave today, and I can't imagine those Aryan girls having thick, dark stubble.

"I'm gonna get beer to watch the sunset," he says. "Want one?"

"No," I say quickly. We're not about to "break beers."

"Well, then, would you mind watching my stuff for just five more minutes?"

"Okay."

Why did I agree, again?

He comes back with two beers.

"I got you one, anyway," he says, handing me a Heineken. "As a *Danke*."

"*Todah*," I say, in my language. The language of the Hebrew Bible.

He opens up his towel and sets it flat on the sand, a few feet away, leaving enough space for conversation. The sky is turning orange over the sparkling waters, and the clouds form puffs that look like the foam atop a good Tel Aviv cappuccino.

We both look toward the horizon, drinking our Heinekens, and I think the impossible is happening: this gorgeous German is picking me up.

"You've been to *Deutschland*?" he asks in a German accent with a domineering voice that must be good for giving orders. I forgot that's what they call it. *Deutschland*.

"No," I say. *And I never will. My mom won't let me, for starters.* "Your first time in Israel?" I ask.

"Uh-huh. I'm here with a delegation for about ten days. We're musicians holding workshops in Israel and Palestine."

Yep. I knew it. For him, the "State of Palestine," already exists—on the land where my parents now live, in Ariel.

"Cool," is all I say. I proceed to get up but only manage to lift my butt off the sand five inches. I sit back down. I settled here first. I'm not going anywhere. Jews are not going anywhere. The sunset is due in a few minutes, and I won't let him make me leave. This beach will never be *Judenrein*, pure of Jews.

Well, I'm not *that* idealistic. I'm simply an admirer of beauty. Watching him is like watching a sunset. He at least owes me that—to provide beautiful scenery in a difficult country that could've saved my grandparents' families seventy years ago had it existed back then.

"Where's the rest of your group?" I ask, despite myself. I really just want to see if they all look like him.

"I took a break from them. Wanted to be alone. We just got here yesterday, and it's been crazy with orientation and settling in, but I'm excited to see the city. I hear they call Tel Aviv 'Berlin by the Sea.'"

"Really?" *I actually didn't know that.*

"Yeah, with all the nightlife, culture, cafés. Recommend any good bars?"

"A lot, actually." *His ancestors killed six million—why am I being so nice to him?* "You have Rothschild with a bunch of places. Dizengoff. Ibn Gabirol."

"Say what?"

"Sorry. They're names of streets."

"Ah. I'm pretty clueless here. I bought a *Time Out*, but there's nothing like a local to point out the hot spots. I mean, you are a local, right? Tel Aviv?"

"Of course." *Ariel doesn't exist to you, anyway.*

"So, what's a good hot spot?" he asks with a wide smile that demands an answer.

I rack my brain quickly. "Kuli Alma. Off Allenby. It's a lounge bar with an indoor and outdoor area. Cool DJs. Try it."

"*Todah,*" he says. *Good. My language. I'm making progress.*

We watch the orange and mauve streaks of the sky turn to gray. Tel Aviv is getting dark, like my feelings. I feel dirty from enjoying the site of this Aryan body and the sound of this damn German accent. His bulbs now radiate onto the sands around us, making the grains sparkle.

"My name is Sebastian, by the way," he says and reaches out his hand.

Sebastian. What an incredibly sexy, non-Jewish name. Rhymes with

Christian. I can see it now: "Hi, Ima! I'm dating a German named Sebastian." Let's just hope his last name isn't Strauss or something like that. Because then his initials would be S.S.

I can't be so rude as to not take his hand. His grip is mildly firm.

"And your name?" he asks.

"Oh." I was too distracted to tell him right away. "It's Nilly, pronounced Nee-ly. Like 'really.'"

Nilly—the acronym for *Netzah Yisrael L'Tiferet*, which means "to the glory of Israel forever."

He takes out his phone. "So what's the name of this place again, and where is it?"

"I'll take you if you want."

And now I hate myself. I'm a self-hating Jew for wanting to see him tonight.

CHAPTER TWO

The Holocaust never seems to escape me, even though I wish it would sometimes. It's just there. Always. Buzzing in the back of my brain. Just as Jew-hatred is in German DNA, the fear of persecution is in Jewish DNA.

My maternal grandparents, Safta and Saba, were Polish Jews who began their "careers" as persecuted Jews at the outbreak of World War II when they were herded into the ghettos of Nazi-occupied Poland.

Safta suffered through the Lodz ghetto until she and her family were deported to Auschwitz where she watched her parents, younger sister, and older brother being forced—their bodies starved, their spirits humiliated—into the gas chambers while she was sent off to slavery for being "able-bodied." Her youngest brother was eleven-years old when a Nazi shot him point blank in the ghetto because he was too weak and sickly to make the roundup in time for deportation.

Ima said it was Safta's *chen*—a charm emanating from her beautiful appearance and determined demeanor—that must have accounted for some grace a Nazi guard bestowed upon her when she churned out ammunition at the Gross-Rosen concentration camp toward the end of the war. He snuck her some bread scraps that kept her going until the Germans liquated the camp by forcing the prisoners on a "death march" to Buchenwald.

Saba worked with his father in the family-owned market before they were all forced into a small ghetto, whose name I forgot. In eighth grade, not long before Saba died of a heart attack, I interviewed him about his war experience for a school assignment, but he told me the story in broad strokes with few details. I recall that he smuggled himself out of the ghetto and, thanks to his light hair and blue eyes (but not as blue as Sebastian's), passed for a Christian Pole and luckily dodged the Nazis posing as a peasant farmer. His parents, two brothers, and two sisters made it out of the war in the chimney of the crematoria.

My paternal grandparents lived through Jewish persecution in another part of the world. My grandfather's cousin, Heskel, had been an underground

Zionist activist who encouraged his fellow Iraqi Jews to immigrate to the land of Israel. He was murdered by an antisemitic mob in the streets of Baghdad in the 1941 pogrom known today as the *Farhud*. This little-known catastrophe was like the Iraqi version of the infamous *"Kristallnacht"* pogrom of November 1938 in which Nazi Stormtroopers murdered over one hundred Jews, looted thousands of Jewish businesses, and destroyed almost all of Germany's synagogues.

Heskel's death convinced my grandfather to one day heed his call to return to "Zion," the biblical name for Jerusalem that also refers more generally to the Jewish homeland. That "one day" came in 1950, after the founding of the State of Israel, when Muslim street violence against Jews evolved into systematic persecution and disenfranchisement by the anti-Israel Iraqi government. My grandfather trekked to Israel on foot with his parents, wife, and siblings. His father asked their friendly neighbors to look over their courtyard villa, to no avail. The Iraqi government seized their property; its fate is unknown even today.

And tonight, I'm going to have a drink with the progeny of the people who pretty much wiped out my mother's family, and who, some say, fed the racist propaganda that incited the Arab Muslim mobs against the Jews of Baghdad.

When I get home from the beach, I make pasta for dinner and log onto an online dating site in search of a Jewish replacement for Sebastian. I open my inbox to the usual boring openers from men I can't imagine even kissing.

-"Hi!"

-"Nice pictures!"

-"If you wanted to ask me any question, any at all—what would it be?"

Why can't you look like Sebastian?

An hour before the date, I call one of my two best friends, Ariella, to talk me out of seeing Sebastian. But, if I really wanted someone to talk me out of it, I'd call my mom.

Politically, Ariella understands me. She supports the "settlements," at least that's what the media calls the Jewish communities built on the biblical heartland of "Judea and Samaria" that Israel conquered (or liberated, depending on whom you ask) during the 1967 Six Day War against the bellicose Arab legions. She even joined me for one day in August 2005 when I spent a week in the Gush Katif settlement bloc in Gaza to protest the expulsion of its 9,000 Jewish residents from their homes by the Israeli army.

Ariella loves Prime Minister Benjamin "Bibi" Netanyahu, not that I do. To me, he's a smooth talker. At first, he voted for the "Disengagement Plan" to make Gaza "*Judenrein*" as a supposed gesture of "peace," but he changed his mind days before the evacuation, probably to ensure the votes of the hard-liners later. For me, the Expulsion (as Gush Katif loyalists calls it) was more than a strategic mistake that led to three mini-wars with Gaza. It was simply immoral and cruel to destroy the lives of good people like that. And I knew: If it could happen to them, it could happen to my family in Ariel.

Ariella's not as much of an activist as I am, probably because her family's home isn't threatened. She grew up in the sleepy Tel Aviv suburb of Ramat Gan in the heart of bona-fide Israeli territory. Today, she lives a few blocks from the beach on Ben Yehuda Street and works as a sales rep for a bio-medical company. We've hardly ever discussed how we feel about modern Germany and Germans. It was never relevant, until now. Her grandparents hail from Russia and Romania.

"What did I get myself into?" I ask her over the phone after telling her about my meeting with Sebastian and, of course, forwarding her his WhatsApp profile picture.

"A shame he's so hot," she says.

"Please don't remind me."

"I mean, I'm not crazy about Germans, and not only because of the Holocaust. Europeans are too Leftie. But even I'll admit you can't not go out with such a beautiful man."

"I know! But what will we talk about? My grandmother? His gallivanting through Palestine?"

"Nilly, I know you. You like to talk politics, but you know how you're not supposed to discuss politics or religion at the dinner table? I wouldn't bring up the Holocaust or Israeli politics as much as I'd like to rip into the Germans sometimes. Not on the first date."

"Is it even a date?"

"Who knows? I mean, I don't know how I'd feel about you dating a German guy, but whatever it is, just find out what he's about. Maybe, by some miracle, he's a *motek neshama*."

Ariella's wish for me is that I ultimately marry a *motek neshama*, which means "sweet soul," a good, nice person of integrity who'll treat me right.

"So, no Holocaust. No politics," I say. "Got it. I could do that."

"Just talk about Israel, generally. You could be our ambassador. Maybe make this a *hasbara* mission."

Hasbara: Israel advocacy.

"A great way to combat Jewish guilt over meeting him," I say.

"Exactly. Maybe through him you'll influence thousands of Germans to become lovers of Israel!"

"*Lovers.* That's what I'm afraid of."

We both laugh.

"But don't sleep with him, okay?" Ariella warns me, as expected. She's more sexually conservative than I am and doesn't engage in casual sex like I sometimes do, usually when I'm drunk. "He has to earn you, and besides, you'll get attached, and he's leaving."

"Okaaaay," I say.

Yes, I think as I brush my wavy hair, in preparation for tonight. *We'll talk about food, travel, music, Tel Aviv, stuff to do in Israel (not including a visit to Yad Vashem, the national Holocaust museum, usually a staple for tourists). I'll be super nice. And hot. So he goes back raving about how beautiful Israeli women are.*

Then again, I can still cancel. Maybe that's the best way to go. The whole prospect of a date—or whatever—with him is already making me so neurotic. It would not be good *hasbara* if all he sees is a neurotic Jewess. *Yes. Cancel.*

Just as I get my phone, I hear the WhatsApp beep.

"Where should we meet?" he asks.

I don't focus on the message but on that picture: a nose that forms a perfect sixty-degree angle in profile, a pronounced jaw bone, and a full head of golden rays.

"10 pm," I write back. "Corner of Allenby and Rothschild."

I'm wearing blue and white, the colors of the Israeli flag, but not on purpose. It's just that these light blue jeans act like a corset tightening my belly while the white tank enhances my modest cleavage over which I hang a necklace with a large golden "O" pendant. *Yes, this outfit will save me from that untamed, subconscious desire he has to kill me.*

We meet at the corner, and he's exactly on time, obviously and refreshingly. While Germans are famous for their punctuality, Israelis are notorious for being late.

But when I see the German (I'd rather not think of him as having a name lest I humanize him), I want to kill *him*. He looks as damn good with a shirt on. The guy knows how to dress. His linen, baby blue button-down relaxes on a body that advertises a healthy, fit lifestyle.

He leans over to offer a polite peck on the cheek—easy, since he's seven inches taller than me. I wish he'd hover over me just a bit longer; I like the scent of his musky cologne.

"You look nice," he says.

"Thank you," I say. *Nice enough for you to have not murdered me?*

"Should I follow you?" he asks, in that killer accent. I wonder what he thinks of mine, not that it's so strong. My English is almost fluent thanks to American cousins, sitcoms, and books. In high school, I applied myself in English class because I knew that the international language would open so many more professional doors. You can't really get by in the world with a language spoken only by some eight million people.

"Yeah," I say. "Follow me." I like giving orders to a German.

We walk down Allenby, one of Tel Aviv's most popular streets. This particular stretch is home to some of the city's trendiest bars and eateries. Further north, Allenby is home to discount clothing shops that cater to people who frequent the seedy bars even further north. With the German by my side, we'll have no problem passing Kuli Alma's selection. *Besides, aren't Germans masters at selection?*

"How's your trip been so far?" I ask, sweetly, as we waltz past the entrance and head down to the urban courtyard.

"It's been good, although this is my real first night out, so *Danke*. It's great that Israel's just an hour ahead, so no jet lag. And I like the vibe of the city. The cafés, the people, the energy. And the women are beautiful."

Is he referring to me or trying to make me jealous? Well, at least I know he's not gay. "You like the Israeli look?"

"I do, actually. I love the dark hair and dark eyes."

That's me.

Kuli Alma is situated in some rundown building, making creative use of useless space. Video montages of nothing in particular—slabs of colors and random images of animals and half-naked people—decorate the cracking cement walls, adding that unmistakable, vanguard Tel Aviv touch.

"Cool place," he says. I don't know why the bar is named such, but "Kuli" must come from the word "cool." The electro music is cool. The dispersed fauna in this sooty space is cool. And the people look cool. The night is still young enough for proper conversation, and that's what we'll have—"proper" conversation—superficial, politically correct...cool.

I take him to the dark, indoor lounge equipped with a long, curved bar and a set of round tables. Kuli Alma is one of those joints that defies the smoking ban, and cigarette smoke mixes with the DJ's jazzy house beats. The cozy dance floor at the far end will fill up toward midnight. We take to a round table in the corner in view of a mural that must have been painted under the influence of LSD with its wacky images of Buddah, ying yangs, and other icons of Eastern spirituality.

A waitress brings us the menu consisting of alcohol and pizza made onsite in an outdoor *tabun*.

"What would you like?" Sebastian asks.

"I'll take a beer," I say.

"Beck? A taste of home."

Great. Another German product for me to consume.

"But second round, we're doing Goldstar—a taste of my home," I insist. The battle of the beers. Although it's no contest. No one imports the mediocre Goldstar unless they're diehard Zionists. But their "unfiltered" brand is making a comeback.

The bottles come right away, and Sebastian expertly pours glasses for each of us.

"*Prost!*" he says, raising his glass.

"*L'chayim,*" I say. "That means 'to life' in Hebrew."

"Cool. L...chhh..."

"*L'chayim,*" I repeat, and he does so, too, satisfactorily. Most non-Jews can't say this throaty "*chet*" sound, but Germans have their own "*chet*" sound, which sounds more like the hiss of a cat.

After our first sips, he asks, "You were born in Tel Aviv?"

"No," I say, about to betray my hometown. "In a small city with a population of about 20,000 in the center of Israel. I doubt you've ever heard of it. I moved to Tel Aviv about four years ago. What about you? Berlin born?"

"No." He hesitates for a moment. "Dresden."

Isn't Dresden the city the Allies rightly pulverized? "Isn't that the city that was bombed in World War II?"

"Yes, a very famous, very controversial bombing," he says, lowering his eyes. This topic probably falls under the categories of "religion and politics." "But it's pretty much rebuilt now and very beautiful."

"Interesting." A "safe" word, definitely safer than: *Well, you deserved it.*

Neither of us seems to want to talk about our respective cities of birth. Or bombs. Not the bombs of Dresden, not the bombs of Gaza.

"So you're a musician?" I ask.

"A producer, too. I play in a band, teach, and produce for commercials, television, and some artists. I'm dabbling in some music-related start-ups, but this stuff, what I'm doing here now, this volunteering—that's for the soul."

I'd rather discuss start-ups than his soul, which his idealistic trip to Israel doesn't render *motek*, sweet.

"There are a lot of start-ups here," I say. "They don't call Israel the 'Start-up Nation' for nothing." The perfect *hasbara* topic!

"Yeah, I know. Berlin is also big on start-ups now. I'd love to check that out, but I won't have time on this trip."

"So what exactly is this program you're on?" I ask after a sip from my half-empty glass.

"Well, a German NGO that deals with conflict resolution started this program for German musicians to give music workshops to Israelis and Palestinians, you know, to foster peace. I saw an ad and applied right away. If we could make peace here, we could make it anywhere!"

Oh no. Is he going to bring it up? Israeli politics. I'm not about to get into it: how the peace process is a sham; how the "State of Palestine" doesn't exist and never existed; how Palestinian "suffering" is exacerbated or even contrived for PR purposes; and how, if they really wanted peace, the Palestinians would follow Israel's example and not set out to destroy her.

"You weren't afraid to come here?" I ask.

Last fall, Israel was hit with a wave of low-tech terror attacks: shootings, stabbings, car-rammings. In June, two Palestinian terrorists went on a shooting spree at the Max Brenner café in the fancy Sarona Market in Tel Aviv, killing four and injuring who knows how many more. The press dubs these terrorists "lone wolves" since no Islamic terrorist group claims responsibility for their attacks, but I don't buy that theory. Palestinian Muslim clerics celebrate these "wolves" as heroes while the Palestinian Authority pays bounties to the Jew-killers and their families.

"Well, it's not really safe anywhere," Sebastian answers. "I mean, you had that attack in France in July. And Germany had its own terrorist attacks this summer, but they weren't politically motivated. Just some frustrated, crazy people. Once a month, I teach guitar to Syrian refugees. They're so against all this violence. It actually hurts them."

He's not a *motek neshama*, a sweet soul, but a *yefe nefesh*, a "nice soul," as some hawkish Israelis mockingly dub those naive do-gooders who think they're saving the world by empathizing with hostile people.

I followed Germany's refugee crisis in passing, skeptical when German Chancellor Angela Merkel opened the country's borders to hundreds of thousands of refugees from Syria and other Arab countries in the name of German "historical responsibility," a clear reference to Germany's xenophobic past. My mother thinks Germany's getting what's coming to them: thousands of jihadists—and not some "crazy people"—ready to engulf their land in Islamic terror.

"Interesting," is all I say, grateful for my safe word.

"My mom was a bit worried," Sebastian continues. "She didn't really want me coming here. I'm an only child, so...But I feel really safe. Actually, it feels normal. I expected to see a lot more army around." He sips from the few ounces of beer that remain. The tempo of the music increases by one beat per minute, and the bar begins to fill up. "What about you?" he asks. "What do you do?"

"I'm an architect," I say, realizing that even my profession is political. These days I'm working on a housing project in Har Homa, which in his "Aryan eyes" is an illegal Jewish settlement in East Jerusalem, but which in most Jewish eyes is part and parcel of Israeli Jerusalem. "I'm a junior architect at a firm in Tel Aviv. Technically, I'm still an 'intern' because Israeli architects must finish three years of interning to get licensed. I'm hoping one day to go out on my own."

"Architecture's cool," he says. "A combination of art and logic."

To my dismay, his appraisal of my profession makes me like him more. The Israeli men I've dated in the past few months seem to have appraised my profession mainly on the basis of its practicality.

"It's cool," I say. "But it's still pretty nine-to-five, so I can't stay out late tonight."

I must prepare an exit. *How much longer can I sit here?* As I watch his strands fall over his golden brows, I find myself not wanting to talk to him anymore and not only because he says stupid things that make me want to argue. My fingers long to twirl those strands.

"I also can't stay out late, but we'll still have that Goldstar, right?"

I look at my beer glass, empty now.

"Let's do it." I say because it's a Zionist beer. "Unfiltered." *Not like our conversation.*

He calls the waitress for our order, and the music volume turns up a notch.

"*Prost*," I say, raising my new beer glass.

"*L'chayim*," he says as our glasses clink together.

"So...what are your plans for the week?" I ask.

"Tomorrow we're in Jaffa. Next day, we're in Haifa. Then, it's Jerusalem and Ramallah."

"So you're teaching music in all those cities?"

"Yeah. To high school students with musical backgrounds. We're producing a type of 'Battle of the Bands'—except it's not a competition. That goes against the spirit of the whole program, which is all about harmony, literally."

"Cool," I say, another safe word.

We sip our beers and take in the sexy, ruptured base lines before I recommend other hot spots in the city. Yes, keep the topic to Tel Aviv—the Jewish sin city—where we Israelis could feel normal, as if we Jews are never hunted down and murdered.

"Do you recommend any spas here?" he asks. "I love spas."

"Well, there's Ga'ash Springs, about twenty minutes north of Tel Aviv by car. They have several pools with water from hot mineral springs below."

"Sounds cool! They have steam rooms and saunas?"

"Yeah. Nothing too luxurious, though."

"Is it co-ed?"

"Yeah."

"But everyone wears a bathing suit?"

"Of course!" *Why would he wonder otherwise?*

"Oh, because in Germany most spas are nude."

"And co-ed?"

"Yep."

"Really? You won't see that here."

"Yeah, it's very common in Germany. Do you like spas?"

"Generally, but I haven't gone to Ga'ash in a while. It gets too crowded, and sometimes they play this loud Greek music. On Saturdays it's filled with families, and everyone is talking and making a mess. But you should go to the Dead Sea. That's like an outdoor spa."

"If only I had more time."

Is he hinting at me to take him to a spa? Even if I wanted to, I wouldn't take him to Ga'ash; it wouldn't be good *hasbara*. When I went there with Alon a few times, we'd jokingly refer to the middle-aged, overweight, and hairy men who frequent the place as "gorillas in the mist." Sebastian wouldn't fit in.

I look at my phone and see a message from Ariella in Hebrew: "How's it going?"

Finally, I quickly finish my beer and muster the strength to say, "Well, I gotta go."

We walk back to the corner where we first met. As we face each other self-consciously, I wonder: Can I at least hug a man whose ancestors murdered six million and who thinks jihadists are just "crazy people?" I certainly can't kiss him, even though the beer—the Beck, not the Goldstar—makes my lips want to.

"This was really nice," he says, looking me up and down, nervously. Is it possible for this Jewish girl to make an Aryan god nervous?

"Can I confide something in you?" he asks.

"Sure," I say.

"You know, as a German, I really wasn't sure how I'd be welcomed here. Maybe it's a complex that we have. You know, because of our history. But you're so nice. You're so welcoming and sweet."

Hah! If only you knew.

"No problem." What he said must be the equivalent of, "*I would've spared your life had we lived seventy years ago.*"

I stand there, ready and excited to dodge the kiss that will surely come my way.

"*Layla tov,*" he says.

I smile at his attempt at Hebrew.

"*Gute Nacht.*" I think that's the only German I know, somehow.

But the attempt at a kiss never comes. Instead, he gives me a tepid hug.

I walk away and call Ariella to tell her what happened and how upset I am—upset that he gave me no romantic overture to refuse...and probably never will.

CHAPTER THREE

I'm shocked and relieved when, the next morning, he texts me: "*Boker tov! Todah* for a great first night in Tel Aviv! S." He has made an overture—romantic or not—that I can ignore.

After work, I fight the prospect of an idle evening at home, which makes me tempted to answer his text, by driving to Safta's old-age home in Rosh Ha'ayin, situated halfway between Tel Aviv and Ariel.

My mother chose the facility not only because it's located in her hometown, where her sister lives, but also because it's one of the best, hence priciest, in the country. My family was able to afford it thanks to compensation checks my mother had finally agreed to accept from the German government.

Ima had debated with Aba whether or not to apply for the "guilt money" due to Safta. The compensation is technically considered a pension for her work as a seamstress in the Lodz ghetto while Poland was under German occupation.

As an accountant, first for the City of Ariel and now for a successful textile factory at the Ariel Industrial Park, my father was able to give us a decent, middle-class life while my mother earned a meager teacher's salary. Our refrigerator was always full, my brothers and I each had our own rooms, and we went on two family vacations annually, one local and one abroad.

But when Safta had a stroke five years ago about the same time that my brother was getting married, the bills piled on, and Israeli government subsidies would cover only basic home care for Safta. My aunt's family didn't have much to contribute, so Ima finally softened to the idea of taking the German "*Geld*"—but not without a fight.

"The Germans will pay to build our Jewish family," Aba told Ima. As a proud Jew, my father harbors resentment toward Germany, but as the son of Iraqi immigrants, the Holocaust played a less dominant, less personal role in his life. "That's better revenge against Hitler."

"At least she should live her last years without any suffering at all," my mother concluded, resigned.

Safta is now the only living Holocaust survivor in my mother's family.

I regret now, more than ever, not speaking to both Safta and Saba in detail about the war years. Both seemed to avoid talking about it, preferring to leave it behind. Safta told Ima the story in one sitting, days before Ima's wedding at age twenty-four. Ima then passed the story onto me, to the best of her recollection, right before my tenth-grade class field trip of former Jewish towns and concentration camps in Poland.

I'll never forget walking into the Auschwitz gas chamber barely preserved after the Nazis tried to destroy all evidence of mass murder. I imagined Safta and Saba's parents, siblings, and cousins inside those chambers as masked Germans situated on the roof (so as not to sully themselves with the stench of Jewish death) dropped pellets of Zyklon B that turned into gas, making innocent Jews writhe and die from painful, protracted suffocation. It was then I empathized with Ima's boycott of all German products.

I so wish Safta could tell me the story now so that I could remember, once again, how awful those Germans were—and why I shouldn't answer Sebastian's text.

I open the wooden door to Safta's suite furnished with a queen-size bed for her and a twin-size bed for her Filipino caregiver, Mary. Safta's sitting in her wheelchair at her usual spot in front of the television while Mary's sitting on her bed glued to her laptop, probably communicating with her young son and daughter still in the Philippines.

I haven't visited Safta for about three weeks, and I feel badly about that. She's clear-headed for a ninety-six-year-old woman, but her memory's fading, and she can hardly talk. Her words come out in nods, *ehs*, and grunts, so I don't know what use it is for me to sit with her and have a conversation that will never be. I feel badly about that, too. I should be in her presence, as long as possible, for her sake, not mine.

But I don't need to talk with Safta as much as I need to feel her. To hug her. To hug her so strongly to counteract my urge to hug that German. I'm hoping, through her infusion, I will get the strength to shoo him away.

She lights up with the smile that always appears when she sees her progeny.

I fall on her and hug her broad frame very hard, so hard that she must be surprised.

"I love you, Safta," I say.

"I uh u…"

She's still so beautiful, Safta. Her lips have thinned but still reveal so much shape. Her high cheekbones are rosy, and her dignified, brunette wig frames a full, soft face that looks much younger than her age.

I sit next to her and hold her hand, caressing her grooves of gray and pink veins. I look into her eyes, once brown and now muted into hazel by cataracts, but still, eyes bright with so much soul—eyes that would love nothing more, after all she's been through, than to see me stand under a *chuppah* with a good man. A good Jewish man.

I entertain her by telling her petty details about my work and mundane news about my siblings. Through my phone gallery, I show her some recent pictures of my niece and nephew. Then, at 8 pm, she turns her attention to the hourly news, even though I'm not sure exactly how much she understands.

It opens with the hot topic of the day: American elections two days away. I haven't been following American elections much. My family in the United States is bitterly divided over the candidates.

I think they're both awful, but I probably prefer that crass, crude businessman over that corrupt, professional politician, woman or not. She would just continue Obama's anti-settlement policy, promoting the myth that Jewish communities in Judea and Samaria are "obstacles to peace." I'm more convinced of my preference when the broadcaster reports how Trump's advisors released a statement that seems to support the settlements, blaming lack of peace on Palestinians' rejection of Israel and incitement to violence.

I don't get my hopes up because he won't win. And, if he does, let's see if this loudmouth would really stand by his promises, especially the one all American presidential candidates make: to move the American embassy from Tel Aviv to our ancestral and modern capital, Jerusalem.

But only one person's opinion matters here.

"You like Trump?" I ask Safta.

She blinks her eyes once. I can't tell if that's a "yes" or a "no."

I take her arm, the one with the "identification" number tattooed by the Nazis to turn her into a product.

"Safta, I want you to dance at my wedding," I say.

Her smile and eyes widen in the hopes that I'm actually announcing an engagement.

"No, Safta. I don't have a boyfriend yet, but soon!" *And he won't be a*

German. "I'll find a good man. A good Jewish man..."

She blinks and nods, and these non-verbal moments with her give me the strength to refuse the German.

I'm proud of myself for not answering Sebastian. I'm even prouder when, the next day, he tries again.

"Hello, *Yafa.* I have a free night tomorrow. Will you be my perfect tour guide again?"

How ironic he calls me "perfect." But these compliments, including calling me "pretty" in Hebrew, are not "perfect" enough to make me answer in kind. Besides, he wants *me* to be *his* tour guide. Rapacious Germans. All they do is take.

"Sorry. I can't. I'm busy." The "perfect" blow off. He should take a hint.

He replies with a sad emoticon.

I don't understand: How could this man—this man who could probably get any girl—want to court me? I mean, Alon always told me how pretty I am, and it's not like I don't get male attention, but this guy's in a different league, unless they all look like that in Germany. Or unless...he sees something more in me, but that's impossible. He knows nothing about me, especially considering how shallow I was on our first "date."

Unfortunately, even my pledge to Safta doesn't have the power to shield my heart against what I feel moments after blowing him off: like a sad emoticon. The sadness accompanies me throughout the day. I sulk over my computer, fine-tuning, without motivation, the placement of the bedrooms on the fifth floor of the Har Homa housing development.

"What's wrong?" asks my colleague in the "cubicle" next to me.

"Nothing," I say.

The more I try not to think about the German, the more I daydream about him. I slap myself as I imagine him ripping off a Nazi uniform from his body so that he could ravage me.

To fight these sick daydreams, I call my other good friend, Dana, as I get into my car to drive home. I had avoided telling her about Sebastian because I didn't want to make him a big issue—and because I knew she'd approve of him.

Born to an American mother and a *sabra* (native Israeli) father, Dana is much more liberal than Ariella. Completely secular, she voted for the Labor Party in the last election to oust Bibi. She is that rare Jew: the kind who never seems to experience Jewish guilt. She eats shrimp, pork, and all that *treif* stuff. She's always up for a night out after a day's work as an account manager for a public relations company.

Like me, she's single at thirty-one, which means we'll soon be spinsters in Israel. It's a Jewish country after all, and family is integral to the culture. Fertility might as well be a Jewish god, and there's an unspoken national calling to repopulate the world with Jews, especially in the Jewish state where anti-Israel Arabs engage in womb warfare.

"Dana, let's go out tonight. To a pick-up bar."

"Why? What's tonight?"

"I'll tell you when we go out."

"Okay. Where?"

"Taylor Made? 10 pm?"

"*Sababa.*"

We meet at Taylor Made, whose facilities are similar to Kuli Alma's, with both an indoor bar and outdoor courtyard, but it's less grungy and more polished with its funky wall decor, shiny wooden bar counters, and a fancy food and cocktail menu. On any given night, a DJ plays mainstream hits or groovy electro for a crowd of well-dressed, young professionals.

Dana and I make a good barhopping duo. With our contrasting appearances, we serve as foils. Dana's straight, dirty blonde hair, light skin, pug nose, and pink lips contrast my wavy brown hair, naturally tanned skin, and full, dark lips. Men who like the willowy, soft type go for her; men who like the darker, strong type go for me.

We sit by the bar and order cocktails for forty-eight shekels each. The price seems to have jumped since I was last here, but I take comfort in the fact that I'm surrounded by Jewish men. I channel Safta. I feel her hug. *Oh, God— the one Jewish God—save me from Sebastian!*

Once the cocktails arrive, I tell Dana about my first date with him, starting, of course, with his profile pic.

"Nilly, you're being silly. If you don't write back to him, I'll send you to a gas chamber, myself!" *Exactly the type of response I expected.* "He's probably not circumcised, though."

"What? I haven't even thought of that." Now I really can't daydream about him. I'm not sure what to picture down "there." "Anyway, it's irrelevant. What can come out of this, anyway? He's going back in a week. We'll never get married."

"Who said anything about marriage? Just enjoy his body."

The advice I so wanted—and didn't. Subconsciously, is this why I invited Dana out tonight?

I look around to browse my single brethren, but the faces and bodies of the Israeli men blur with an image of a shirtless Sebastian—his pants on—holding them all up in his strong arms, ready to hurl them to the side of the road. *Oh, God*! It's terrible. I don't resent Sebastian but rather those Jewish men—those who would let this German outmatch them in physical strength, in brute force.

"Anyway, what makes you think he's not circumcised?" I ask, resenting myself.

"Most Europeans aren't."

"Have you been with an uncircumcised guy?"

"Once. That Dutch guy I screwed when I was traveling in South America."

"How was it?"

"A bit weird at first, but when he was inside me, I couldn't tell the difference."

"Forget it. I'm not getting into this. I can't sleep with a German."

"Nilly, he's not a Nazi."

"His grandfathers were."

"How do you know? Did you ask?"

"No, and I don't plan to. But they were all Nazis. They had to be!"

"So let's say his grandfathers were Nazis. Doesn't make him one."

She has a good point. "Fine, then he's a leftist. He must think I'm an 'obstacle to peace.'"

"Well, you are."

"Stop it!" My chastisement is half-playful, half-serious.

"Most Europeans are anti-settlement," she says. "But, maybe, if you get to know each other, he'll see that you're nothing but a...crazy settler!"

I fake slap her upper arm. "Stop. You're just as bad as him." Truth is, I don't discuss Israeli politics with Dana, either, and we're still great friends.

Dana turns serious. "A cousin of mine from Haifa lived in Berlin for a few years. She was part of that 'Milky Generation.' Got a job at a real estate company, in sales, I think. Israelis are apparently making a killing in real estate there."

"What's the 'Milky Generation?'"

"Oh, you didn't hear about that controversy? Made headlines."

She explains how, a few years ago, an Israeli Berliner compared grocery receipts from a Berlin and Tel Aviv supermarket on a Facebook page, encouraging Israelis to make "*aliyah*" to Berlin. It was a provocation; "*aliyah*" is the term used to describe the immigration, "ascent," to Israel. Judging by the cost of "Milky," Israel's famous chocolate pudding brand served with whipped cream on top, Berlin is three times cheaper than the Jewish state. Some Israeli parliamentarians called the leader of the Milky movement a "traitor," but frustrated Israelis sympathized.

I'm more familiar with another controversial dairy product. I loosely participated in the "cottage cheese protest" of 2011 when Israelis went out into Rabin Square and Rothschild Street for a grassroots march against the rising cost of living in Israel, judging by the cottage cheese price index. A bucket of cottage cheese had doubled in the span of three years.

These days I live from month to month on my 8,000 shekels net salary. Rent eats up almost half. I work long hours with twelve vacation days a year. My parents contribute toward my automotive and telephone bills. I barely manage to set aside 300 shekels a month for that "rainy day." My boss turned me down for a raise last year.

The "cottage cheese protest" seems to have completely failed, especially considering the cost of my cocktail. I catch myself wondering: How much does cottage cheese cost in Berlin?

"We talked about it last year at the Rosh HaShanah dinner table," Dana continues. "She got flak for the move, but she said she didn't hold this generation responsible for the Holocaust. They weren't born when it happened. Also, I remember her saying that Germans are so nice because of all the guilt."

"Maybe that's why Sebastian is so nice to me," I say. "Maybe he wants me to be his own guilt-reducing project."

"You better take him up on it!"

"Stop. I can't. I wonder if he even recognizes how despicable his nation was."

"That's another thing my cousin said. They learn about it all the time. It's in their curriculum. They have Holocaust memorials all over the place.

They even have these little brass stones built into the sidewalks near buildings where Jews used to live. Jewish institutions are guarded like crazy. It's like the safest place for Jews in Europe right now."

"Really?" I say without enthusiasm, trying not to be convinced.

"Point is: They can't let anything bad happen to Jews...again. Look, we're constantly reminded of it, too. Like with *Yom HaShoah* when everything is fucking closed at night." She's right. Our Holocaust Day is sandwiched between Passover and Israel's Independence Day, giving us no respite from holidays. "How we're so obsessed with 'Never Again.' How we live here, always thinking, 'out of the ashes of the Holocaust.' Well, I don't. At least I try not to. We have a historical bond with Germans, even though it's twisted."

When Dana gets philosophical, she actually makes sense. I wonder if I'd feel as attracted to Sebastian had he been Swedish or Swiss, or if there's something about his "German-ness" that intrigues me.

Finally, the alcohol kicks in, and I feel loose—loose enough to smile at a guy who looks reasonably cute, sitting in the corner with a friend. As the night wears on, Dana and I get up in the aisles with our second drinks. My eye contact induces his approach.

Too bad he gets up. No longer hidden by the bar, I can see that he's only two inches taller than me, and I've learned from dating Alon that I'm simply a stereotypical, shallow woman who's attracted to tall men. Is it terrible of me to notice that he has a slight, oh-very-slight, hooked nose?

But no! I'll see past that. I'll look at his character, his personality...his race and religion.

"What's your name?" he asks.

"Nilly. Yours?"

"Yossi." A nickname for Yosef. *A good Jewish, biblical name.*

"You from Tel Aviv?" I ask Yossi.

"Yeah, and you?"

"I'm originally from Ariel." To most Israelis, Ariel is not a "settlement," thanks in part to my *alma mater*. Ariel University's accreditation as a public university in 2013 normalized the city in the eyes of the general public.

"Oh, I'm sorry," Yossi says. "It must be boring there."

At least it's not political hostility like Sebastian's.

"Well, it's getting cooler with the growing student population," I say. "Like a university town."

"What do you do?" he asks.

"I'm an architect."

"Ah, cool. What field?"

"Mostly residential. And you?"

"Hi-tech."

"Ah, cool. What field?"

"Computer programming."

Why couldn't he be gallivanting around some third-world or conflicted country, trying to save it?

"Do you live alone or with roommates?" he asks. I hate that question. Is he testing how one-night-stand-able I am?

"Alone."

"How old are you?" he continues.

"What is this, an interrogation?"

"I just want to get to know you."

I turn to Dana and grimace, not caring if he notices. He's actually pushing me into the stronger arms of Sebastian.

I remember why I've hardly dated since breaking up with Alon. The Israeli men I've dated in the past few months didn't seem to want to get to know me in a way that counts. The dates felt like interviews in which we compared basic personal information to determine if we're a practical fit, whether for a one-night-stand, dating, or marriage.

Maybe we Israeli Jews do not need to delve into each other's souls. I mean, the depth of our existence here, on this small piece of earth, fighting for it against all odds, is self-evident. We don't have to talk about saving the world because we're saving it just by living here on the frontline of freedom, as brothers and sisters in arms.

So all this unstated idealism leads to his final, mundane question: "Do you have parking where you live?"

As my response to Yossi, I take out my phone, scroll to Sebastian's message, and, in my tipsiness, write: "I'm free Wednesday eve."

CHAPTER FOUR

At 9 pm we meet at Miznon, one of the city's trendiest fast food joints famous for its gourmet pitas and *balagan*, slang for "mess." A long line is already stretching to the pavement of Ibn Gabirol Street, if you could call it a "line."

No one is standing in any particular order, but that's okay because it's fun to look over the open kitchen where hipsters stuff pitas with all these goodies—lamb *kubbahs*, hamburgers, chicken livers—sautéing them with the perfect mix of salt and spices and then dousing them in *tehina* to create the most delicious pita feasts in Israel.

"Ofir!" "Michael!" "Orit!" are some of the customer names cooks shout over the pop music.

Sebastian is already in line, just as beautiful as I remember him, maybe even more so. He's wearing a white T-shirt with an immaculately, deliberately torn collar. Its light cotton fabric reveals the contours of his chest muscles. His jeans seem custom tailored to accentuate his well-endowed manhood. Yes, I notice. I wonder if the foreskin adds to the mass.

"Fun place!" Sebastian enthuses and steals a light squeeze of my arm, making this wait so much more bearable—and agonizing. His touch causes me to spasm for a split second.

I get the English menus, hand written on recycled fragments of brown paper bags, a testament to the establishment's care for the environment. Fresh, whole cauliflower heads beautify the wooden shelves as the main décor of the shack-like interior.

"No shrimp or pork here?" he asks as he looks at the list of items divided into sea, land, and sky categories.

"Not so common in Israel," I say. "That's, like, really not kosher."

"What's 'kosher' exactly, anyway?"

So how do I explain this? "Well, there are certain animals Jews can't eat, and those we can have to be slaughtered in a certain way."

"So it's not about a rabbi blessing the food?"

"No, that's a myth."

"But some Tel Aviv restaurants serve pork and shrimp," I explain. "It's a very secular city."

"Do you eat kosher?" he asks.

"Not really. I grew up traditional, but I went to a religious elementary school—not too religious, not like ultra-Orthodox, you know, with the black hats and stuff, but I learned about it. I didn't grow up eating shrimp and pork, so I never really developed a taste for it. I don't eat meat so often, but when I do, I try to eat kosher meat, but not strictly."

"Too bad. You're missing out," he says. *I'm missing out on a lot of unkosher flesh, it seems.* "But the minute steak with egg sounds fantastic. Two beers?"

"Yeah. Beer is totally kosher."

I instruct him to grab a newly empty table as I continue to wait in line so I can order. I think you have to be Israeli to order in this *balagan*, not a polite European.

"I'll take care of this," he says and hands me cash, which I happily take. I am, after all, offering the services of a "perfect tour guide."

After putting in our pita orders to include a side of cauliflower they so famously grill, I go to the mini salad bar in the corner and fill small plates with pita ends, *tehina*, pickle wedges, and tomato sauce.

"Cool!" Sebastian says as I put the free appetizers on the table.

"They don't waste food this way," I say, for the perfect *hasbara*. Israel is humanitarian for finding a solution to that age-old dilemma of what to do with pita ends. "A culinary ecosystem."

Our beers and cauliflower are first to leave the kitchen, allowing us time to munch, drink, and talk while we wait for our meatier orders.

"So, how were your first few days?" I ask after we take our first bites and I teach him the word "*ta'im*," meaning "tasty."

"They were great. We went to Haifa today and met with Jewish and Arab students—Muslims, Christians, and also Druze. I was impressed with their talent, but then again, we accepted musical people. What we're doing is really cool. We're having each group write different songs using the same chord progression. Then we'll mix everyone up into different bands, and they'll perform each other's songs at the 'Battle of the Bands.' It's nice to be part of something bigger than yourself."

How noble. How cliché.

"Why Israel?" I ask, wiping the last pita end into the remaining, delicious *tehina*. "I mean, there are so many conflict zones in the world. You could make a difference in so many other places."

"Good question. I mean, I'd love to work with children in Thailand or Vietnam, too, but I've been hearing a lot about Israel. A friend of mine came to Tel Aviv last year. Israel's always in the German media. There were a lot of articles this year about Israel and Germany celebrating fifty years of diplomatic relations. It's a big deal because of our history, you know. We learn a lot about the Holocaust in high school. So I guess you could say Israel's on my radar."

Boom. He dropped the H-bomb first.

What Dana said might really be true. We are connected in some twisted way by our tragic history.

"We also have a lot of Holocaust education," I offer. "I mean, *a lot.* Actually, a lot of my education comes from my family." I retaliate against his H-bomb with the A-bomb. I take a deep breath before I press the button. "My grandparents are Holocaust survivors. My grandmother survived Auschwitz."

He looks at me with both surprise and sadness. "Oh, wow. I'm so sorry."

"I hope that doesn't make you uncomfortable," I say. *This is exactly why Jews waltzed right into the gas chambers—the need to make sure people don't feel bad about murdering them.* I take three more sips of beer.

"Not at all," he says as he also takes to his glass.

"But my mother was born in Iraq," I say, taking us out of Europe.

"Iraq?"

"Yeah, Baghdad. There was a big Jewish community there, probably one of the oldest in the world." But I won't get into how they were forced to flee because of Nazi-inspired pogroms. The A-bomb has caused enough damage.

"That's cool," he says, bringing us to safety.

Our conversation is thankfully interrupted with: "Nilly!" Our pitas are ready. He offers to get them. The A-bomb has harmed my appetite, but when Sebastian hands me my pita stuffed with sautéed chicken liver, Auschwitz becomes ancient history.

"This looks great," Sebastian says, beholding his thin, minute steak pita stuffed with grilled onions and peppers, topped with an egg yolk that oozes over the fleshy yumminess. He takes a huge, manly bite, like a hungry animal eating its prey.

"*Ta'im!*" he says and finishes the sandwich in only six bites.

I'm already tipsy around 10 pm when I suggest we walk across the street to Toma, a garden bar spread over a large deck located adjacent to the ZOA House, the former headquarters of the Zionist Organization of America that today serves as an events center.

He takes my hand as we walk across. The bombs have claimed no casualties.

I feel privileged walking with such a hunk. *Wait a minute? Shouldn't he feel privileged to be walking with me, especially after what his ancestors did to mine?*

Now I really resent all of my formal and informal Holocaust education because I don't like having to relate his every move to the Holocaust. Why can't I just think about how nice his thick, soft hands feel against mine?

I haven't had a real romance since Alon. My last date took place a few weeks ago with a moderately attractive thirty-five-year-old real estate lawyer. Since he worked in a related field, I thought we'd have much to discuss, but the conversation focused on the rising prices of Israeli real estate and how housing laws are changing to discourage foreign investors. The date felt like a business course.

But I wanted to give him a chance, so I accepted his offer to walk me home from the bar to my apartment. He didn't reach for my hand to hold, but when we got to my place, he asked, "Do you have coffee?"

In Israel, that's a code phrase for: "Do you have sex?"

"I don't drink coffee," I lied and wished him goodnight.

Sebastian sadly lets go of my hand when we get to the bar stools. A cheerful bartender takes our orders.

"Beer again?" I ask.

"Let's."

I want—no, *need*—something strong. "Do they have Maredsous in Germany?" I ask. "I think it's Spanish or something. It's really popular in Israel."

With a high alcohol content of 10 percent, Maredsous is the beer of choice among many of my friends for offering drunken value for money.

"I actually never had it," Sebastian says.

I normally order a third; tonight, I get half a liter.

"So you grew up in Dresden?" One large sip of the cherry-syrup tasting Maredsous gives me the courage to pry into his family's past. Dana's right. I can't just assume they were Nazis. Maybe his grandparents were "Righteous

Among the Nations," those who saved Jewish lives, and my whole neurosis is for naught.

"Born and raised," he answers. "But, actually, it was a different country then. It was the German Democratic Republic. The GDR. East Germany."

Did I even know that? "So you grew up under Communism?"

"Yeah, until I was eight."

"What year did the Wall fall again?"

I completely forgot this part of Germany's post-war history: the division between East and West. I had first learned about it watching the Olympics as a child when the West and East each had their own gymnastics teams. My German studies consisted of, almost exclusively, the Holocaust.

"November 1989."

I do the math quickly. He must be around 35. "And how was your childhood?" I ask.

"I guess you could say it was normal. I didn't really know what I was missing. We couldn't leave the East. We played outside a lot, especially by the river when it was warm out. Dresden wasn't as built up back then. The GDR didn't have the money to restore the bombed-out parts. We didn't even have Western television because Dresden's located in a valley—the Valley of the River Elbe—and the antenna signals didn't catch American television, not like in other East German cities. They called us the 'Valley of the Clueless.'

"So we were stuck with only radio, but that's when I knew I was missing something: MTV. I heard David Bowie, Michael Jackson, and 'The Boss' on the radio, but I couldn't watch the music videos. When the Wall fell, my first thought was: Finally, I get to watch 'Born in the USA' and 'Thriller.'

"After that we got to travel west, to Austria, Switzerland, and I got to see how much more people had."

"Who did your travel with?"

"My mother. My father left my mother not long after the Wall fell."

"Oh, I'm sorry."

"It's okay." He waves his hands dismissively, but his eyes drop in sadness.

"Did your grandparents also live in Dresden?" *I'm getting closer.*

"From my mother's side." He pauses, as if he's debating whether or not to press another button. "Actually, my grandfather died in the bombing. He worked in a Dresden factory making camera lenses. My grandmother, who died a few years ago, survived the bombing because she moved to the countryside with family when she was pregnant with my mother."

"Oh, God. I'm so sorry."

Or am I? Actually, he reacted with an "I'm so sorry" to my A-bomb, so it's only right I reply in kind to the actual D-bomb—but no, I refuse to draw any moral equivalence between a death camp and the bombing of a Nazi city. If the D-bomb contributed to the end of Auschwitz, then I might even have to raise this Maredsous in celebration. Instead, I take a sip, feeling drunk enough to ask, as a warning flare for the N-bomb, "Was he a civilian or a soldier?"

"You mean, was he a Nazi?" There, he put out the flare. "It's okay. You can ask." He speaks, looking straight ahead at the liquor on the shelves. "I mean, there was only one party." *Take that, Dana!* "My father's father...he was a soldier. Fought in North Africa with the Wehrmacht." I forgot the Nazis didn't only ransack Poland. "Honestly, I don't even know if they joined the Nazi party."

"Weren't you all forced to be Nazis?"

"Well, it depends what you mean by that. Everyone was forcibly drafted, but I think only the SS had to be members of the party. Thank God, my grandparents weren't in the SS. Truth is, my family didn't talk about World War II. My mother said her mother didn't know about the Holocaust until later. Anyway, I don't really see myself as part of that generation."

I'm both comforted and not by this distinction, new to me. On the one hand, his grandfathers may not have been directly involved in Jewish genocide; on the other, he never really bothered to find out. Then again, right now, I don't want to see him as part of that generation, either. I just want to see him as an amazingly good-looking, sweet, smart man I like talking to but who might not like talking to me if this line of questioning turns into a *blitzkrieg*.

"So when did you move to Berlin?" I ask.

"After high school. I went there to study music. I mostly taught myself music production because I wanted to produce pop and electronic music and maybe film scores, and not only play the classical music my father pushed. Berlin was really cheap at the time, cheaper than today."

How could chocolate pudding get any cheaper?

"And your parents? They're still in Dresden?" I ask.

"My mother's there. My father lives near Hannover. He was a drunk who never really amounted to anything in life, and he used to hit my mom."

"Oh, yikes."

"Yeah. I'm hardly in touch with him." He frowns and changes the subject.

"What about your family? Siblings?"

"Well, my parents are together. I have two brothers, one older and one younger."

"The middle child."

"Yep."

I look at our glasses. Almost empty. I'm surprised I've downed more beer than him.

"And where do they live?" he asks.

"In that small town I grew up in." I'm not drunk enough to drop another A-bomb: Ariel. I guess he's not the only coward here.

"How'd you get into architecture?"

"Well, I've always liked art, and I was good at math, so, like you said, this is the perfect combo. You know, in Israel, it's not easy to be an artist—so don't think about moving here. I mean, we're a developed country and all, but we're small and people don't make so much money, so they don't really spend it on art. They'd much rather spend on vacations."

"Did you ever think of leaving Israel?"

"Not really. I have relatives in the US, but I guess you could say I always felt connected to this place."

"I could understand that. It's a very deep place."

Now I'm comforted.

"Did you serve in the army?" he asks.

"Yes. The intelligence corps." I speak with dramatic flair. "Analyzed maps to look for terrorist and weapons hideouts."

"So you're a spy?"

"Exactly. So you better be careful." *Actually, he really should be.*

"I come from East Germany." He winks. "We're used to spies."

He grabs a strand of my hair and looks at me with his striking blue diamonds. I shake his fingers off by taking two sips of beer. Then I catch his gaze and smile meekly. I'm scared because the adage goes that you can see a person's soul by looking into his eyes and...I don't see one.

"Can I kiss you?" he asks, catching me off guard. *What kind of man these days asks a woman before he kisses her? I guess a German.*

I'm upset that he asked because now I'm forced to make a choice. Should I let this grandson of a "civilian" maybe-Nazi and a "Wehrmacht" maybe-Nazi kiss me? As I struggle with the answer, his face appears in a blur. I taste the digested chicken liver at the top of my throat.

"Are you okay?" he asks, concerned.

"I feel a little sick," I say.

"Can't hold your beer like a German," he jokes, but I can't laugh. "Shit. Your face is turning blue. Let's get you some air."

He puts his arms around my shoulders to stabilize me as we walk toward a bench on the sidewalk where I can sit in the open air.

"Wait here," he says. "I'll pay and get water." He comes back with a bottle. I take small sips to settle my stomach.

"Let me take you home," he offers. "You live around here?"

"Yeah," I say as my vision returns.

"I'll get a cab."

He hails a cab and gets inside with me. In the back seat, I lean my head on his arm, exploiting my abating queasiness to justify this closeness. He walks me to my apartment building entrance while the meter is running.

Standing by the door, I keep my arms at my sides. He takes hold of my elbows. "Are you going to be okay?"

"Yes, I feel better." But now I'm emotionally queasy. I stare at his kiss-able lips. "You're not coming in for coffee, okay?"

"What? Whoever said anything about coffee? I just want you to rest. I'll check in with you in the morning."

"Really?" I say.

"Don't be silly."

My residual drunkenness gives way to courage, this time not to ask any more questions but to answer his, belatedly, with a kiss. Our lips touch for only two seconds, but it's confirmed: Unlike his eyes, his lips are full of soul.

When Sebastian doesn't check in as promised, I call Ariella after work, on the verge of tears.

"I don't know what I've done," I cry.

"The German?" she asks.

"Yes. I'm such a mess."

"Do you want to come over?"

"Yes."

Ariella lives in a one and a half room apartment. It's half-refurbished,

which means the floor tiles are new but the old-fashioned layout of the apartment makes no sense. Its hallway breaks into a four-walled kitchen with a small service porch and a bedroom with an indoor balcony. As an architect, I imagine how I'd knock down the walls to create open space and light, but a fully refurbished Tel Aviv pad would cost at least a third more.

"Why did I get sick when he asked to kiss me? I'm such a freak," I say, sitting over tea on a beat-up sofa in the indoor balcony enclosed by clumsy blinds.

"You know what? You can't ask those questions," Ariella says in her spiritual way.

Ariella's one of the least materialistic people I know. She likes to think she's a tomboy and often wears sneakers (definitely no heels) with jeans or jean shorts. If she tweezed her eyebrows, groomed her messy hair, and put on makeup more diligently, she'd be a knockout. "I truly believe that you say and do exactly what you're supposed to say and do in the moment. God is guiding us all the time."

Her talk of God comforts my agnostic, Jewish soul.

"Finally, a man comes into my life, and I sabotage it," I say.

"You didn't sabotage anything. If it's meant to be, he'll come back. But it's probably not because it's complicated, and you know that deep down. That's why you got sick."

"Then why did I kiss *him* at the end?"

"Because he's hot, and you were drunk."

"Yeah, I guess that's a good enough reason." Then I think: *No!* There must be a deeper reason. "Why do I have to deny him, really? Will denying him bring back the lives of my relatives? Wouldn't it be a greater act of vengeance to let this German give me pleasure?"

"Don't look at it that way. Don't look at him as 'vengeance' or 'not vengeance.' Maybe it's just a matter of you finding the right guy, and he's not right for you. You can't be with someone that you're always walking on eggshells with. I really want to see you with a *motek neshama*."

"A *motek neshama* I'm attracted to," I say. "Will I ever meet him? I've tried all year since I broke up with Alon and turned up dry."

"Of course you will. You just have to be patient and keep the faith."

"Thanks, Ariellush," I say with my term of endearment.

I go home, feeling comforted but still not at peace. I lay my head on my pillow, feeling an urge to say the *Shema*, the prayer to the one God that Jews historically recited on the path to affliction, including to the gas chambers. But now I want to say it as a Jewess suffering on her path to love. Isn't that a more noble cause?

"Listen, O Israel, *Hashem* is our God, *Hashem* is one, and you shall love *Hashem* your God with all your heart and with all your soul and with all your being."

Then I add my own words.

Please, Hashem, *the God of my forefathers—and foremothers. Will you even grant me what I want, because you didn't hear the prayers of my ancestors when they pleaded with you not to let them suffer and die. And I want to live, to live to the fullest. And now I have a chance they never had, not only to live here freely in the land of Israel but to go out with a German. A German! So is it so wrong that I ask you to have him call me?*

Before shutting off my phone for bedtime, I peek at handsome Sebastian's picture—those soulless eyes and soulful lips. I can't write to him after last night. He must initiate so that I know I didn't scare him away.

I see movement. *Typing...*He's writing something to me!

But no words appear, just a video.

And there he is, holding a guitar, his muscular arms gliding gracefully yet potently over the strings as he sings in a very sexy voice:

Nilly, Nilly, she's sometimes silly
Nilly, Nilly, pretty like a lily
So here I am, singing this ditty
Cuz I already miss you, silly Nilly

Two Arab teenagers gather around him in what appears to be a classroom and shout, "Hi Nilly!" on his cue. "You're so pretty!"

Then he writes, "How are you feeling?"

Could a German man indeed be a god? Because this is one of the godliest things I've ever beheld. I replay the song and see something I couldn't see before, which appears even through my telephone screen: His eyes have soul. A vibrant soul. A good soul. Maybe even a sweet soul.

I listen, O Israel, to my new lullaby—the answer to my prayer.

CHAPTER FIVE

In the morning, I respond with, "I feel much better, thanks to your perfect song!"

I don't tell him another reason I feel better.

I woke up to a text from Ariella announcing that Donald Trump has won the American elections against all odds. I'm happier than I thought I would be. If the bozo actually stands by his pledges, I'll have to worry less that my family's home will be sacrificed for the sake of "peace."

But more than that, his completely unexpected victory revives my belief in miracles. *If Trump could win, Sebastian could convert to Judaism!*

"Glad to hear," Sebastian writes back with cheerful emoticons. "But now you owe me another tour!"

This time, I feel like God gave me his blessing. "I could make it up to you tomorrow night."

"Perfect, silly Nilly."

I deserve that nickname. I really was silly. This time, I'll take charge and really be the "perfect tour guide."

I pick him up from his hotel around 8:30 pm. As he steps into my beat-up Renault hatchback, I'm jealous of the sun. It passionately kissed his hair, on his head and arms. His eyes radiate even more against his newly tanned skin. I faintly pucker up, but he kisses me on the cheek.

I drive to Taqueria, Tel Aviv's coolest Mexican place, located just around the corner from Kuli Alma. I'm annoyed that I have to circle around a few times to find parking. Traffic in the city has gotten worse ever since they started building a Tel Aviv subway, forcing many city streets to close.

The place is so packed, we're put on the waiting list. As we wait outside in pleasant evening weather, I tell Sebastian how I read that, until Taqueria came along, Mexican food never really took off in Israel. Mexican black beans, in comparison to hummus' garbanzo, are too heavy for the Israeli stomach, especially during the sticky summer. Taqueria managed to tone down the heaviness of Tex-Mex to create crispy tortillas, refreshing salsa, and light bean dips that satisfy the discerning Israeli palette.

After a seven-minute wait, we take our seats in the cramped restaurant made to feel denser with a mural featuring a large picture of a Mexican-styled Jesus surrounded by vintage movie and concert posters.

"I could see a place like this in Berlin," Sebastian says then tosses his eyes to the table a few inches away from us. "People just wouldn't be so squished together. Germans like their personal space."

"Well, as an architect, I can tell you that, as a small country, we have to make maximum use of space."

We order nachos grande and fish tacos to share. He gets the classic margarita—me, passionfruit. I'm not afraid of getting tipsy with him again. Looking back, I realize my nausea came not from the alcohol or his question. My gut simply couldn't handle my holding back so much about myself.

"How was your week?" I ask, sincerely eager to hear more about his experience in Israel.

"Well, aside from Trump winning the American elections, it was good. Never thought I'd be grateful to be a German."

"Yeah, pretty crazy," I say with a slight smile betraying my unexpected joy. As much as I don't want to hold back, Trump is not my crusade. As an Israeli, he's not my leader.

"But funny," Sebastian says. "We asked the Palestinians in our class what they thought of Trump, and they said they don't care who's the American president. To them, they're all the same. The Bushes, the Clintons. If they can't be too bothered, I guess I shouldn't be, either."

"Interesting." The safe word. "What Palestinians? From what city?"

"Today we met Palestinians from East Jerusalem at the YMCA in West Jerusalem." Maybe it's a German habit for more reasons than one to differentiate between the "East" and "West" sides of a city. To most Israelis, Jerusalem is united.

"So you met with Palestinians or Israeli Arabs?"

"What's the difference?"

"Well, 'Israeli Arabs' hold Israeli citizenship while Palestinians live in the Palestinian Authority and hold Palestinian ID cards."

"Well, they're from East Jerusalem, so that makes them both, right? They identify themselves as Palestinians, even though some of them have Israeli citizenship, but not all."

"You've done your homework!"

"Well, we had some prep coming in. Israel annexed the Golan Heights and East Jerusalem after the Six-Day War, but the Palestinians in East Jerusalem didn't want to become Israeli citizens, so they became permanent residents and got those blue Israeli ID cards. Last night, we split up for home hospitality with families in East Jerusalem, and my host, Ismael, a moderator in our program, showed us his blue ID card and his Israeli passport. He got Israeli citizenship so he could travel abroad more easily. He really wants to come to Germany. Maybe I'll host him."

"Cool that you got to go to dinner there," I say, meaning it. As a German, Sebastian could tour parts of Israel that I could never really see up close, like some "East Jerusalem" neighborhoods.

I'm not surprised his group hangs out more on the Palestinian side. We hardly ever hosted Europeans in Ariel. My mother would argue that it's because Germans sympathize more with Jew-haters. I wonder if Germans sympathize more with Palestinians because they're just more hospitable to Germans, although not necessarily for the right reasons. Germans probably don't realize many Palestinians embrace them for their Jew-hating past.

"Where in East Jerusalem does he live?" I ask.

"Jabel Mukaber." My stomach tightens. Jabel Mukaber is well known as a jihadi hotbed that spawned a few of the "lone wolves" who stabbed or ran over Israelis, including last year when an Arab employee of Israel's telephone company rammed his company car into a rabbi, killing him.

"Honestly, I wouldn't feel safe there. Some terrorists come from that neighborhood." *I'm making progress.*

"Well, the Mansour family was cool. Our program is against violence, so I knew they wouldn't set us up with people who support terror. I asked them what they thought about all those stabbings and stuff. Ismael said he thinks the Occupation should end through peaceful means."

There. He dropped it, nonchalantly. The O-bomb. "Occupation." I should make a deal: If he won't drop the O-bomb, I won't drop the H-bomb. Oh, no. That's not a good idea because it will feed sick Palestinian propaganda that equates Israel's "occupation" of "Palestine" with the Holocaust. My stomach hardens into a cannonball, preparing for the right time to strike.

"But most of the time, we just ate. Check this out." Sebastian takes out his phone to show me pictures of platters of lamb kabob, stuffed grape leaves, and homemade hummus with pine nuts. In the background he points out Ismael, his sister in a flowery hijab, and the lady of the house in a black hijab. "The mom's an incredible cook."

"There's nothing like Arab hospitality," I say. *This much is true.*

Our food comes, and his bulbs open wide in delight. "You people know what you're doing with food in this country!" He takes a huge man-bite from his taco. "*Ta'im!*"

"And what did you do yesterday during the day?" I ask, my stomach softening to his compliment, which seems to include East Jerusalem into "this country," and to the *ta'im* nachos.

"Ramallah."

"And how was that?" I ask, truly curious. I had often passed Ramallah on Route 60 when I travelled from Ariel to Jerusalem. It's just a thirty-minute drive away from my hometown. Sometimes, I wished I could simply turn into the Palestinian "Tel Aviv" for some hummus or shopping like we did when I was little. After the bloody second *intifada* of 2000 to 2003, in which Palestinians blew up Israelis every other week in cafés, bus stops, and nightclubs, the checkpoints went up. Now, a big red sign by the Ramallah "border" announces it's illegal and unsafe for Israelis to enter.

But my German (yes, he's my German now) is serving as a window into this forbidden world.

"Here, I'll show you." He takes out his phone and shows me pictures of Arab teenagers, mostly boys, playing guitars, smiling. I actually recognize one of the boys from the video he sent me.

"Did you film the song there?"

"Yeah."

"Oh, my God, that's so precious." First Trump, and now a Ramallah boy appearing in my serenade. *Miracles really could happen!*

"Are they even allowed to play music with Israelis?" I ask him. I know the former mayor of Ariel once invited neighboring Palestinian towns to be hooked up to the city's electricity grid for more efficient energy, but the Palestinian Authority forbade them from collaborating with Ariel.

"Seems so," Sebastian says. "The program director had to fight with both authorities. He had to get permits from the Israelis to let the Palestinians— those from Ramallah—to come to Tel Aviv for the 'Battle of the Bands.' The Palestinian Authority made sure no settler groups were involved, but we weren't going to involve them, anyway."

I was about to sip my margarita but put the glass down. My stomach recoils and hardens. The counterattack begins. "Settler groups? What's that?"

"Settlers or groups that support settlements, I guess." The eggshells littered around him look very sharp, but then I realize: I've got shoes. To be his "perfect tour guide," I must walk on eggshells for us to move forward.

"What if I told you I'm a 'settler group?'" The sound of the crackling eggshells is actually refreshing.

His expression is sincerely confused. "What do you mean?"

"I was born in what you'd call a 'settlement.' My family lives there."

"What?" He's shocked.

Why does it feel like I'm stepping not on eggshells but on corpses?

"Did you pass by a place called Ariel?" I ask.

"Yeah. On the bus. Saw the red roofs from a distance. Our tour guide said it's a huge Jewish settlement right smack dab in Palestinian territory that will ruin the chances for a Palestinian state. They said there was a concert hall there or something that some artists boycotted."

"Yeah, the Ariel Regional Center for Performing Arts. It's a really nice theater. I saw some good concerts there."

"Hmm," he says, a safe mumble. The waiter comes by and Sebastian orders another margarita, either to stall for time to think or to digest my revelation with more alcohol. "I can't believe you're a settler. You don't look like one. You're so cool and fun. You're not religious."

Most Europeans probably buy into the image of "settlers" as religious extremists in Jewish garb carrying guns with which to shoot Palestinians.

"I'm sorry if I don't fit into stereotypes," I say. "Maybe if you were allowed to work with 'settler groups,' you'd find out how diverse we are. Ariel is actually 85 percent secular. They even sell pork there. I should have told you earlier, but 'settlers' are so stigmatized. It seems so stupid to be judged so harshly just because of where you were born. Makes me feel like I'm wearing a sign that reads: 'Product of the Occupied Territories.'"

He nods sympathetically, but I can tell he's choosing his words cautiously. I've laid down *my* eggshells. "So you're illegal?" he asks.

"And very dangerous."

"Lucky for you I like danger," he says. Our margaritas come, and he takes a sip in relief. "You know, I was kind of curious when we passed by the settlements. I mean, we hear so much about them, but we didn't go into any. We just know that they were built on Palestinian land and make life hard for the Palestinians, using up their water, cutting off their roads."

I roll my eyes. "Lies and smears. It's not that simple. But how could you know the truth if you're not allowed to talk to 'settler groups?'"

"Well, I won't boycott you. I'm not into boycotts. I have one friend who's very anti-settlement. Thinks we should boycott them, especially because of our past, saying Germans especially can't support any kind of nationalist aggression. But I'm a musician. I'll play music to whoever wants to hear. When 'The Boss' performed by the Berlin Wall, he said he wasn't playing for any government but for whoever loves rock n' roll because music breaks down barriers. That's inspiring."

"I'm not crazy about walls either," I say. "Most 'settlers' actually don't like the security barrier separating Israelis and Palestinians. It breaks up the beautiful landscape and creates all these divisions. I believe we could live together. So does my father. He works for a textile factory at the industrial park in Ariel. It employs hundreds of Palestinians. They earn a good living. Get Israeli social and welfare benefits. If people boycott his plant or force it to close because of its location on this or that side of the wall, they'd all lose their jobs."

"Really?"

"Yeah, but you won't know that if you don't talk to 'settlers.'"

"Well, I'm talking to one now," he says.

"I even graduated from Ariel University, one of the most boycotted universities on the planet. One of my design partners was an Arab girl—a 'Palestinian' from an Arab-Israeli town called Tira. We were part of a team that designed a medical clinic for an international student competition. The organizers didn't accept our submission because it came from the 'Occupied Territories.' Our skill, our achievements, our plan—all that didn't matter. Only our geography did. We could have helped build a medical clinic."

His forehead crinkles. "If there's anything I've learned in life, it's not to judge people from where they're born or where they live." He sighs. "After all the havoc we wreaked in the world, I'm not proud telling people I'm from Germany. It's like I also wear a label: 'Product of Germany,' especially here."

"Yeah, some Jews, at least the older generation, still have problems buying German cars." I don't mention my mother.

"And Dresden has its own stigmas, not only because of the bombing, but people think it's filled with all these neo-Nazis because this far-right, anti-immigration movement holds rallies there every Monday. Sometimes you just want to be seen for you and not your nationality or race or religion."

I never thought I'd receive an ethics lesson from a German, but, at this moment, he's not "a German," a leftist, a non-Jew—the grandson of maybe-Nazis. He's an intriguing, idealistic man who's trying, in his own way, to make the world a better place. And who might actually like me.

And with that I raise the margarita glass. "*Prost.* To breaking down barriers."

"*Le'chayim.*"

After dinner, we walk to Neve Tzedek, a slum in the early days of the State that has since gentrified to become one of the city's most opulent, charming neighborhoods with its refurbished tenements now showcasing luscious balconies and gardens. Down Shabazi Road, past its posh boutiques, we stop at a *gelateria*, and I introduce Sebastian to the "*halva,*" sweet sesame, ice cream flavor.

"*Ta'im,*" he enthuses after he tastes a sample.

He teaches me how to say *ta'im* in German.

"*Lecker,*" I repeat as I try the raisin and rum flavor.

We order a mix of flavors in two cups and share.

I probably know more German than I think. My grandparents sometimes spoke Yiddish, the German-Hebrew dialect, to each other but never to me and rarely to their children. Still, some Yiddish words found their way across our Shabbat table.

Sebastian holds my hand intermittently as we pass "The Station," a British-mandate-era, beachside train station that was recently converted into a sparkly entertainment hub. From here, I point to the stone minaret signaling the Jaffa port, explaining how Jaffa, the biblical port city, was once an Arab stronghold. Most Arabs stayed in Jaffa during the outbreak of the War of Independence. Ever since Jaffa and Tel Aviv united, the neighborhood has become home to a rising Arab middle class, hipsters, and upwardly-mobile families who don't want to feel too bourgeoisie. Jaffa's exotic Ottoman-style homes contrast the sleek skyscrapers and simplistic Bauhaus architecture for which Tel Aviv is known.

Even though I'm wearing flats, my feet are getting tired from all this walking, so I suggest we sit somewhere on the promenade connecting Tel Aviv and Jaffa.

"Do you have a beach in Germany?" I ask, feeling ignorant.

"Up north. The Baltic Sea, but it's far out and cold most of the time. But Berlin has the Spree, the river, and there are some really nice lakes around Berlin in Brandenburg where Berliners like to go in the summer when it gets dark really late. We have something called 'Spätis.' *Spät* means 'late' in German. They're like late-night kiosks where you can buy cheap beer, so instead of sitting at pubs, people get beer from Spätis and take walks along the river. Do you have things like Spätis?"

"Yeah, I guess. Our 'kiosks.' For drinks, cigarettes, snacks, that sort of thing."

"So let's find a 'Späti,' get a beer, and sit by the water."

"Great idea." *And romantic.*

We find a Späti on the seam of Jaffa and Tel Aviv and, with beers in tow, find a stretch of flat stone overlooking the shore. Sebastian unfurls his sweater over the stone as a cushion. The salt of the ocean mixes with the sweet sesame lingering on my tongue. We make a toast then face the ocean in silence until he exhales in delight and says, "Come here."

He signals me to lean on his shoulder. I feel tipsy from his touch as his strong arms envelop me. He strokes my arm over my sweater, making me feel both relaxed and nervous, as I sink further into his hard torso. Then he begins playing with my dark, wavy hair, clearing enjoying what, for him, must be an exotic part of my body.

Thankfully, he doesn't ask to kiss me this time. He simply starts with my neck, moving up closer to my ear and then approaching my lips. I turn my face toward him as my full permission. His lips are not only soulful but skilled. He starts softly until his tongue tastes mine. He might as well be tasting me below, where I begin to tingle.

I pull back before we kiss too heavily because my thoughts now wander to the F-word.

Foreskin.

His most exotic body part.

I reluctantly sit back up and inch away from him. Finding out if he's circumcised without checking personally might be trickier than finding out if his grandparents were Nazis. I sip beer to ease back into the conversation. *We've survived the A-bomb, the H-Bomb, the N-bomb, the O-bomb. What about the F-bomb?*

"Did you have any religious upbringing?" I ask, my maneuver. "Or did you grow up completely secular?"

"Well, my grandparents on my father's side were Christian, but, truth is, we didn't grow up with any religion," he answers easily, naturally, clearly not annoyed by my shift from kissing to talking. "We lived under communism, which basically banned religion. A lot of churches from the Renaissance period were destroyed in Dresden, and the Soviets never bothered to rebuild them. I think most Germans were Christian before the war. I wasn't baptized, though."

"What does that mean?"

"Christians become Christians, I guess you could say, when they're baptized. It's a type of ritual dipping into water."

"At what age?"

"Different ages, I think."

"So you mean you're not really Christian if you weren't baptized? I thought if you believed in Jesus, that's enough."

"I don't know so much about Christianity, but if you officially want to become Christian, I think you have to dunk yourself in the water."

I laugh. "Like in Judaism. If someone wants to convert to Judaism, they have to dunk themselves in something called a *mikveh*, ritual waters. That's probably where baptism comes from."

"Probably." This talk of Jewish and Christian bodies dunking in water causes my mind—and eyes—to wander to the F-bomb. My next spying maneuver: "Don't some Christians also circumcise their sons?"

"Not in Germany." *I got my answer.* "In Israel you do, right?"

"Definitely. At eight-days-old."

"Ouch!" He instinctually covers his crotch. "Why do you people do it?"

I won't interpret his "you people" remark as antisemitic. It's a fair question.

I'll start with the rational reasons I can conjure. "Some doctors say it's healthier," I say.

"I'm not sure," he says and places his palm over my knee. "Don't take this the wrong way, but the whole chop-chop thing, well, seems so primitive."

I flash back to the "chop-chop" of my nephew three years ago when the rabbi made the blessing over his circumcision: "Blessed are You, Lord our God, King of the universe, Who has sanctified us with His commandments and commanded us to enter him into the Covenant of Abraham, our father."

"We're actually taught the opposite. That you're the heathens." I punch him lightly on the side in jest and because I want an excuse to touch him, at least anywhere except his F-bomb. "Abraham, you know, was the first monotheist. Everyone around him was an immoral pagan, so he made a covenant with God to start a new way of looking at the world."

"But why like that?"

"Well," I'm coming up with this on the spot, "what's the one thing that symbolizes a covenant between a man and a woman—that one unbreakable rule?"

"You mean faithfulness?"

"Yeah. So in Judaism, man makes a covenant with God by sacrificing a part of his, how shall I say, sex. The removal of the foreskin is like the seal. This covenant means you have control over your primitive instincts, your urges, so that you can live a life with a higher purpose."

He moves his hand toward my inner thigh and squeezes. "Then I'm glad I'm pagan," he says. Next, he brings his hand to my cheek and kisses me deeper, longer than before.

I push him away, nervous now because his skillful kissing is making me curious about his skin-full sex. I must control my urges. *Can I even touch one of Judaism's greatest taboos? The symbol of everything we don't want to be?*

While he may not be circumcised, he's certainly controlling his urges quite well. If he were a secular Israeli, his hands would have already attempted to slip under my shirt. Despite being members of the covenant, my countrymen are not the most sexually patient. Sebastian seems perfectly happy transitioning from kissing to teasing to talking to kissing to teasing to talking. I wonder if German men generally take it slow or if something is holding him back, like a girlfriend.

I devolve our heavy lip lock into sweet, short kisses, and we face the ocean again. The ocean breeze turns colder, but I'm heated by his body.

"I take it you don't have a covenant with anyone back in Germany?" I ask.

He's confused. "You mean, am I an atheist?"

"No. I mean, are you single?"

"Yes. And an atheist. And you?"

"You mean, am I an atheist?"

"No, I mean, are you single?"

"Yes, and I guess you could say I'm agnostic. God to me is not a personal God, more like some sort of a higher power that represents right and wrong."

"So when was your last relationship?" he asks. "I mean with a man."

I laugh. "About ten months ago. Actually, we were engaged, but I broke it off not long after."

"Why?"

"He was a good guy. Nice and supportive, but, honestly, I never felt fully attracted to him. No real passion. He was circumcised, but I guess you could say I didn't have enough urges to control for him."

"Ouch."

"Yeah. And what about you? When was your last relationship?"

"About six months ago. We dated for almost year. She was about to move in, but then I realized I wasn't ready for that kind of commitment. I still wanted to be free to travel and perform and do what I'm doing right now."

He kisses me again, and just when I'm ready for him to act like an impatient Israeli, he pulls away, controlling his urges, even though at this point I'm not even sure he has them for me. *Could my Jewishness be as much of a barrier for him as his foreskin is for me? Is teasing a Jewish woman the modern form of antisemitism?*

"So, what else do you have in store for me, dear tour guide?" he asks. "I don't want this night to end just yet. I still gotta see more of Tel Aviv nightlife."

"Dancing?"

"Yes."

We take a cab to Jimmy Who, a pick-up dance bar on Rothschild off Allenby that plays electro, which Sebastian tells me he loves. When I'd go to Jimmy Who once every few months, I'd see a lot of foreigners drawn to its state-of-the-art sound system and industrial decor that puts it on par with the world's best clubs.

Outside, I spot a few light-skinned foreigners—Germans?—trying to pass selection. I hold Sebastian's hand and raise the other to get the selector's attention. She quickly asks me how many.

"Two," I answer.

She unlatches the chain for us right away. No self-respecting Israeli establishment would refuse a man as beautiful as Sebastian.

We squeeze our way through the loud, packed corridor to the main bar, and this time, unencumbered by the prospect of conversation, we each down a whiskey shot.

On the main, tight dance floor near the DJ booth, the electro bass lines, alcohol, and close quarters gradually induce us into dirty dancing. Finally, he puts his hands on my hips and raises them toward my breasts. His tongue cuts deeper than before into my throat. My hands soar over his shoulders, his back, his chest. I relish in the sensation of every bump and dent of his body, except for the most important one.

I make sure to keep our crotches at least an inch apart. Even as I get more drunk and aroused, I tell myself to be like Abraham—to control my urges. I can't explode the F-bomb.

Finally, he pulls me closer to him, pressing his primitive area against mine. I gather my monotheistic strength.

"I just want you to know," I say, drunk, "I'm not sleeping with you."

"Whoever said anything about sleeping with you, silly Nilly?"

"I just thought—"

"It's fun just dancing with you."

I'm both pleased and annoyed by his patience, but not long after our crotch-free dirty dancing, he suggests we go home.

He calls a cab and holds me in the backseat.

"I'm out with the group tomorrow, but beach on Saturday afternoon?" he asks from inside the cab as he lets me off.

"Yes," I say before kissing him good night.

I go up to my apartment alone, thinking how this uncircumcised man who did not ask to come up for coffee for the second time might as well be a Jew, as holy as Abraham.

CHAPTER SIX

Once in a while, Ima reminds me that Safta and Saba never bought German products and that she proudly continues their tradition. Before heading to Ariel for Shabbat dinner with the family, I decide to test this ban.

After a strong morning coffee, I stop off at a Tel Aviv electronics store for a new blender. I remember having complained to her this summer as I tried to make fruit shakes that our blender was leaking. While we're now well into autumn, I'm going to feel like making a shake today.

"What blenders are made in Germany?" I ask the short, middle-aged man who's the stereotypical Israeli image of an electronics salesman—slicked-back hair, a body that speaks of little ambition, and a smile that says, "Don't worry, I won't *really* cheat you."

"Well, most are made in China, but the parent companies are German."

"Which ones?"

He takes me to the aisle with the blenders. "There's Braun."

"That's a German company?"

"Seems so, from the name. Why does it matter?"

"Oh, well, it's just that their products are better, no?" *Including their men?*

"They used to be better until they started making them in China. There's also Grundig, but I think it's owned by a Turkish company now."

Oh no. Are there no more bona-fide German blenders?

China and Turkey will not work, especially not Turkey, which has been an ass to Israel ever since it got that new Muslim dictator. Turkey was behind that "Marmara" flotilla that had attempted to break Israel's maritime blockade on Gaza by posing as a humanitarian delivery. After the passengers rebuffed the offer of the Israel Defense Forces to dock in Ashkelon for inspection, a group of IDF commandos commandeered the ship, armed only with paint guns, believing the humanitarian claim. The "humanitarians" viciously attacked the soldiers with knives and clubs. More IDF commandos came on board, this time with live ammunition. The IDF killed nine people, only to be labeled "war criminals" by the Turkish government and other Israel-hating regimes.

I check online. Braun is now owned by Proctor & Gamble, an American company. Actually, this commercial globalism works well because, if Ima wants to ban a product for its German name, I could simply tell her it's not *really* German...

"Let's go with Braun."

My family lives on a quiet street in Ariel next to a brand new park and about a fifteen-minute walk from the city center, which consists of government offices housed in pre-fab structures and a bunch of nondescript shops and eateries.

My father was one of the city's pioneers, part of the 6,000 recruits nicknamed "nucleus Tel Aviv." These adventurous, secular Jews gave up a more comfortable life in the metropolitan Tel Aviv area to build "the city of Samaria" on biblical mountaintops, driven by a call to claim the literal high ground of the Land of Israel as a security measure. Thirty-five years later, the hills of Ariel serve as a geographic watchtower overlooking the populous Sharon coast just forty-five miles away by car.

We moved into our current home when I was four-years-old. As the city expanded, so did the house. A few years ago, my parents renovated it, adding a top floor and turning the basement into a rental unit that is currently rented to an Ariel University student.

My mother's in the kitchen when I come in. She's wearing her flower-printed apron over her ever-expanding waistline, cutting vegetables for tonight's chicken soup, my "hangover cure." In the last few years, she has evolved from a spritely, active middle-aged woman into a buxom sixty-year-old homemaker whose main purpose in life is to cook and care for her third generation. This year, she reduced her teaching hours to part time.

I place the box with the blender on the granite island.

"Ima, I finally got a blender," I say. "On sale."

I take the blender out of the box.

"Braun. Is that a good brand?" Almost on cue, she says, with a scowl, "I think it's a German brand. Sounds German."

She continues to move about preparing food.

"I don't know," I say.

"You know we don't have German products in this house. Those killers."

That was fast.

"I didn't even think about it," I said. "The guy just told me it was a good blender." *Sebastian is already making me lie.* "Actually, isn't Braun a German-Jewish name? Maybe it was a German-Jewish factory?" *And taunt her.*

I pretend I'm looking up its nationality on my phone. "It's American, Ima. The original company was German. Is that okay?" I speak casually to hide the importance of the greater issue at hand.

"I would've preferred Israeli."

"Yeah, but our Electra blender fell apart!" *Just like our men.* I sigh in exasperation. "Ima, even if it were German, don't you think we can lift the ban on German products? I mean, a lot of time has passed. It's a new generation. Israel and Germany are celebrating the jubilee of diplomatic relations."

"Never! Not after what those animals did to Saba and Safta, the Jewish people, the world. Let them and their children pay for decades to come, if not forever."

No wonder Jews hardly intermarry. They have Jewish mothers. And if I were to follow her lead and deny myself this German pleasure—and blender— I'd become like her, ensuring my children live by a self-denial that my mother considers self-preservation and self-respect.

In defiance of her, I open the blender and make a shake with whatever fruits I can find. The apple-pear-date shake is disgusting, but I drink it anyway.

We've always celebrated a traditional Friday night dinner as quality family time. But, unlike our Orthodox co-religionists who completely "unplug" by refraining from using electronic appliances on Shabbat, we generally gather around the television after dinner. Usually, when I don't have plans, I crash in my old bedroom, now a guest room.

Sometimes, we invite friends and guests, like tonight. At the last minute, my brother Arik invited his relatively new colleague, a thirty-five-year-old *oleh* to Israel named Aviram. My brother had wanted to set us up last month, but I was in no mood for a blind date, so I gave him permission to invite Aviram for Shabbat dinner for a more organic meeting.

With the Shabbat candles illuminating our dining room, I feel the spiritual coziness that Shabbat always brings. The familiar, comforting aromas of the chicken soup, roasted potatoes, garlic chicken, and meatloaf remind me why Jews fought to keep this special day in non-Jewish countries. I feel blessed to look forward to a delicious meal, bound to a tradition that keeps families together.

My parents sent me to the religious, Zionist state elementary school in Ariel to give me a strong Jewish education. Secular schools in Israel teach the Bible as a work of literature, but at the religious-state schools, we learn the Torah as the base of a living religion. But, come high school, I didn't want to attend a religious school, mostly because I hated the dress code requiring long skirts. Still, I developed an appreciation for Jewish tradition. I would know how to practice Orthodox Judaism if I wanted to.

As I watch my father pick up the silver goblet of wine to recite *kiddush*, the blessing ushering in the "seventh day of rest," I realize I'd probably have to give up this beloved tradition if I ever married a man like Sebastian. He can't read Hebrew, let alone recite *kiddush*. He'd no doubt think this ritual is just as weird as circumcision—all of us standing, bearing "witness" to God's creation of the universe in six days and his resting on the seventh.

Marrying a non-Jew, however gorgeous, would be another type of "settling."

I smile sweetly at our guest sitting across from me. With Aviram, I wouldn't have to compromise this tradition. He's not bad looking, just not particularly good looking. Then again, most men are not good looking compared to Sebastian. Aviram's facial features, below a receding hairline, are pleasantly symmetrical aside from one feature. This hooked-Jewish-nose thing is not just a Nazi myth.

As we get to the chicken soup, Aviram, prompted by Aba's inquiry, begins to explain in "Heblish"—a mix of Hebrew and English—how he made *aliyah* from Los Angeles as "Abe." Upon moving to Israel two years ago, he Hebraisized his name. Thanks to *ulpan* classes and practice, he achieved Hebrew fluency, building on the base he received in Jewish elementary school.

"So why did you make *aliyah*?" I ask.

"Well, luckily I came to a job at a start-up, so that helps. But, really, how could I pass up a chance to live in the Jewish state in my lifetime? It's hard to give up the quality of life in America, especially Los Angeles, which my father likes to joke is the capital of '*olam hazeh*.'"

We all laugh. "*Olam hazeh*" is a reference to "this world," the material life, as opposed to *olam habah*, the spiritual "world to come."

"What did you study?" I probe awkwardly, feeling like I'm on a date with my family watching. I'm sure my mother would love for me to go out with him, but she knows better than to nudge. I've already told her quite forcefully after I broke up with Alon, which she regrets, never to ask me or pressure me about my love life. Come to think of it, pleasing her must have played a role in my agreeing to Alon's proposal.

"Finance and marketing," Aviram says.

"He's our new MarCom director," Arik says, sitting next to his wife, Dorit. "Smart guy and easy to get along with."

Arik, my brother, completed his MBA at Ariel University a few years ago and now works as an executive at a software company in Petach Tikva near Tel Aviv. Dorit, a social worker, recently gave birth to a girl who, along with my three-year-old nephew, is asleep. My younger brother, Yaron, an engineering student at Hebrew University, is with friends in Jerusalem this weekend.

"So you like it here?" Dorit asks.

"Love it! Arik's company is great. Tel Aviv is so vibrant. It's changed a lot since my junior year abroad at Tel Aviv University. So many restaurants, bars. And all these new parking and GPS apps make it much easier to get around. And it's cool to be so close to Europe. I took ski trips to Austria and summer trips to Spain and Hungary. Can't do that so easily from Los Angeles."

How much easier life would be with a man like him! He loves Israel, Tel Aviv, and Arik told me he even had no issues with driving into a "settlement." He's obviously financially stable. We'd live a good life, traveling to Europe as proud Jews who deeply understand the crimes perpetrated on that continent.

"So, is there nightlife in Ariel?" Aviram asks me after dessert while Ima is in the kitchen cleaning up with my sister-in-law. "It's a university town I hear, so I assume there are pubs and stuff."

"Yeah, there are pubs, and some are even open tonight, but they're mostly for students. Honestly," I say, meaning it, "I wouldn't really recommend them. They have nothing on Tel Aviv."

"Are you going back to Tel Aviv tonight?" he asks.

"I don't think so. I'm kind of hungover, so I was thinking of crashing."

"I just think it would be cool to go to a bar in a so-called settlement."

I should feel refreshed by his curiosity about my hometown. I could be his "perfect" Ariel tour guide, but I'm completely apathetic. It's a coin toss. Heads, I take him out. Tails, I stay in.

"Let me think about it. Can you excuse me for a few minutes?"

"Sure," he says.

I leave him to toss a coin privately. But when I pick up my phone, I get my "head"—Sebastian's head appearing next to a text that reads, "Shabbat Shalom. See you tomorrow!"

"Shabbat Shalom," I answer back. Aviram is out of luck. "And *Danke.*"

CHAPTER SEVEN

We agree to meet at 2 pm at the same sandy spot where we first met.

I bring my beach blanket but not my Kindle. Finally, a book won't be my companion. Days are getting shorter; the sun, cooler. But today is still in the mid-70s, and the sands are full of people lying out or playing *matkot*, catching the last bits of autumn sun. The cobalt blue sky is streaked with a few jagged clouds.

At 2:05 pm, he still hasn't shown up, atypical for a German. I should've come fashionably late. As three more minutes go by, I convince myself that he stood me up. He was never interested. He's just a cruel Nazi playing games with my Jewish heart.

While I wait on the blanket, I respond to my brother's text asking me if he could give Aviram my number.

"Sure," I answer, happier than I was last night to have Aviram as an option.

I text Ariella to complain about Sebastian's tardiness.

"At least you didn't sleep with him," she writes.

"Is 'everything but' okay?" I write back.

"Under one condition."

"What?"

"You really, really can't help it."

I reply with an "LOL" emoticon.

Then, at 2:11, I feel a cold, wet tap on my shoulder. I turn to see the bottom of a Goldstar bottle. I look at Sebastian above, wearing his swim shorts and a T-shirt.

"Sorry I'm late, but there was a line at the Späti, and I'm having reception problems."

Acceptable excuse.

I stand up, wipe the sand off my summer dress, and kiss him lightly on the lips. As I look into his icy eyes melting from the Tel Aviv sun, he pulls me to him, placing his hands right above my ass while my arms reach over his shoulders.

"Thanks for bringing the blanket," he says after letting go.

"Thanks for the beers."

We sit, side by side, drinking our Goldstars. My not-so-dainty feet look like they belong to a delicate princess's next to his brawny, manly ones; my shaven, tanned calves are so feminine against his bulky calves spread with blonde butter. During our small talk, I look at couples walking hand in hand by the shore, feeling lucky to be here, finally, with a man I really want to touch.

"I can't be out too late because I have rehearsals at six," Sebastian says. "Can you make it to the show tomorrow night?"

"I think so," I say, flattered he would want to share that moment with me, however Leftie. Maybe I mean more to him than just an Israeli fling.

"So how's the water?" he asks.

"Haven't touched it."

"Well, let's go find out."

We ask our neighbors to watch our stuff, and then my mind processes him taking off his T-shirt in slow motion. He crumbles the cotton like a piece of paper and tosses it to the sand. His perfect pecs beg me to feel them up, the way a man would a woman's breasts. I then focus on the gentle line of hair leading to his erogenous, no-go zone.

I take off my summer dress and look down at my fit body—not as fit as his. I try to work out three times a week, but it usually ends up being two. I'm wearing my favorite white bikini, pick-up-bra style so that my B cup looks more like a C cup.

Sebastian looks me up and down, satisfied.

"Ready?" he asks.

"Yes."

He takes my hand and leads the way, stepping first into the waters. "A bit chilly, but if we jump in, we'll get used to it," he says.

He dives horizontally into the shallow, without any fear, this god who has control over the elements. Meanwhile, I walk in timidly, afraid of the cold and of ingesting salt water.

"Come on!" he shouts.

"I can't swim as well as you!"

I tread slowly in the shallow, gradually getting used to the cool temperature. He comes back for me, puts his arm under my legs to lift me, and glides me over the water. We're like Adam and Eve in paradise, until he throws me into the deep. I ingest salt water through my nose and cough.

"That's mean!" I say. *The real German is coming out.*

I punch him in retaliation—an act of anger as much as flirtation. My fist on his shoulder feels like straw banging on a piece of metal.

"I could've gotten hurt, asshole."

There. I'm getting out my aggression and suspicion.

He takes hold of my shoulders. "Hey, chill out. Sometimes you just need to dive in."

Even more of an asshole for using that metaphor because he's not just referring to the water but of diving into him—or of him diving into me.

His touch turns tender as he wipes the water from my face and kisses me with his salty lips.

"Sorry," he says.

In response, I swim out a few yards away from him to assert my independence. The water temperature feels good now, alternating from hot to cold every few patches, just like my feelings for Sebastian.

He screams in elation. "I love Tel Aviv!"

I swim near him and smile now, and he pulls me toward him until my legs wrap around his. His feet are still touching the ocean floor while mine rely on his body as an anchor. The lifeguard warns swimmers to stay near the shore, accentuating the sense of danger.

With my body steadying over his, we kiss. The salt in the water acts like a lubricant for my hands to glide over his muscled contours. I look around. Another couple is kissing—or having underwater sex?—about ten meters away from us. This moment becomes not only one of the most torturous of my life but also the most erotic.

My feet stay locked around his, and I feel a light stab near my crotch. I move my crotch away instinctively as if it's shielded against an unchosen cock. That piece of skin that must occupy no more than a square inch of area now occupies an entire world in my mind.

I break away. He catches up to me quickly.

"Everything okay?" he asks. I turn to him, flapping, and he grips my sides. "You're shaking."

"I'm cold," I lie and swim away again.

"What's the matter?" he asks, swimming after me.

I can't hide from him. Germans always manage to catch the Jew.

"I'm nervous," I say as we paddle face to face.

"Why?"

"Well, uh, I've never been with a man like you."

"What do you mean?" he says, pulling me close to him, our crotches barely touching.

"You're so, well, uh, German."

"What's that supposed to mean?" he asks a tad angrily, probably fearful of my prejudice against him as much as I'm fearful of his prejudice against me.

I must limit my prejudice to that one part of his body. "I mean, you're so, uh...uncircumcised."

"Oh, so you're afraid of my—how do you call it?" He rubs his crotch against mine. "My foreskin?"

I gasp. Again, he pleasantly surprises me by how much he correctly anticipates—and correctly touches me.

"Exactly," I say.

His left hand reaches for my ass while his right reaches inside my crotch. His knuckles brush against my clit and then clasp the lips protecting it.

"Foreskins are nothing to be afraid of. You have one, too."

I protest in pleasure. "Yeah, but that's different."

"How so?" he asks, now rubbing his finger against my clit.

"My foreskin is very, very necessary for pleasure." I barely manage to get the words out.

"And mine isn't?"

"No."

"Well, how would you know?"

Is that a challenge?

He's right. I don't know.

"It won't bite," he says.

Goaded by my pleasure and the cover provided by the water, I lay my hand flat on his abdomen and slip it under his swim shorts. I pet the length of his cock as it expands against my touch. He leans his head back. I circle my forefinger around the head searching for the foreskin, but I can't feel this unnecessary layer. I brave the tip, but it's smooth and soft, like a Jew's. Pleasure drips from his blue eyes, making him appear the most human I've ever seen him.

"I don't even feel it," I say.

"What?" he whispers.

"Your foreskin," I say and remove my hand.

He steadies his breath and says, "It requires a manual for new users. Do you live alone or with roommates?"

Finally, he's starting to sound like a circumcised Israeli!

"Alone."

"Should we go to your place? I'll show you exactly how it works."

I can't help it. My foreskin persuades me. "Yes."

I don't know how I manage to parallel park in the blue-white permit zone right near my place; my hands keep shaking on the wheel at the prospect of him coming over.

I live in a large studio apartment off Rabin Square. When I moved here last year, I had debated whether or not to save money by living with roommates, but it was worth living solo for a moment like this.

I excuse myself to go to the bathroom so that I can physically and mentally prepare for it. I look in the mirror. My face is bronzed by today's sun, and the salt has softened my skin and reduced my hair's frizz. My waterproof eyeliner has not smudged although my lip gloss is gone, not that I need any. I splash water on my face to wake me from what feels like a surreal dream. My stomach feels light, as if it's hollow, with only those proverbial butterflies flapping around inside.

As I come out, he's standing by my home office near the sofa across from the corner nook consisting of my bed. He looks at my work table topped with some blueprints, sketches, and a bunch of office supplies.

He opens a folded blueprint as I approach him. "What's this?"

"It's a floor of a residential building I'm working on," is all I say.

I'm not about to explain how it belongs to the Har Homa residential complex. Talk of settlements would be such a buzz kill. I'm interested in other protrusions.

What kind of architecture went into this man? I want to take a pencil and follow it along his masterful body. I want to learn from him how something should be made, as an organic, vital creature. He seems to hold up the human form exactly as it should be: proud and strong.

Fuck, I'm starting to sound like Hitler!

But is the mark of his non-Jewishness the stain on this physically splendid structure?

"Can I get you a drink?" I ask.

"No. I want you."

He kisses me while pushing me toward the sofa. He takes off my summer dress, leaving me in my bikini. I'm now sitting on the sofa, legs closed, while he opens his legs around mine, kneeling over me. I take off his shirt and grab onto his sides as he bows his head to trace the edge of my bikini top with his lips, sneaking his tongue along my nipples. Then, he unfastens my top and sucks each breast with equal time and pressure so that neither is envious. My desire moistens as his lips glide to my neck and mouth.

He pulls my bikini bottom down to my knees to pet that extra piece of flesh whose sole purpose is to give a woman pleasure. While rubbing, he sneaks a few pokes into the crevice.

"Oh, man, you're so wet," he says in delight.

He lays me down so that one leg is hooked over the sofa while my head is on the armrest. With one hand petting my inner thigh, he inserts the middle finger of the other hand inside me. His finger goes deeper than any man's has ever gone, as if it is being suctioned inside. He presses onto one spot against my vaginal wall. My G-spot? This acute pleasure is new to me.

"What are you doing?" I ask through a moan.

"Maybe I don't bite, but you do. I can't take my finger out."

Can there be a threshold to female pleasure? It's unfamiliar, intense, and agonizing. I grab his arm to pull his finger out, but he pries my hand off by the wrist so that I cannot interfere. He then holds both my wrists together, like a handcuff, while he inserts another finger, which a spring inside me now wants to eject.

"Oh, my God," I cry. "What are you doing?"

"Why? Your foreskin can't take it?" he says, continuing to finger me.

"No," I say through a literal snob. "It's cruel!"

But he disregards my protests and continues.

"Stop!" I yell.

He removes his fingers quickly and looks me in the eye. "You really want me to stop?" he asks, looking slightly concerned, disappointed.

Now I'm angry at him for really stopping. "No. I give you permission to grab my pussy."

He laughs at my obvious reference to the famous Trump hot-mic scandal in which he bragged about "grabbing pussy."

"Good, because I wouldn't grab it any other way. Do you need a safe word if it gets too much?"

"Trump?"

"I'd really rather not hear his name in bed."

"Is 'Nazi' better?" I dare to say.

"Same difference, but that would do the trick," he says and thankfully gets back to grabbing.

No way I can shout out "Nazi"; he seems to be making a painstaking effort to repent for his ancestors by making me scream in unbearable pleasure.

"Oh, my God! Stop! Oh, my God!" I cry as he alternates between fingering me and rubbing my clit. The butterflies have moved from the hollow of my stomach to my newly hollowed-out brain as he presses on this one spot, which makes me squirm even as my entire body vibrates.

I sink my teeth into his shoulder as I jerk from this heartless beating up of pleasure. This time, I pry his hands off me once and for all. I really can't take anymore. I've come, probably more than once.

I close my legs and lay on my back, completely spent, flushing out this horrifying titillation with deep, heavy breathing.

My ancestors once had to beg Germans to stop them from causing so much pain. Here I am, begging a German to stop causing me so much pleasure. *This can't be wrong.*

He carries me to the bed where I rest in a fetal position. He caresses my back during what must have been the most peaceful, calm nap I've ever known. I open my eyes and turn on my back to see him looking down at me, his shirt off but his shorts still on.

I look at the clock. 4:26 pm. His rehearsals are in an hour and a half. Not much time. I push him down so that he's lying on his back. My strong belief in the biblical concept of measure for measure—or in this case, pleasure for pleasure—prompts me to brave his uncut glory.

I climb on top of him, camping my legs over his upper thighs that belong more to a warrior than to a musician. I slide my hands down from his shoulders toward the edge of his shorts. I lift their elastic and snap it back, a warning to us both. Under the fabric, his gentile manhood seems to be wiggling, anxious for freedom, another biblical concept.

My right hand cautiously, curiously rubs it over his shorts. He remains silent, but I'm not interested in his reaction. I'm now a biologist examining a new species of animal. Scientific inquiry is also a hallmark of Jewish tradition.

After a few minutes of massaging his length, I count "1-2-3" in my head and pull down his shorts.

"Oh, my God," I say, but not because of the godless foreskin. His cock has shot straight up, beautiful and large, its head fully exposed, all perfectly proportioned with the rest of his body.

"Everything okay?" he asks, noticing my puzzled look.

"Yeah," I say, fascinated. "Are you sure you're not circumcised? There's no foreskin!"

"Now for the tutorial?"

He rubs the head of his cock and grasps for the loose skin.

"It retracts when I'm hard," he says, pulling the stretchy, fleshy fabric over the penis head. I see it now! *So this is the piece of skin responsible for dividing Jews from the rest of humanity?*

I take over and trace my fingers up and down the shaft, underneath the ring. Then I, too, stretch the foreskin over the head, following his example.

"Does this hurt?"

"Not at all. It's quite sturdy. You could even stick your fingers inside it. Actually, if you rub me using the skin, it feels really good. "

Now I'm like a little girl playing with a new toy she got for Hannukah. *What are the rules? How many players? How do you win?*

He's quiet as I take hold and massage his shaft, sometimes using the foreskin as a type of polishing cloth. Fascinated, I hold up the extra layer of skin and insert my finger in between the foreskin and the head. His eyes twitch and his lips form an ecstatic pout from my explorations, as if there's something spiritual to this physical friction.

As I continue burnishing the length with one hand, I cup his balls hanging neatly below with the other. I would never have imagined that one day I'd be holding the German life source in the palm of my hands. No sooner does he convulse in a way I've never seen before in a man.

The F-bomb has exploded.

CHAPTER EIGHT

I drive to work on Sunday with sore legs and slight bruises on my wrists, feeling like a different person. Is there something about a Jewess touching an uncircumcised German penis that biologically and metaphysically changes her? Have my cells morphed, somehow making me less racially Jewish?

I feel lightheaded, even giddy, as I walk through the lobby of the skyscraper located in the Diamond District of Ramat Gan. Our offices occupy the thirtieth floor of this very corporate tower. The firm, Zimmerman and Associates, consists of executive offices and three large rooms—one for the concept team, one for the execution team, and one for the logistics team.

My firm is probably one of the few in Tel Aviv that designs for commercial and residential projects in Judea and Samaria—one reason I applied. It wasn't my first choice, but it was a safer one, given my degree from Ariel University.

I had applied to two other Tel Aviv firms. While neither said so outright, I think they preferred students who didn't study at the Israeli university in the "territories," despite my good marks and capable portfolio. I discovered later that the owner of one of those firms is active with Peace Now, the Jewish left-wing group that leads boycotts against Jewish institutions in Judea and Samaria. *And here I am complaining about Europeans?*

My boss, Tal Zimmerman, is not a right-wing ideologue but a good businessman who saw opportunity in the growing "settler" market, one of the fastest growing populations in Israel, despite all the bans, thanks in part to natural growth, particularly among Orthodox families.

When I get to my desk in the "execution" room, my giddiness from last night turns into exasperation. I turn on the computer to finish up measurements on the Har Homa complex.

The project had been victim to the temporary settlement freeze imposed by the Obama administration. I like defying world opinion by building homes for Jews in their modern and ancestral capital, but even before meeting Sebastian, the Har Homa complex didn't satisfy me. Jews should live in Jerusalem with panache, but this complex, like many others, is a mere technical, commercial endeavor rendering every unit—and every inhabitant—a product. It was designed according to a template for massive residential complexes being built across Israel but adapted to Jerusalem, whose buildings are required to be outfitted with the Jerusalem stone that gives the "City of Gold" its unmistakable antique charm.

When I visited the virgin construction site—situated on a mountaintop overlooking Bethlehem and the settlement bloc of Gush Etsion—I reveled in the beauty of the Judean Hills. It pains me to know that we had to chop the hill, as if with a saw, to make the land conform to the building's design. This cookie-cutter complex belongs on the abused land as much as...a foreskin belongs on a penis.

I envisioned a residential complex built organically upon the hill with each individual unit designed to preserve and maximize the beauty and variations of the natural landscape. I never shared my vision with my boss. I knew my place as an executioner—of that gorgeous hill.

But last night, in which I defied social and religious conventions, has given me the courage to walk into Zimmerman's office to do what I've dreamed of doing since I started working here about three years ago.

We get niceties out of the way, and I ask: "I'm curious, what other projects are coming in?"

"Why?" the bespectacled Zimmerman asks. He's a tall man whose angular features remind me of a skyscraper. His button-down shirt, tucked neatly under a belt fastened over meticulously hemmed pants, serves to separate his body into very clear levels. His polished shoes form triangles at the tips. His perfectly groomed, brown goatee adds the only real artistic flourish.

"Well, when the Har Homa project is over, I would very much like to go in from the ground up with the concept team."

"Why?"

"An intellectual, creative challenge."

"You know the concept team is not for interns," he says, sitting across from me, his desk clean of paperwork he quickly delegates to his assistant.

"I know, but I'm almost done with my internship." I muster the courage I felt with Sebastian and ask, "Could you just try me out? In lieu of the raise I didn't get."

He sighs, clearly guilted. "Well, our concept team is already established. We don't necessarily need fresh blood."

Normally, I would have accepted this limit. "So can I just sit in on the meetings?"

"I suppose. Let me check with them."

"I prefer something in the *shtachim*." The "territories."

"We've just secured a tender for Ma'ale Adumim. Does that count?"

"It depends who you ask," I say, smirking, thinking Sebastian and his German friends would probably consider this well-established Jerusalem suburb a "settlement." Like Ariel, Ma'ale Adumim is a city that most Europeans resent as a formidable obstacle to a contiguous Palestinian state. Working on such a project would be an apt counterbalance to Sebastian's foreskin. "I'd be very grateful. Thank you."

CHAPTER NINE

Nalaga'at is a joint Arab-Jewish events center located in Jaffa. It means, "Please Touch"—appropriately. I still want to touch Sebastian even if the "Battle of the Bands" is a typical Leftie event where they'll probably bash the settlements.

The auditorium stage is set up with a slew of instruments and microphones for the joint Arab-Israeli performances, although the touchy-feely, co-existence model hasn't extended to the families. Visibly Jewish Israelis sit on one side of the auditorium while visibly Muslim Arabs sit on the other, as if an apartheid wall separated them. The Arabs are distinguished by their darker appearance, more formal wear, and women's hijabs. The Jewish Israelis appear more diverse in skin tone and style, with most wearing jeans. Only one man is wearing a *kippah*.

A completely different group sits in the first few rows: the Germans, identifiable by their height, light tones, and precise, relaxed movements. Here, they're looked up to by all sides. I find Sebastian and give him a "break-a-leg" hug.

The emcees of the evening are two students: a Jewish girl and an Arab boy, both sixteen. They take to the microphones dressed like models for junior wear. I wouldn't be able to tell who was Jewish and who was Arab if not for their accents articulating English words.

They introduce the founder of the "Music for Peace" program, an aging German rocker named Axl Riemer. Upon semi-retirement, Riemer decided to start a foundation dedicated to promoting peace around the world. His first destination: Israel-Palestine. Next year, he hopes to bring the program to other conflict areas, like Syria or Iraq. No wonder he started in Israel; it's peaceful enough to host them.

Riemer takes the stage, his straggly, gray-blonde hair up in a ponytail.

"Thank you all for welcoming us to your cities, your homes, and your hearts," he says in a strong German accent, carrying himself with cool rocker charisma. "We spent the week in Haifa, Tel Aviv-Jaffa, East Jerusalem, West

Jerusalem, and Ramallah. We'd like to thank the Israeli authorities for granting permits to the parents and children of Ramallah so that they could be here for this historic concert.

"People say peace isn't possible here, but judging from how well these young musicians play together, we know it is. Even though the Palestinians from the West Bank and the Israelis couldn't meet during the week, we found a place where they could: music. Our idea was simple. We didn't only give these students practical tools for writing a song and performing in a band. We wanted to show them how we, like music, are all built from the same 'flesh and blood,' which, in the case of music, is scales and chords.

"The four groups composed pop-rock songs using the classic pop chord progression: first, fourth, and fifth. We chose to compose in the key of C major because, as musicians here know, that's the happiest scale, and we're optimistic about the possibilities for peace.

"In writing the songs, our team of very talented musicians from Germany, Israel, and Palestine, as well as a joint Israeli-Palestinian team of mediators, led discussions on the Palestinian-Israeli conflict—the fear of terror on the Israeli side and the fear of dispossession and disenfranchisement on the Palestinian side.

"Today we spent the entire day rehearsing, mixing the teams up to form new bands, so that they could learn each other's' languages, musical and beyond. We know that Israel is still coping from last year's surge in terror attacks. And we know Palestinians continue to feel desperation living under occupation. But we hope this event teaches everyone to reject the cycle of violence. There's a better way to make a change: using our voices.

"As Germans, we know the importance of peace and the horrors of war. We had an incredible experience being in this amazing country, built out of the ashes of the Holocaust, doing what we can to make this world still an even better place, where hatred and racism are a thing of the past."

The crowd claps, not so enthusiastically, but they clap.

"*Danke. Shokran. Todah.* Thank you."

Riemer has confirmed the theme of the songs: equalizing Israelis and Palestinians, leveling their respective grievances to the same moral ground. Characterizing the conflict as a "cycle of violence" renders all of us beasts. Israeli soldiers monitoring Palestinian towns are no different than the Palestinian terrorists they seek to find and stop.

Still, in the spirit of the event, I keep a hopeful mind as the emcees come back and introduce "Learn," originating in Haifa.

The stage quickly becomes crowded with a total of eight Jewish and Arab players and singers, although it's still hard to tell who is what, except for the light, tall Germans accompanying them, like Sebastian.

He calls out "one, two, three," to introduce a cheesy, but sweet, pop-rock song that starts with:

Learn, learn, learn
Learn to change, Learn to grow
Hear my side, and I'll hear yours

Learn, learn, learn,
We dream of peace, the end of war
Just hear my side, and I'll hear yours

Stylistically, the song is well executed with catchy melodies and harmonies. Some of the teenagers are smiling, clearly enjoying themselves. Others appear nervous. A few seem like they don't even know what they're singing, not that I pay much attention to the teens. My focus is on Sebastian and those very capable fingers strumming that guitar. When the song's over, the young performers walk off stage, giggling in triumph. The Jewish side claps more enthusiastically than the Arab side.

The emcees introduce "Love," originating in Tel Aviv:

We all have mouths, mouths that speak
We all have hands, hands that play
Voices that sing, sing of a world of love

A world of love, is that so hard?
A world of love, with open hearts

Love, love, love, it's all we ask
Love, love, love, an easy task

Then comes "Dream" from Ramallah. The emcees explain how the Tel

Aviv team had contributed a rap to the song since Palestinians couldn't host Israelis.

> *We dream of doors, not walls*
> *We dream of songs, not guns*
> *We dream, dream, dream, of that time when we are free*
> *Free to roam together by the sea*

A young rapper in gansta gear waltzes on stage with:

> *We've built enough walls b'tween our land, our hearts*
> *Let's knock 'em down, and make a new start*
> *We're all afraid, but we can overcome*
> *To talk with the other, to dream on the run*

With each successive performance, the applause increases in volume and genuineness. "Peace" from Jerusalem closes the show.

> *Two different people, walking side by side*
> *On the road to peace, there's nowhere to hide*
> *We're here together, we have no choice*
> *An eternal city, the birthplace of hope*

> *Nowhere to hide, we're both here*
> *The sun is shining, the paths are clear*
> *Nowhere to hide, so take my hand*
> *We'll build together this beautiful land*

Finally, a standing ovation, but I, like half the audience, stay seated.

If I were an average do-gooder, my heart would be filled with so much awe at this spectacle. Muslims and Jews, Palestinians and Israelis, singing together about "love and peace!" But the entire event has boycotted the people who stand to be violently uprooted, maligned, and discriminated against by this learning, loving, dreaming, peace-ing.

I approach Sebastian at the foot of the stage where he is unplugging equipment.

"You're so talented," I say, focusing on style not substance. "Very professional performances! You groomed some real stars there."

"*Todah!* We're cleaning up a bit, and then I'll meet you upstairs and introduce you to people."

In the lobby, where refreshments are being served, families and students mingle about, all proud and excited. In the corner, a television crew is conducting interviews. As I wait for Sebastian, Aviram texts me.

"Great meeting you on Friday night! Feeling spontaneous? A new bar opened on Ibn Gabirol. Wanna check it out with me later?"

"So sorry. Normally I would, but I have plans tonight," I answer, wondering if his message is a sign to abandon the leftist Sebastian. "Another night?"

"Sure."

About fifteen minutes later, Sebastian takes me by the arm, as if to show me off to his friends. He introduces me first to Lukas, the bassist. An inch taller than Sebastian, with blue eyes and brown hair, Lukas is also handsome but not as handsome as "my German." I wonder if I should set up his friends with Ariella or Dana. *Let us each have our own private German!*

"This is Nilly, my private Israeli tour guide I told you about," Sebastian says. *How else did he describe me? Did he objectify me to his friends the way I objectified him—his own private "settler?"*

"Nice to meet you," Lukas says, shaking my hand. "He told me about some great places you took him to. I have to come back and try them. What's that place called? 'Mazo?'"

"Miznon," I say.

"Yeah. Sounds great."

"You should definitely try it," I say. "You had a good time here?"

"Amazing. There's so much to see, and the people are so friendly. And this program—I learned so much."

The drummer, Tim, looks like a Viking with his 6'5" husky frame and blonde, triangular beard.

"Nice to meet you!" Tim says after our introduction.

"You're a great drummer," I say, sticking to the truth.

"*Danke,*" he says.

Benjamin, the keyboardist, comes over. He's a hipster type with long hair and an arm plastered with tattoos.

"Are you going to steal Sebastian from us again tonight?" he asks. *They all seem to know about me.*

"I see you enough in Berlin," Sebastian tells him.

Now for the women. They're not as hot as the men, but then again, German women don't interest me.

"Nice meeting you," says Anka, a vocal coach, through crooked teeth. She's pale and dainty to the point of looking fragile.

"Great meeting you," says Janin, a guitarist, who, unlike Anka, comes off masculine with her deep voice and bulky build.

I answer in kind—the extent of our conversation.

Before we leave, Sebastian introduces me to the Mansour family, his new friends from East Jerusalem. The parents, Nabil and Hanin, must be in their mid-fifties. The father puts his palm on his chest in lieu of shaking my hand while Hanin shakes my hand limply. She's wearing a traditional Muslim dress hiding the body of a woman who clearly eats well while Nabil looks distinguished in a brown button-down and sports jacket.

Sebastian is particularly keen on introducing me to Ismael, their twenty-seven-year-old son. Wearing jeans and a T-shirt, the dark-skinned, black-eyed handsome Ismael could pass for a Mizrahi Jew—a Jew hailing from a Middle Eastern country. He doesn't properly shake my hand but clasps it quickly. I have no idea if religious Muslim men are even allowed to shake a woman's hand, let alone a "settler's."

"He might come over for Christmas," Sebastian tells me and puts his arm around Ismael. I'm jealous of Sebastian's touch—and an invitation to Berlin that Sebastian hasn't extended to me.

"I'll really try, bro," Ismael says.

A young woman standing a few feet away is looking at us, scornfully, from the corner of her eye. Ismael calls her over and introduces her as his older sister, Amira. She has a pretty face with hazel eyes that sparkle against the glittered edges of a flower-printed hijab. Her attempt at trendy Muslim style comes in the form of fitted jeans and a beige tunic.

"*Ahalan*," Amira says to me, suspicion in her gaze.

"Are you also a musician?" I ask Amira.

"No, no. I studied nursing. I work at a clinic in Jerusalem."

"Ah. Very nice."

Normally, I like conversing with everyday Israeli Arabs. Jews and Muslim Arabs interact almost daily, in business and at universities, for a kind of real, grassroots, unmoderated peace. My Arab study partner at Ariel University was always kind to me, once donating to me a sketchbook and even inviting me to her house for the *Iftar*, the break-the-fast feast after Ramadan. But Amira's guarded demeanor doesn't encourage me to continue the conversation.

The crowd begins to disperse. The Germans, filled with self-congratulation, get ready to celebrate over beers at some bar in Jaffa.

"You should go with them," I tell Sebastian, knowing that if we meet, I would not be able to hold back my true thoughts about the show. Besides, I have Aviram as a backup.

"Why? This is our last night together."

"Are you sure?" I ask, feeling like I should warn him.

"Don't be silly, Nilly."

We hardly speak as I drive to my neighborhood for drinks near my house. I take us to Landwer, a restaurant-café chain designed with warm, wooden tones, suggesting a place where people can talk intimately.

"Is this place German owned?" Sebastian asks after he orders a beer and chicken nuggets. I suffice with tea. I have no appetite.

"Why?"

"I think 'Landwer' is a German name. In German, the 'w' is pronounced like a 'v.'"

"I have no idea," I say with an unintended edge to my voice. I look at the menus. "'Founded 1919.'"

He asks the waitress, and, indeed, the original café was founded in Berlin by a German Jew who fled Nazi Germany and started a coffee-roasting company in Tel Aviv. This German-Israel connection could either be auspicious—or foreboding. I choose the latter. This will be his send-off back to his friends, back to Germany.

"What's bothering you?" Sebastian asks.

"It's just that you're leaving tomorrow," I say. I can't believe that even after I exploded the F-bomb, I still feel a need to filter my words.

"I know," he says after biting into a nugget. "You sure you don't want?" he asks.

"Yeah," I say. *Sharing food is too romantic.*

"So what did you really think of tonight?" *He reads me too well.*

I take a sip of tea as I say, my heart tense, "It was cute."

"Only cute?"

I pause before letting out my next words, heavily, "Fine. It was worse than cute. It was predictable, naive, cliché. First of all, if this is supposed to be a program about peace, why weren't 'settler groups' invited to participate? Why didn't you go to a place like Ariel, for example, and make some songs with them?"

"I told you. We don't go into Jewish settlements as a matter of policy. A lot of people think they're 'obstacles to peace.'"

"If we're 'obstacles to peace,' shouldn't we be the stars of the show?" This time, I count myself as a "settler." "I mean, peace is made between enemies. And if Palestinians and settlers are enemies, they're the ones who should be singing together, who should work things out the most."

"According to the international community, they're illegal."

"That same law-abiding, international community that stood idly by as the Nazis gassed Jews in Auschwitz?"

The A-bomb has stunned him. He stops eating and purses his lips. *This will be over soon.*

"They're not illegal," I continue. "At best, they're disputed. But if all you do is sing about love and peace, you'll muffle the truth. You won't learn how Jews are indigenous to the land of Israel, especially Judea, having lived here continuously for over 2,000 years. How the Balfour Declaration of 1917 and the San Remo Conference of 1920 pledged these lands to the Jewish people. How the Jordanians handed out land deeds like candy when they illegally occupied the West Bank between 1950 and 1967, an occupation that didn't seem to bother the 'international community.' How the Arab war against Jews in these lands started way before the 'settlements' existed, way before Israel's victory in the Six-Day War. Actually, it started even before the founding of the State of Israel."

He sits back and puts his hands on his lap, which I know would rather cover his face from shrapnel.

"That's all way over their heads," he says. "And, honestly, way over my head. It's hard enough to get Palestinians to sing with 'regular' Israelis. We have to start somewhere."

"You're being played, you Germans."

"What do you mean, 'us Germans?'"

"They feed off your German guilt to make you feel like you're the good guys making a difference. Finally, you Germans aren't the bad guys anymore; you're the saviors. But this *kumbaya* means nothing if you keep scapegoating the settlements. Talk about a 'show.' The Arabs couldn't defeat us in conventional war, so they're trying to defeat us in the war of public opinion, making us out to be aggressors, occupiers, 'colonialists,' no better than Nazis."

"And you Jews think that just because you went through horrible murder you get a moral blank check to do what you want."

Woah. Did he just say something antisemitic? I think that's bona-fide antisemitic. The truth comes out. *That's it. I've had enough.* I take out my wallet from my purse and throw twenty shekels onto the table to pay for my tea. "I had a great time with you, but 'we Jews' don't need a lecture in morality from you Germans."

I leave, something I probably should have done last week. Now I'll go out with an American-Israeli man with whom I'll need no filter.

Walking on the empty pavement, I put on my scarf. The temperature has dropped by a few degrees in the last hour.

With no destination in mind, I text Aviram: "My plans were cut short. You still going to the bar?"

"I'm there now!" He texts me the address, within walking distance. I continue along Ibn Gabirol, feeling pleased and even amazed by my courage in speaking my mind and getting up.

Just as I'm about to text Aviram that I'm on my way, Sebastian comes up from behind near a "Späti" and a burger joint. Tel Aviv bats are flying overhead, inside and out of the trees lining the pavement.

"Nilly, I'm sorry," he calls out. I turn around to face him. "That came out really bad. I didn't mean that. This is so intense. I was not prepared for this conversation. I really thought you'd be inspired, impressed. I didn't realize how sensitive you are about these issues. I didn't mean to lecture you. For the record, I'm not naive. I don't let them compare Israelis to Nazis. I think I was upset that you attacked me as a German, so I hit back."

This is the most soulful I've seen his eyes, more soulful than when he sang that lullaby.

I sigh, easily surrendering, and not only because his short speech has convinced me that he doesn't hate Israel or Jews. I'm not so noble. Deep down, I probably wanted him to chase me. I wanted a German to chase a Jew in abject apology.

"It's okay," I say. "I'm sorry, too. I know you mean well, and I'm sure the program does some good, but it's just—argh—I'm so sick of people ganging up on Israel, especially the settlements, with all these lies and accusations. Especially Germans. I mean, I hope you don't mind my saying, but you really should know better. Don't you have your own problems to deal with in Germany? I mean, it's very sweet that you're trying to help, but this our shit."

"You're right. We have our own problems. Our own shit. The refugee crisis. The rise of the far right. I suppose it's easier to deal with another country's problems." He pulls me by the arms while I roll my eyes. "You see. I'm learning from you, Nilly. That's why I like you. You're different. Interesting. You make me think. You're more than just a holiday flirt. You really made my time here very special."

"You're also interesting," I say. "And different. Very different. And very beautiful. Did I ever tell you that? Well, now I have. Not that it matters because I still think it's better we part ways. This is impossible. You live in Germany. I live in Israel. I'm Jewish. You're not. You hang out with people who think I'm an 'obstacle to peace.' Not only that, but I didn't tell you: I design apartments for those 'obstacles to peace.' My firm builds in Judea and Samaria, 'Occupied Territory.' We'll only butt heads. And last night was…wow. But this can't go anywhere. You should be with your friends tonight."

"I don't know where this will go either, but I do know that I don't want to be with them. I want to be with you." He pushes me closer and examines my face. "Did I ever tell you how much I love your…nose." He kisses it.

"My Jewish nose?"

"Yes."

He kisses it again. I can't help but crack up. *I want to be with him, too.*

"And I love your Aryan eyes," I say.

"Don't talk to me like that," he says, grabbing me by the neck in a light chokehold. "Actually, don't talk at all."

He kisses me forcefully to shut me up. I forget to text Aviram as he pushes me by the ass toward my apartment, another apt correction to history. A German making sure a Jew finds her way home.

CHAPTER TEN

As we climb the two floors to my place, he grabs my crotch from behind until we get to the door. Inside, he quickly takes off my dress and shoves me on the bed so that I'm lying on my back in just my bra, panties, and silk scarf.

"What are you do—" I manage to say, not in protest but curiosity.

"I told you: no talking," he says, covering my mouth. "Stay here and don't move." I'm a horrible—or good—Jew and obey his orders. They turn me on.

Keeping one hand on my stomach, forcing me down, he reaches for the sleeping mask on my nightstand and places it firmly over my eyes so that I can't see anything, not even through the slits. He then takes off my scarf and ties it over my mouth to gag me.

Blinded, I hear him unfasten his belt, and I wonder if I'll need a safe word more than ever. *What if he whips me with it?* But he uses the belt to tie my wrists together and then moves my cuffed hands over my head.

I hear his footsteps against the hardwood floor. *Where is he going? The bathroom? His friends? Is he going to punish me for not fawning over his noble quest for peace? Is he taking out his hatred of Israeli policies on me?* A true act of cruelty would be to leave me like this.

I'm relieved when I hear him fussing with some sort of object near the sofa. His feet stomp near me again. He unzips his pants. I feel a sharp poke at the base of my right foot. *A stick? A pen? A tool he hid in his jacket? Maybe he's into BDSM. Maybe Berliners are into kinky stuff.*

I can literally feel my heart pounding from within because my attention is forced inward. He trails the stick, or whatever it is, up my ankle, along my outer shin, slowly, upward to my inner thigh, forcing my legs apart. I feel my hair stand up on end as he brings the stick into the nook between my thighs, over the wet cotton of my panties.

Will he stick that unknown object inside me? I kind of want him to, but, unfortunately, the stick goes no deeper, and he leaves me to writhe in uncertainty. I long to scratch the tingles I feel all over my body, but when I try to break my hands free from the belt, he grabs them and holds them together.

With the object, he presses down on my left nipple from underneath my bra, hard enough to elicit a muffled cry of pain. He repeats the procedure on my right nipple.

Finally, a popping noise. *A cap!* It must be a marker he took from my desk. He pulls down my panties to write something on my lower abs. The felt of the marker tickles me.

I sense him hovering over me. He takes his pants off.

I know if I wanted him to stop, I'd find a way. But I don't. In fact, I've wanted him to take me from the moment I saw him.

I hear a tear. A condom wrapper. He removes my panties, and a hard object presses against my crotch—and it's not the marker. His uncircumcised baton presses slowly, deep inside me, and I'm completely entrapped by his body and my desire for him.

As he trespasses inside, I scream and moan through the loosening scarf until he slams a pillow over my head. Completely blinded and nearing suffocation, I focus on the baton whipping me up from the inside, making my body quiver. His force on the pillow weakens, but my yells still come out suppressed, which is good because the entire building would hear me otherwise.

His chest is firmly pressed against mine, and he removes the pillow just as he's about to come. My eye mask has fallen off, and I look into his eyes. Now they have a soul—a cruel one. As he finishes off, I shake, violently, along with the entire room.

Finally, he unshackles me. I look down at the words on my abs: "Occupied Territory." An arrow points to my crotch.

"I don't boycott the Occupied Territories," he says getting up, looking satisfied. "I conquer them."

I fall asleep on his warm, sweaty chest, utterly defeated.

But once morning light seeps through the window, my strength returns. I must retaliate.

I reach for his groin underneath the covers. It's not yet erect, allowing me to feel his loose foreskin. To "remove" it, I wrap my hand around his cock. The foreskin retracts as his weapon against me hardens. He then reaches for my clit, but I quickly grab his hand and push it away. This isn't a duel.

I find the mask and put it over his eyes, but I have no patience for the other tools, not that I need them for him. He is a willing victim.

Mimicking his technique, I haul the covers off him and navigate his body with the marker, tracing his foot, his inner legs, then bringing it around his balls, around his upright shaft, and up to his chest, where I poke his pecs. Finally, I bring it back down to his abdomen. The felt glides on his smooth skin. I find a condom.

He doesn't resist as I saddle over him. I rock back and forth on him like a soldier on horseback racing to victory, holding onto his pecs like they're handles. I normally don't orgasm from this position, but the friction of his foreskin must be causing extra stimulation, and I come quickly, as does he.

I dismount from my ride.

He looks down and reads: "Product of Germany."

We call a truce as I turn my back to him and fall asleep again.

We wake up at 9 am, and I don't care that I'm late for work.

"Come to Berlin," he says to my relief. At this moment, I couldn't bear the thought of not seeing him again. If he had "conquered" me to ensure I'd feel bound to follow him to Berlin, he has succeeded. Ariella was right. Sleeping with him has made me feel attached. I'm his prisoner of war.

"Is that an official invitation?"

"Yes. You could stay with me. I have a cute little apartment in a neighborhood called Prenzlauer Berg. It's kind of like Neve Tzedek. Used to be slums, but now it has a lot of cute shops and cafés. This time, I'll be your perfect tour guide. Show you around, even cook you dinner. Don't worry, it'll be kosher. I'll make my killer gnocchi without shrimp. You'll have so much fun you won't want to leave."

That's what I'm afraid of.

"I'll think about it," I say.

After a quick cup of instant coffee, he orders a cab. I sadly hug and kiss him goodbye near my door.

"What's your Facebook," he asks.

"Nilly Haddad," I say. "And yours?"

"Sebastian Schröder," he says, explaining how he usually spells his name with an umlaut.

S.S.

"Let me know when you land, okay?" I ask.

"Of course, silly, sweet, pretty, crazy, sexy, settler Nilly."

"Thank you, SS," I say mockingly, in retaliation, but he doesn't laugh. "I hope you don't mind if I make Holocaust jokes sometimes."

"You can make them, but I can't." he says. "Most Germans can't, so I won't always laugh, either."

In lieu of laughter, he kisses me on my Jewish nose.

I close the door after him, sad but also elated. He doesn't hate me. Actually, this German, this man, Sebastian—SS—likes me. He really likes me!

CHAPTER ELEVEN

After work, I meet Dana at my apartment to tell her my war story and show her the scene of the "conquest."

Sitting on my sofa, which I feel like Sebastian christened, we check out his Facebook page. It's filled mostly with pictures of him at various performances. His most recent post is a group picture taken in Jaffa with all program participants.

"He's so hot," Dana says.

"Don't remind me." I sigh. "So should I go to Berlin?"

"Of course you should."

I look at my phone. He must have landed by now, but he hasn't been online since this morning.

"What should I tell my mom?" I ask. "Lie?"

"Yes."

"Oh, God. This is so stupid. I'm thirty-one-fucking-years old!"

"I know."

"It shouldn't be like this. Judaism shouldn't make us have to lie to our parents." I feel like Esau who rejected his birthright for a simple pleasure: the red stew that Jacob, his younger twin brother, had cooked for him, in a ruse. Jacob knew that Esau, weary from one of his hunting excursions, would trade his first-born rights for a delicious meal. Sebastian is my red stew.

"Why open up this can of worms when it's not serious?" Dana advises.

"And never will be," I mutter. "If I want to start a family, I can't do so in Germany. It has to be here, with an Israeli, a Jewish guy."

"Why?"

"Because that's just how it is," I say and sip tea in confusion. I don't have a more exact answer.

"Well, good luck with that, Nilly." Dana shakes her pretty, dirty blonde head. "You know how awful the situation is here. The man market is really bad. Maybe it's our age. While you were having the most erotic week of your life, I went out on two dates. One of them just got out of a divorce with two kids. He kept talking about his ex-wife like I was his therapist.

"This other guy lives with his mother because he's in between jobs. He cut the date short, and I think it's because I ordered an expensive cocktail, and he didn't want to pay for another. He didn't tip the waitress because he said she was rude, and then, of course, he wanted to come up for 'coffee.'

"I think I'm going to give up dating here and, worse case, have a baby on my own. It's a supply and demand thing. The good ones get married young, like after the army. The single guys our age are either fucked up or on their chapter two—not that there's anything wrong with that, but it's more complicated. So, if you won't go for yourself, go for me. And bring back a German for me!"

"Well, he did have a pretty cute friend, Lukas. The bassist."

"Now you tell me!"

"Okay, okay, I'll go! So, what should I tell my mom?"

"Tell her you need to go there for work," Dana says. "Truth is, your profession is international. Tell her they're sending you to work on some Israeli housing development there."

"Not a bad idea."

We check out flights together. Round trips cost only $200 in December.

"Now I just have to coordinate with Sebastian. I hope he writes to me soon." I pick up the phone from the coffee table to check it again. He was last online at 7:33 pm.

At around 9 pm, Dana leaves, and still no text.

I binge on a new television show about Vikings to get my mind off him, but the conquests of these blonde Nordic hunks only make me miss him more. I check my phone again. He was online ten minutes ago.

Now I'm left to Google him, which exacerbates my longing. He appears mostly in concert announcements, looking sexy with his guitar. No doubt he has a ton of groupies. Maybe he didn't mean the invitation. Or maybe he was offended by my SS comment. Maybe I should not have made that Holocaust joke.

Finally, at 9:21 pm, I notice he's online. I wait for movement to indicate he's "typing" to me. None.

By 10 pm, I'm glad I called him "SS" because that's what he is—a mean Nazi who wants to ravage a Jewish body and then kick it to the curb.

"Ariella, he's a total *schmuk*," I say to her over the phone close to midnight, knowing she'd be less forgiving of him than Dana.

"Why? What happened?"

I pause in shame. "We had sex last night," I say, without going into the details I'm not yet sure she'd appreciate. "I haven't heard from him since he left this morning."

"Nilly, now I get to say 'I told you so.' Now you're attached. And now he won't rush to text you because he's already conquered you."

I smile. "In more ways than one." Now, I go into the details.

"That's hot, Nilly," Ariella says, begrudgingly. "Even I admit. Listen, I think you just have to look at this as an experience. I'm sure he'll write to you eventually, but maybe it's better this falls off. You go to Berlin, you'll just get more involved, and it will get complicated. Your life's here. Your career's here. Your family."

"Yeah, maybe he'll do me a favor by not writing to me," I say, although I can't resist rehashing. "Do you think he was offended that I called him 'SS'?"

"If he is, then he's a baby. You can't worry about that. You really have to stop second guessing yourself. He doesn't deserve it."

As much as I try to convince myself that I'm better off not hearing from him, I cry myself to sleep, angry at myself for surrendering to him, angry at my country for always reminding me about the Holocaust, and angry at the Holocaust—not for murdering so many millions—but for making my relationship with a German man I like so difficult, so impossible.

I wake up to the alarm at 7:30 am after a shoddy night's sleep, and there I see it! A message from him, like morning dew on my phone. Suddenly, I'm wide awake and energized.

He left no words, only a video. This can't be good. He's too nice to break up with me over a text, so he'll let me down via video.

There he is, as hot as red stew, holding his guitar on a sofa in that place called Prenzlauer Berg.

"Hi, Nilly, I'm back. It's been an exhausting day, but I stayed up to write this ditty. I hope you like it."

He strums a few chords with the happy, cute melody of a children's song.

Silly Nilly, we met on the beach
Silly Nilly, I thought wow—she's out of my reach
Silly Nilly, oh so pretty
Silly Nilly, so I wrote this ditty

To see if she'll come to Germany

Silly Nilly, what a nice surprise
Silly Nilly, let's watch the sunrise
Silly Nilly, from Ariel
Silly Nilly, with the body of a bell

But now there's one thing I ask, pretty Nilly
Will you please come here and touch my willy?

I'm giddy with laughter, even though the last line makes me want to punch him. *Is that the only reason he wants me there?* Actually, no. After that song, I don't want to punch him. I want to do exactly what his last line requests.

"I'm convinced!" I write back. "Should we chat over WhatsApp to make a plan?"

"Do you have Skype?"

"Yes, but I don't use it much. I'll turn it on for you…"

"Yeah, baby."

We make a plan to Skype on Thursday night. Knowing I'll see him, even if only through a screen, calms me for the rest of the week.

I perform well at work. I sit in on a conception meeting for the Ma'ale Adumim housing project, taking the "fly-on-the-wall" approach to understand why they chose the template they chose and how they plan to modify the plan to suit the site, whose natural hills have already been flattened, which is a shame given I'm feeling more imaginative than ever.

On Wednesday, Zimmerman gives me approval to redeem my five remaining vacation days for early December, provided I complete some assignments on the Har Homa project.

Since he left, I imagine Sebastian beside me every night before going to sleep—on top of me and inside me—so I'm actually frustrated when I see him in front of me, through a computer screen, speaking from his kitchen table, the table where I might soon eat and drink with him. He looks so squeezable in a sweatshirt, his dirty blonde bangs messy.

We spend the first few minutes staring at each other and smiling, interspersed with small talk. Finally, we compare schedules.

"What about the second week of December?" I ask.

"That won't work," he says.

My heart sinks. "Why not?"

"It's too long to wait. Can't you come earlier?"

I sigh in relief. "I have some work to finish. It's the earliest I could come."

He opens his phone and checks his calendar. "So far, I have a gig that week and some rehearsals and guitar lessons, but I'll try to take off as much as I can. December is a great time to be here. The Christmas markets will be open."

"Christmas markets?" *From foreskins to Christmas markets.*

"Yeah, they're awesome. You'll see."

"Ok. So I'll get the tickets. You sure?" I ask myself as much as him.

"Don't be silly, Nilly."

The next day, I call my mother from my office line.

"Ima, I have some news that I'm not sure will make you happy, but it should."

"What? You dating a *goy*?" A non-Jew.

How does she know? She doesn't, really. It's just her way of reminding me of her worst fear.

"No!" I feel like a Jew hiding a German in the basement. I wish I could have a *sichat nefesh*, a heart-to-heart talk, with her and confide that I have a crush on a German man. Maybe, if she were accepting, I'd actually be wiser in my interactions with Sebastian.

"Work wants to send me to Berlin," I say.

"What? Since when do you travel for work?"

"I guess it's a promotion. They like my work and want me to meet with some developers there who want to build something in Berlin." I speak with fake calm to hide that I'm lying. A promotion should induce much more enthusiasm.

"Can't they send someone else?" she asks, clearly irritated.

"I don't want them to send someone else. It's a cool opportunity."

"I would never step foot in there."

The sneer in her voice grates on me. "Ima, it's a new generation. Can we blame the people who weren't born when the Holocaust happened?"

"Doesn't it occur to you how much Jewish blood is flowing in the streets of that country?"

"Actually, most of the blood flowed in Poland." I don't know if I'm being sarcastic. "But that was seventy years ago. If we don't want them to boycott us, then shouldn't we not boycott them?"

"You can't even compare. The boycott of us is antisemitic. The boycott of them is against antisemitism. Let them feel scarred for years to come. Let their grandchildren suffer, too. The Torah says the sins of the fathers visit upon the third and fourth generations."

"So what does that mean? They're all guilty?"

"Yes."

"But Germany's a friend of Israel now. I mean, didn't Merkel say that Israel's security is a *raison d'ê·tre* for Germany?"

I recently read that somewhere.

"She's a fake friend who'll turn on us in a heartbeat," Ima says. "Look what she's doing now, letting all those Muslims in. They traded Jews for Muslims. I guess they deserve it."

I don't argue because I share her concern that opening borders to hundreds of thousands of refugees from Muslim countries steeped in hatred for Israel will increase antisemitism and bring to European soil the merciless terror attacks that I don't wish even upon my enemies, let alone contemporary Germans.

"Ima, what if I go to Holocaust museums and stuff?" I say, in my defense. "Understand more of what Saba and Safta went through."

"I'd never give them money, not even to their Holocaust museums—their crocodile tears."

Should I understand her? Should I feel that resentment, even hatred? I mean, part of me thinks I should. The Nazi generation committed what may have been the greatest crime in human history, certainly the greatest crime against the Jewish people. Maybe we're too easy on even this generation. Let Germany be forever reminded of their sins with a perpetual boycott.

Ah! What a burden! Being a Jew! The burden of history, the burden of ethics, the burden of memory—and now the burden of great, unrequited desire. I wonder what kind of burden Germans feel and what's worse: the burden of extreme victimhood or of extreme aggression.

Then I think how we Jews have our own kind of "racism." Germans weren't allowed to marry Jews under Hitler, but today some Jews aren't allowed to marry Germans. Granted, I wouldn't be executed or jailed if I were to marry Sebastian (thinking too far ahead), but my own mother would probably shun me while my father might learn to live with it, eventually.

I've asked for courage to be honest with Sebastian—should I also ask for courage to honest with my mother?

"Ima, this isn't a high school field trip for which I need your permission."

"Fine. I'm not happy about it, but if you must go, then be careful. Too many Muslims there. Europe is not safe for Jews anymore."

"Okay, Ima," I say. "Not that Israel's so safe for us either these days. More Jews died here than in Germany in the last few years."

"It's because they hardly have any Jews left."

CHAPTER TWELVE

The world has become one large waiting room. To ease the agony, I learn Sebastian's language. Yes, I'm learning the language of the Nazis. I'm learning the language that ordered the liquidation of my grandmother's ghetto and the cold-blooded murder of my great uncle. Yes, I'm learning the language that murdered six million.

It's easy with the Duolingo language app. And surprisingly exhilarating.

Guten Tag. Good day.

Danke. Thank you.

Ich bin Nilly. I am Nilly

Du bist Sebastian. You are Sebastian.

Ich bin Jude.

Du bist Deutscher.

Ich bin Israelin.

Du bist Nazi.

The next time I scream in pleasure, it will be in German. "*Sehr gut!*" und "*Mehr.*"

We've started counting down the four weeks until T: "Touchdown."

On T-23, we have our second Skype call. He gives me a tour of his apartment: his modern kitchen with its well-stocked liquor cabinet, his living room/studio with a huge sofa, and, of course, his bedroom with a queen-sized bed. I feel as excited as a toddler discovering a new park with a shiny, state-of-the-art monkey bar playset.

On T-20, he sends me another ditty: *Twenty days to Berlin/Twenty days 'til the fun begins/Twenty days 'til you're here/Twenty days 'til you're near.*

On T-16, we discuss plans but most of the time just stare at each other.

On T-14, he sends me a picture of him and his mom in front of the Elbe River in Dresden. He went to his hometown so that he could borrow his mother's car for our week together. I'm touched that he told her about me and jealous that he could. He must really like me, and I hope enough to take me to Dresden; the landscape behind him looks beautiful.

In return, I send him a picture of the bare mountains surrounding Ariel, with the caption: "Occupied Territory." He leaves that unanswered.

On T-9, he sings to me again, this time bare-chested: *Nine days to Berlin/ Nine days 'til the fun begins/Nine days 'til you're here/Nine days 'til you're near.* Nine days until my hands crawl up that chest.

For the first time in my life, I fantasize about having phone sex, but I don't suggest it, mostly because I'm too prudish for that but also because I don't want to set up my visit as a sex holiday, not that it could be one. Unfortunately, I'm probably getting my period right before I land, and I don't like having sex on my period.

On T-7, Safta is diagnosed with pneumonia, and I must go to the hospital. With medication and rest, she's expected to recover, even though pneumonia at her age is risky.

I inform Sebastian over text, and he lovingly replies: "*Gute besserung!* I'm sure your visit will make her feel better. She's so lucky to have you, and soon I will be, too!"

In the hospital room, Safta looks at peace on her bed, being fed through an IV. As usual, her face lights up when she sees me. I take her by the hand, so soft and warm, and tell her about my new professional venture in Ma'ale Adumim. She nods, presses my hand, tries to say something but doesn't succeed.

This time, I don't tacitly bring up Sebastian. Safta and Sebastian must learn to co-exist.

After the visit, I'm inspired to send Sebastian a selfie of me and Safta. I write: "She'll make it through. She's a fighter. After all, she survived Auschwitz."

He dodges that A-bomb.

On T-6, he recovers with a picture of a white sheet of paper with "T-6" written in blue marker flanked by two blue stripes from above and below, mimicking the flag of Israel. A message of peace.

On T-4 to T-2, we suffice with sweet nothings and emoticons.

On T-2, I get my period, which means I won't have sex until it's over. In Jewish Orthodox law, married couples aren't even allowed to have sex until ten days after a woman's period, at which point she ritually cleanses herself in the *mikveh*. I never planned to keep that marital law, but learning about this method of temporary abstinence has conditioned me toward period-free sex. Ariella advises me not to tell him in advance but to take my period as an opportunity to develop our non-sexual relationship.

Finally, T-1! He sends a video of him in front of a famous Berlin landmark. "Me and the TV Tower are waiting for you!" he says and, to close this twenty-eight-day waiting period, the countdown song: *One day to Berlin....*

PART TWO

BERLIN

CHAPTER ONE

Touchdown.

As I'm ushered to border control after landing with El Al, I want to call my mom and cry: *Ima, this is a miracle! A Jew coming to Berlin with an Israeli passport to be stamped by a German! Who would've thought seventy years ago!*

Instead, I just text her to let her know I landed.

After getting my luggage, I duck into the bathroom to refresh my make-up. I exit baggage claim—my heart racing, my hands shaking—and there he is, standing in the waiting area wearing a sturdy black jacket, a handsome winter look for him, holding up a cardboard sign that reads: "Silly Nilly."

I laugh and run to him like in the movies. His polite kiss heals the sore that had developed in my heart from his absence. Toward the exit of the Berlin Schönefeld Airport terminal, away from the crowds, we kiss less politely.

When we step outside, I feel an unfamiliar gust of cold, and I put on the winter coat I bought especially for Berlin. He holds my hand as we drive in his mother's Audi, but I really just want to climb on top of him so that I'm driving two German products at once.

Fortunately or not, I don't because I have my period.

Sebastian lives on a street called Danziger Strasse—*Strasse* for "street," of course. I'm surprised how so many English words have their roots in German. Cognates and some Yiddish expressions I know make German easier for me to learn.

His street is so pretty with this *Altbau*, "old building," architecture dating from the turn of the 20th century. The exteriors are much more decorative than Tel Aviv's popular Bauhaus architectural style that focuses on the marriage between form and function. Ironically, Bauhaus originated in Germany and was imported to Israel by German Jews. While some refurbished Bauhaus buildings in Tel Aviv are quite charming with their clean and curvy lines, most grate on my aesthetic sensibilities.

But, as we drive down his *Strasse*, I can't help but wonder what kind of Nazi marches took place on this street, how many swastikas decorated the balconies of these pretty *Altbau* complexes, and how many Jews had been kicked out of them.

Well, some Jews have come back. As we go up the spacious staircase, Sebastian points out a neighbor whose landlord is Israeli. International real estate investors are snatching up properties in Berlin, which are much cheaper compared to apartments in other European capitals and especially Tel Aviv.

I already feel at home in his apartment of hardwood floors and pretty window panes. The place I've seen only through Skype comes to life: his modern kitchen with quality granite counters; his bedroom with that queen-sized bed and fluffy pillows; and his cozy living room/studio with that huge sofa, an entertainment system, some plants, and studio equipment and guitars in the corner.

His unit was not built with the stinginess common to modern Israeli apartments. Once, in the early days of the State, Tel Aviv apartments would accommodate three large bedrooms over 100 square meters. Today, to maximize profit, developers convert the same square area to six-room apartments with tiny bedrooms and cheap finishing.

"What an amazing apartment," I say as I put my luggage down in his bedroom. "I know this is rude, but do you mind if I ask how much you pay?"

What a typical Israeli question. We're always nosy about others' salaries and rents.

"It's okay. Germans always ask that." *Good to know.* "I pay 1,000 Euro."

"Wow. That's almost what I pay for my stupid studio!"

"That's Berlin."

"No wonder so many Israelis choose to move here."

"Yeah, but rents are going up. If I leave, I'm sure the landlord will ask for more. So I don't really want to leave."

"I wouldn't want to either," I say as I begin to open my suitcase. "Can I take a shower?"

"Sure. In the meantime, I'll make my famous gnocchi."

"Yummy!"

"Veggie, no shrimp."

"*Ata motek.*" You're a sweetheart.

I step out of the shower, wearing leggings, a T-shirt, and a jersey sweater, and lean on the doorpost of his kitchen, admiring his adept movements as he expertly cuts spinach. Eric Clapton is playing from an iPad secured into a holster on a liquor cabinet featuring a fine selection of whiskeys, brandies, and herbal liquors.

I go back to the bedroom for an addition to the collection: a bottle of Har Bracha wine.

"Here you go: a product from the West Bank."

"You're a good salesperson for them," he says, then smacks my ass.

"Actually, I brought it because it's delicious. Won many awards."

"One way to find out!"

He takes out two wine glasses, and we sit on the small dining table against the wall. He pours and tips his glass toward mine.

"*Ta'im!*" he says after his first sip.

I happily sip the "settler" wine as I watch him fry garlic in olive oil, adding spinach and capers. Once the gnocchi is ready, he lights two tea light candles on the table and takes out two large plates to serve the meal. He tops the finished dishes with freshly grated Parmesan.

"*Lecker!*" I say after my first delicious bite, enhanced by the wine.

I look up on the wall at a bulletin board tacked with pictures. As we eat, he points out who's who: friends trekking in Vietnam and India, his mother and stepfather, his divorced stepsister and her two children.

"No pictures of your father?"

"No," he says, his tone cold. "We hardly talk, and, if we do, it's mostly for administrative family stuff. I think I told you he wasn't good to my mom. I always had this feeling I had to protect her from him. But he's the one, more than my mom, who really pushed me to be a musician. Said I could be the 'next Wagner.' I don't really understand why because he was more into business, but he was brutal in how often he made me practice piano and, later, guitar. I wonder if I would've been a musician if not for him."

"So, he did some good," I say. "For that I thank him. You *are* very talented."

"Hmm. Thanks. He also let my mother keep the house in Dresden when he met another woman and left. Fortunately, my mother met Alex, my stepdad, when I was sixteen." He points to the large man with a mustache, his arms enveloped over Sebastian's dainty, blonde mother. "A great guy. He was like my father ever since, which is good because I didn't want to be the man of the house anymore. I wanted to travel, see the world."

"Where are your father's parents?" I ask—and not to determine if they were Nazis.

"Only my grandfather's alive, but he has dementia. He lives with my uncle in Rostock, up north, where my father was born. I hardly spent time with him growing up."

"Was he also a drinker?"

"Not that I know of, but," he raises his glass, "I should probably watch my alcohol intake anyway. Don't want to end up like my father."

"You won't," I say, meaning it.

"I know," he says, touched. "And this wine really *is* good!"

"Well, I also have dessert," I say and stand to get it.

"From the West Bank?"

"Of course."

"Because I wouldn't want dessert from anywhere else." He smacks my ass again.

I bring back a gourmet chocolate bar made in the Hebron Hills and sit on his lap. I break off two squares, one for him and one for me, but the slightly sweetened squares soon mesh into one as we kiss. The settlements should market their products as aphrodisiacs, although I can't imagine the more religious settlers wanting them to serve this purpose. My body melts with the "settler" chocolate. He places his hand over the smooth cotton of my leggings toward my inner thigh.

I become even more conscious of my desire because I must curb it. I pull my lips away from his but then lick a drop of chocolate from his lower lip.

"You're finally here," he says, happily.

"Finally, but..." I stammer. I'm about to serve an antidote to the aphrodisiac. "I have some news."

"Uh-oh."

"No, it's not bad. I mean it's bad, but not tragic."

"You have to leave Berlin early?"

"No, no." I sigh in annoyance. I say it quickly, "I have my period. It's the fourth day. It should be totally done the day after tomorrow."

"Oh, that's all?" he asks, unfazed.

"Yeah, I just thought...you wanted me to 'touch your willy.'"

"Well, you still can."

I slap his shoulder gently. "You know what I mean."

"Well, I don't mind. We could use towels."

"No. I don't like having sex when I have my period."

"It's okay. We don't have to have sex tonight. We can just cuddle. My willy can wait."

"Really?" I ask, relieved. I forgot: He knows how to control his urges.

"Really, Silly Nilly. You tired?"

"A bit. It's an hour ahead for me."

"Then I'll tuck you in."

He clears up some of the dishes and literally lifts me up to carry me to his bed. He lays my head on the velvet-colored, silky pillowcase matching the sheets. From the kitchen, he brings back the candles and puts them on his nightstand.

He takes off his jeans and T-shirt so that he's wearing only boxers. The candlelight casts him in stark dark and light shadows, as if he's a model for a Caravaggio painting. He rolls up next to me, and we lie on our sides, facing each other. He places his hands on my upper thigh, and I put my hand on the triangle of hair on his chest. His skin is hot, as if he had lain out all day in the sun. It calms me like a fireplace.

"I don't know how I'll get through the night in the same bed with you," I say.

"Actually, it's better this way. We'll build up the tension. We're good at that."

I turn on my side as he holds me from behind. He's not Abraham but Jacob, rejecting the "red stew" for a greater reward.

CHAPTER TWO

I wake up, well rested from his cuddles, and he's already out of bed. I step into the well-heated living room. The window reveals dreary, gray clouds and unfriendly red brick, but I'm warm and cozy in just a tank. He's on the sofa, in sweats and a T-shirt, fiddling with some chords on his guitar. I don't let him know I'm there so that he doesn't stop playing. The pleasing melodies are the soundtrack of our budding romance.

"Hey, pretty," he says when he finally notices me.

"Do you have to stop?" I ask.

He gets up. "Yes. For this." He kisses me.

"I didn't brush my teeth," I say.

"I don't care."

"When did you wake up?" I ask.

"About a half hour ago. Didn't want to have breakfast without you, so rehearsing for my show on Thursday, which you'll come to. I thought today we'd do a free walking tour of Berlin—well, you just need to tip them. It's not supposed to rain until the evening. They take you to the old Berlin Wall, Checkpoint Charlie, some Nazi buildings, and the Holocaust Memorial." He says "Holocaust Memorial" nonchalantly, as if it's a run-of-the-mill tourist attraction, like an art museum. "And when I go to rehearsals, you could explore on your own. Maybe you want to see the Jewish Museum? I was there a few years ago. Very impressive."

"Good idea. *Ata motek.*" He really is a sweetheart for suggesting the Jewish Museum.

"Come, I'll make some coffee." I follow him to the dim kitchen.

"What would you like to eat?" he asks.

"What do you have?"

"Honestly, I don't eat much for breakfast." He looks through the fridge. "Bread, cheese. I could make toast."

"That sounds good. First, I'll brush my teeth."

I come back from the bathroom to find him in one of my new favorite poses: making coffee with an Italian espresso maker. Usually, I suffice with instant. I sit down at the table with a mug of his refined, strong coffee, reveling in his spoiling me. He plates toast, slices of cheese, and olives on a decorative, wooden tray.

I make an open-faced sandwich and bite into one of the most delicious cheeses I've ever tasted.

"*Lecker!* Such good cheese. What kind is it?"

He hands me the package. Gruyère from Switzerland. 2.99 Euro. Swiss cheese like this would never cost so little in Israel. My country really has to get its act together with "milky" products.

I put on several layers to brave the cold: a tank, a long-sleeve shirt, a knitted sweater, tights, and jeans, all sealed with boots and my new winter jacket. I'm snug. To mark my first day in Berlin, I don my Jewish star pendant, thinking of Safta.

At the door, ready to leave, Sebastian lifts the pendant and says, simply, "Nice."

He drives us to a boulevard called Unter den Linden near Brandenburg Gate, one of the most iconic city "gates" with its Doric columns and an imposing statue of a chariot atop the frieze. We join about twenty people for the "free tour."

Our tour guide is an American named Walter who's been living in Berlin for two years. He asks everyone where they're from: Canada, Australia, Brazil, China, India, and even Malaysia. I say, unapologetically, "Israel."

"What I love about this city is its diversity," Walter says, explaining his reasons for moving here. "And you'll see throughout the tour, it's a city and country that has no shame in admitting: 'I was wrong.' That it's dealing with its horrible past, a huge stain on its history. All this makes it an interesting place to be."

Indeed.

Who knew that German history began before 1933, the year Hitler took power? Walter goes into historical facts about Germany I never knew, like how it first became a modern nation-state in 1871 when the prime minister of one Germanic state, Prussia, united other Germanic states to form the Federal Republic of Germany, which today consists of sixteen states, including Berlin, a city-state.

The first memorial we visit is the most important to me: The Holocaust

Memorial, taking up one city block, appearing like a series of gray, metallic tombstones. *A cemetery?*

"It's called the Memorial to the Murdered Jews of Europe in no uncertain terms," Walter explains on the sidewalk at one end of the memorial. "The German government didn't want to sugarcoat what happened. The Jews were murdered. The Nazis murdered them.

"It was designed by Jewish architect Peter Eisenman and is made up of 2,711 concrete stelae over a sloped ground. The designer did not give any interpretation, leaving it to you. Just walk through and interpret as you wish, but notice that wherever you go, you'll always see a bit of the city."

Sebastian holds my hand as we walk through.

"I don't see graves but buildings," I tell him. "Buildings reaching up to the sky because the people that Hitler destroyed could have built so much. Who knows how many creators—great architects and musicians—he murdered. It doesn't make sense. None at all."

He kisses me on the forehead. "No, it doesn't."

We make our way through the maze, holding hands, and reach a spot where we're engulfed by concrete slabs that must extend twelve feet high.

Finally, he slams me against a stele. After making sure no one is looking, he presses his hands under my shirt and grabs my breasts over my bra, squeezing them. He pushes his body close until I feel his erection. I push him off. We can't have sex here! *But he persists, and I give in because his body overpowers my desire to honor and remember. I reach my hand under his shirt to feel his abs.*

Woah! I must shake off this daydream. *How could I fantasize about Sebastian here? It's so wrong!* Maybe the architect shouldn't have made such a structure, where couples could hide and make out—or wait—is *this* my interpretation?

In Nazi times, people had to hide what they truly loved, what they truly wanted, like if a German loved a Jew, or a Jew loved a German. This *is* supposed to remind us of a cemetery but one for souls: the desires, ambitions, dreams, and loves that people were forced to hide and never fulfill.

Comforted by my new interpretation, I continue to hold Sebastian's hand, guilt-free, as we reach the other side.

We continue on to a plaza near Humboldt University, Albert Einstein's *alma mater.*

"Welcome to Bebelplatz, to a memorial commemorating the infamous book burning of 1933 in which Hitler's thugs burned 20,000 books by authors deemed hostile to the 'German spirit.' These included communists, socialists, classic liberals, pacifists, and, of course, Jews like Sigmund Freud, Karl Marx, and the great German poet, a Jewish convert to Christianity, Heinrich Heine, whose prophetic words are quoted here." He translates the German quote written on a plaque: *That was only a prelude/Wherever they burn books/In the end they burn people. 1820.*

I look through a square, glass plate set into the stone ground. Through my reflection, I see a series of white, empty bookshelves.

"This memorial, called 'The Library,' was designed by Israeli artist Micha Ullman," Walter continues. "Its shelves could have housed all those books that Hitler burned."

The country really has come a long way, hiring an Israeli artist to call attention to this Nazi crime. While the Nazis may have burned books and people, the Jewish artistic spirit lives.

At Checkpoint Charlie, the former main checkpoint between East and West Berlin, I remember again how, after the war, Germany was divided into the capitalistic West and communist East.

Standing in front of a map of Germany hanging near an old stretch of the Berlin Wall, Walter explains how the Allies agreed to divide Germany after World War II between the Russians, Americans, British, and French. While Berlin was an island situated in the heart of East Germany, the Western Allies weren't ready to concede it due to its political and cultural significance. West Berlin served as the only gateway for East Germans seeking to escape to the free, more prosperous West, and millions did.

We walk along remnants of the Berlin Wall constructed around West Berlin by the GDR in August 1961 to prevent this massive brain drain. The Wall became the icon of the Cold War, separating people and ideologies. Hundreds of East Germans died crossing the "death strip" where border police were ordered to shoot to kill anyone who attempted to cross. I never realized how much Germans must have suffered after the war, with their land divided, not that I feel too bad for them, especially considering how German politicians now seek to divide my land into a free Israel and a totalitarian "Palestine."

One remnant of the wall sits alongside the site of the former SS headquarters, today the Topography of Terror museum chronicling the rise of Adolf Hitler and Nazi Germany. The only Nazi building to survive the devastating Allied bombing of Berlin is the former headquarters of the Luftwaffe, the Nazi air force. Walter jokes how it now serves as the headquarters of a different "terror organization," the Finance Ministry.

I wonder why Walter takes us next to a mundane parking lot on a residential street, but Hitler's bunker is underneath our feet. I can't believe I'm standing on the site where Hitler committed suicide with Nazi comrades and Eva Braun, the girlfriend he was wise enough to marry hours before he shot himself and she took a cyanide pill. The Germans and Allies didn't mark the spot of his demise lest it become a neo-Nazi shrine. I wonder how people can live in the apartments above, knowing one of the world's most evil men lived and died in these grounds.

The Holocaust is no longer a horror I see in documentaries. I'm in the heart of where Hitler planned the genocide of Jews and, essentially, the murder of humanity. It's all around me. Yet, so are cafés and restaurants where I can enter freely, not only as a Jew, but also as an Israeli, a Jew with my own state. I wish I could call Ima and say, "See, the Germans really are making amends!"

Walter ends the tour at a *shwarma* joint, his recommendation for lunch.

"The owners here are Lebanese, but they employ Syrian refugees," Walter explains. "And while the refugee issue is a hot topic here, no one would disagree that the Middle Eastern immigrants make the best *shwarma* in the city!"

Best *shwarma* or not, I clutch my Jewish star pendant, sensing I should hide it. The place reminds me of falafel and *shwarma* joints in unfriendly Arab Israeli towns. Above the menu on the wall is a framed photograph of the Temple Mount, the symbol of Palestinian sovereignty over the land of Israel. Two Arabic-looking men place their order, and I can't help but get an eerie feeling that the Holocaust Memorial and Germany's new Muslim population cancel each other out.

"Do you mind if we eat somewhere else?" I ask Sebastian. "I didn't come to Berlin for falafel."

"No problem. You want to try Berlin's famous currywurst?"

"What's that?"

"A classic Berlin food. Invented in the 1950s, I think, for all the construction workers rebuilding West Berlin. Basically, it's a sausage topped with a ketchup-y sauce and curry powder."

"But it's pork, right?"

"Yeah." He pauses to think. "But it's called 'God's Food.'"

"Why?"

"Because only God knows what's in it."

I laugh at his corny joke.

"But we'll find a place with veggie options," he says.

After eating my first—and last—vegan currywurst, Sebastian drops me off at the Jewish Museum.

At the vast museum chronicling the rise and fall of Jewish life in Germany, I focus on images less familiar to me: the vibrant Jewish German community that once was, with its ornate synagogues, Jewish schools, and rabbinical seminaries, even intellectual salons founded by Jewish women.

I read about great German Jewish minds (aside from Einstein): rationalist philosopher Moses Mendelssohn and mystic philosopher Martin Buber; composers Felix Mendelssohn (Moses' grandson), Gustav Mahler, and Arnold Schoenberg (assuming Austrians and/or Christian converts count); and even sex researchers, like scholar of homosexuality Magnus Hirschfeld and sex therapist Dr. Ruth Westheimer, who had been saved from Hitler's clutches by the *Kindertransport* that transported thousands of Jewish children to safety in Britain.

German Jewish history ends with the Holocaust. The final room tells tales of German Jews who stayed or returned: a minuscule seed left for Jewish renewal.

The museum has reminded me how central this country is to my Jewish identity, for better or worse. Being in Berlin is much more profound than I thought it would be. And I have a gorgeous German man to thank for asking a neurotic Jewess to watch his stuff.

I find my way back to his apartment easily using the subway and let myself in with an extra set of keys.

I embrace him tightly when he walks in, wet from the rain, holding a bag of groceries. I feel like a dog thrilled to see her owner after a long absence. I guess that makes me a "bitch." My mom would probably think I am for feeling strangely happy and at home here.

We had already decided to avoid the cold by eating in tonight. As he bakes salmon and I make salad, embracing each other from behind in between, I feel like we're a bona fide couple. After dinner, we snuggle up on his huge sofa and watch a stupid Hollywood movie on his large flat screen. I made sure to wear tight leggings as a lock to what has become my no-go zone.

"T-1 until your period is over, right?" he asks as I lean on his thigh to watch the movie.

"I should be all clean by tomorrow afternoon."

"Good," he says, playing with my hair.

I fall asleep in the middle of the movie. When it's over, he carries me to his bed, and I dream about concrete slabs.

CHAPTER THREE

I feel his goodbye kiss at 8:30 am when he leaves for a guitar lesson followed by a songwriting session, this one for a car commercial. A lasting source of income, he told me, comes from rare and coveted commercial gigs.

"I'll be back around 2 pm," he says.

I officially wake up about an hour and a half after he leaves.

He sends me via text some suggestions for nearby cafés for breakfast, and I walk around to check them out, despite it being a bit colder than yesterday.

This Prenzlauer Berg place is so charming! I pass by high-end boutiques, cafés, and restaurants, the kind I'd see in Tel Aviv's nicest neighborhoods, all filled with well-dressed, yuppie people and women with strollers.

I'm drawn to a spacious, corner café called Spreegold for its inviting cushioned booths. I must have a sixth sense for anything Jewish because I open the menu to familiar Israeli foods like *hummus* and *shakshuka.* I wonder if it's owned by Israelis, but the *shakshuka* is not made Tel Aviv style. Instead of fried eggs over a spicy tomato sauce, this version comes with poached eggs topped over chunky salsa. I enjoy it nevertheless.

With about an hour to kill when I get back to his apartment, I browse online for stuff to do in Berlin and come across a "Jewish Berlin" tour in Hebrew. I order one for tomorrow morning. I turn on German radio and do some housework—wash the dishes, clean the kitchen, and even fold his laundry. I like pretending to be his housewife.

"Are you naked?" he writes to me at 1:45 pm.

"No."

"Well get ready to be. I'll be back in 20 minutes."

After restraining ourselves because of my period, he must, thankfully, feel the same way I do: Let's not waste time undressing. Playing along, I wait for him on the bed, completely nude except for my Jewish star. But when he enters the bedroom, he just laughs and quickly scans my body without any lust whatsoever.

"Put your clothes on," he demands.

"What?" I feel totally ashamed. "I thought you wanted me to get naked."

"I do, but not here."

"What the fuck?"

"Just put your clothes on." He takes my jeans from the floor and throws them at me. *The brute is coming out.*

While getting dressed, I feel annoyed enough to be snarky and say, "SS is deporting me."

He laughs, too evil of a laugh for someone not comfortable with Holocaust jokes. "Something like that."

I don't laugh in kind.

We get into the Audi, and I'm nervous. We reach a main street with many more visible Muslims than I've seen in Prenzlauer Berg. *Shit. Is he setting me up?* We park the car in a neighborhood that looks much more rundown than his. I'm sincerely frightened but don't ask any questions.

He leads me to some sort of park that looks abandoned. *He's taking me to an alley. He's going to gang rape me with Muslim refugees!*

"Where are we going?" I ask in an unfriendly tone, my body tightening.

He points to a two-story building in the distance.

"There."

As we approach, I see a glass entrance decorated with a sign of curvy letters: "Vabali."

He opens the door for me, and we enter a long, glass, tranquil corridor flanked by a Japanese garden of gravel grounds, metallic lanterns, and sculptures of some jolly, fat man, probably Buddha.

"A spa?" I ask, feeling like an idiot for being so fearful.

"Not just any spa. A nude spa. So are you ready to get naked? Actually, you have no choice."

"It's co-ed?"

"Yes."

"You mean, I can't wear a bathing suit even if I wanted to?" My body tightens again.

"No. It's forbidden."

"100 percent?"

"100 percent."

"Oh, my God! I can't believe you brought me here."

"That's why I didn't ask your permission. I really think you should try it. You'll love it. It's an experience, but if you're really uncomfortable, we can leave."

My fear has turned into trust—and intrigue. Anyway, I won't see anyone I know here. "Well, this is a once-in-a-lifetime opportunity, so...okay."

At the cashier counter, he orders entry for two, and we receive watch-like bands that serve as the key to our lockers and as payment processors to rent robes and towels at the wooden-accented lobby that feels like a warm, luxurious cabin.

We enter a co-ed locker room, and I'm weirded out when I see a naked man putting on his boxers, right in front of me! I can't help but notice (or maybe I can) that he's uncircumcised. If I ever wanted to build immunity from the shock of the uncircumcised penis, I've come to the right place. I'm about to be surrounded by a lot of foreskin.

"So, strip," Sebastian demands as we get to our lockers, side by side.

"Here? But there are men around."

"Don't worry. No one cares here."

I focus on him instead and keenly watch him undress as I peel off my own winter layers. As he takes off his shirt, revealing the elastic of his briefs through his jeans, I want to dig my fingernails into his waist, but this is a place where I must continue to practice the same discipline I had while I was on my period.

We pull our pants and underwear off at the same time. Finally, I see him in his full, uncircumcised glory. With his penis un-erect, it looks like, to use an apt German analogy, a "wurst" in a blanket. The head is completely covered with a layer of skin that forms a "nipple" at the end. This "blanket" makes his "wurst" look worse, stifling my desire to hold onto it, which helps in a place like this.

I take off my jewelry, including my star pendant, and we put on our snuggly terrycloth robes before entering spa facilities that smell like healing herbs.

This Vabali place is a wonderland! The main hall is like a sanctuary of wellness, with a square pool in the center flanked by plush lounge chairs and a *chuppah*-like canopy sheltering a cushioned bed. Curtains dangle over the perimeter of the pool, hanging from the ceiling of the upper floor. The black metalwork of the lamps over lounge chairs interlaces to form Stars of David. *A sign of God's approval?*

Sebastian holds my arm over the terrycloth as he escorts me to the sauna area where a chalkboard announces times for various treatments.

"The treatments in the saunas are actually called 'Aufguss,' which means something like 'from the pour.' *Auf*, meaning 'from,' and *Guss*, from the word '*giessen*,' to pour. Because when you pour the herbal water over the hot stones, it creates aromatic steam. It's a German tradition."

"You mean it's a gas chamber? I know that tradition very well, SS."

He looks at me admonishingly. I sometimes can't help these Holocaust jokes, although maybe I should.

He points to the board. "Each sauna room has a different 'flavor.' You see, at 3 pm we could do the honey peel. Then at 4 is the 'fresh mint' Aufguss. But we could also just hang out in the pool and jacuzzi." He motions toward the pool. "Actually, let's start there."

We hang up our towels and robes and step into the main indoor pool completely nude, but we might as well be wearing bathing suits judging by how absolutely no one looks our way. This place is ripe for an orgy, but it feels more like a hospital.

It takes me a few minutes to ease into the room-temperature water. Sebastian embraces me from behind, loose enough so that our bottom halves don't touch, reminding me of our "underwater" experience in the ocean. But I try not to remember; it makes me want to repeat that experience.

"This is paradise," I say. Actually, we are literally in the Garden of Eden, feeling no shame in our nakedness.

"I knew you'd like it," he says.

"I do."

I swim away to the other side of the pool, enjoying the tingling of the water ripples against my bare skin. He follows me. We lean back on the edge, and I put my hand on his back to feel around his shoulder blades. Swimming together like this, unable to make out, is more erotic an experience than doing it in the water. This takes Jewish purity laws to a whole new level.

"Ready for the Aufguss?" he asks. "It's starting in a few minutes."

"I never thought I'd say it, but I'm ready for the gas chamber."

This time he cracks up. I'm glad he's getting more comfortable with Holocaust jokes. "Silly Nilly," he says.

I punch his arm. "Silly you." I'll spare him "SS."

Outside, a huge garden is equipped with dozens more lounge chairs, an outdoor pool that looks more like a lagoon, a small jacuzzi, and several "gas chambers." Under Sebastian's direction, I rush into the warm corridor of our first "chamber" where we take off our robes yet again.

Inside the special sauna room, we sit on our towels, as required, and wait for the "Aufguss Führer"—the gas chamber commandant?

"So he'll come with a bucket filled with the water and pour it over the stones over there." He points to what looks like an open furnace that could cremate bodies. "He'll do it three times, and each pour will create hot steam that he'll fan over us to make us very sweaty. After the second pour, we'll get some sort of honey mask to put over our bodies. He'll do the last pour with the honey all over us."

"*Süss*," I say. Sweet.

I look around and examine the other bodies around me—easy. I notice another hottie or two but also your odd, pot-bellied man. What most of these Germans share in common is an astounding lack of body hair, at least on their bodies. German men seem to bald less than Israeli men. I spot one dark, hairy man (on his head and body) sitting across from me. He must be Middle Eastern, maybe Israeli, because he's circumcised. But when he opens his legs far wider than the other men, I think how even those Israeli "gorillas in the mist" wouldn't be so impolite as to show off their lack of foreskin this proudly.

I think back to last New Year's when groups of Muslim migrants sexually assaulted women during celebrations in Cologne. *Should they allow some sort of selection here?* Not based on their able bodies, but their motivations? Who's here for the gas, and who's here for the ass? I don't ask Sebastian. He might call me "racist" for even suggesting any type of "selection."

As the wooden ledges fill up, the "Aufguss Führer" comes in wearing a checkered fabric that forms a skirt—the kind worn in Turkish *hammams*—but it doesn't make him look any less masculine. I'm in awe of his build, calling to mind the stereotypical Aryan superiority. He must have zero body fat on his smooth, six-foot frame made up of shards of muscle. I wonder if Sebastian really isn't that special. These German men are stunning.

And mean. He shuts the door, but two women try to enter a few seconds later.

"*Raus! Geh raus!*" the Führer yells. Get out. Exactly how Germans must have spoken to Jews. I'm the only one who appears perturbed. Sebastian kisses my moist shoulder.

I don't understand the Führer as he explains the Aufguss procedure, so I take Sebastian's lead. The water sizzles, and the steam rises with the Führer's first pour over the hot stones. With a towel, the Führer starts fanning the steam over us, section by section. I breathe in the sweetness that fills the chamber. My body relaxes. But when the Führer repeats the process, I feel a bit woozy. My body temperature spikes. I hold Sebastian's thigh to steady me.

"It's getting hot," I whisper. "I think I'm going to faint."

He holds onto my kneecap. "We're having a short break for the peel, but do you want to leave?"

"I'll hold out a little longer." *I can't miss this.*

The Führer opens the door, providing some respite from the heat, and brings back a tray of small bowls containing some sort of honey mixture. He instructs us to rub it over our bodies.

"Let me do it for you," Sebastian says as he scoops some of the honey peel with his fingers. He rubs it on my back, letting it mix in with all the sweat. No wonder we're required to sit on a towel; another type of honey is flowing beneath me. Then, through the lingering steam, I notice the Middle Eastern guy rubbing his inner thighs. I think he has an erection! I look away. *Creepy!*

I don't say anything to Sebastian, not yet. Now it's my turn to rub some of the honey onto him, but I've already lost some of my sex drive because of Creepy Guy.

With honey all over my body, and the Führer pouring a third round of gas, my only concern now is making it out alive. As the Führer fans the heat yet again, my body feeling even slimier, I gasp for oxygen. I'm about to die in a gas chamber in Germany.

Finally, it's over. Everyone claps, but I can't get out fast enough.

Outside, my body temperature has risen enough to feel hot even in the cold air. I rush to the open shower stall of mint-green stone. People stand around me as I sip lukewarm water and wipe the honey off. I don't feel sexualized by anyone, until Creepy Guy approaches the stall and stares at me. I immediately turn off the water. I step out and lunge for my towel on a hook right next to him.

"Where are you from?" Creepy Guy asks in what sounds like an Arabic accent as I quickly wrap the towel around me.

"I'm from here, with my boyfriend," I say and then stare at Sebastian, who's now showering. Man, do I sexualize him as he wipes the honey off his body. Once Sebastian is done, I quickly follow him.

"I need to sit," I tell him.

"Let's try the jacuzzi?" he asks.

"Okay."

We sit in the corner of the rectangular jacuzzi next to another couple, bamboo plants overhead. I look around, by instinct, for Creepy Guy.

"Did you notice a man with an erection in the Aufguss?" I ask.

"The guy sitting across from us?"

"Yeah."

"Well, I didn't look down there, but I saw he was a bit weird."

"I think he was Arab. He asked me where I was from. Do men hit on women here?"

"I hardly see it. Most Germans probably wouldn't hit on a girl here out of all places because that's really creepy. But one time I came here with an ex-girlfriend, and some guy—a German guy—offered to rub the peel on her back."

Was he at least cute? I wonder but don't ask. I think I'm becoming positively racist of German men. "Anyway, creeped me out."

"Don't worry, I'll protect you," he says, putting his arm around me, although I'd feel more protected had he been more judgmental of Creepy Guy.

"Do they have nudist colonies or beaches in Israel?" he asks.

"I don't think so. Maybe in some circles."

"Why not?"

"Well, it's a Jewish country, so we have more of a tradition of modesty," I say as our calves intertwine in the hot, but not too hot, water. "In my Orthodox day school, I had to wear skirts that reached below my knees and shirts with sleeves. That was too much for me. How is this nude thing so normal here?"

"I'm not 100 percent sure," Sebastian asks. "Germany's more secular, I suppose. Maybe it goes back to our pagan roots. This is how they must have warmed up during the winter. Also, East Germany had something called *Freikörperkultur*, which means 'free body culture.' Maybe has something to do with communism seeing men and women as equal. But there's also the practical aspect. It's much easier to rub honey on yourself in the nude and probably more hygienic."

I wonder if this comfort with nudity in co-ed environments actually represents a higher level of civilization. Here we are, dozens of men and women, respecting each other's bodies, engaging in no inappropriate sexual behavior or innuendo—well, except for Creepy Guy.

Next, we enter a meditative sauna where Sebastian and I massage each other, but Abraham's foreskin remains intact.

We take a smoothie break at the in-house restaurant, and I'm relaxed enough to ask him about his songwriting session.

"It was good. I've worked with this writer for a while, and we wrote some good music and jingles together, but it's always a gamble. Sometimes we write on spec, sometimes we get paid a fee even if they don't use our music. So we'll see. You never know when you'll get the call. That's why I also do other stuff—teach, studio sessions. You have to be very versatile as a musician here, or anywhere."

"Well, you're so talented. You come up with these songs so quickly."

"It was hard when I first started out, but it gets easier with time. And it helps to have good inspiration." He takes my hand and smiles, implying I'm his muse. *Paradise keeps getting better.*

Before we leave, we enter another "gas chamber," this one infused with coconut, and I leave the spa feeling the most relaxed, healthiest—and may I dare say—happiest I've ever felt in my life.

How amazing that I've come to Germany, and the only gas chambers I experience are those that heal me.

We drive back to his apartment, knowing our non-nude state is temporary.

"You know, now that you just finished your period, you can't get pregnant," he says in the Audi.

"What are you saying?"

He looks at me, this time with lust. "I could feel you."

I tense up. I didn't expect him to request unprotected sex. "What about STDs?"

"My last relationship was six months ago," he says, then pauses. I sense hesitation. "We got checked when we were together. I've only had protected sex since. Interesting fact: Men with foreskins have to be careful. It's easier for bacteria to get caught in there. So Judaism may be right about the health issue."

"All the more reason for us to use a condom," I say, now even more uncomfortable.

"Nilly, I'm clean."

"How do you know I am?"

"Are you?"

"As far as I know. I've also always used condoms when I wasn't in a relationship." I'm not about to go into my sexual history, including how some of my casual Israeli partners were condomphobes who asked to pull out. Maybe they feel more confident without that piece of bacteria-prone skin.

He puts his hand on my lower thigh and squeezes it. "No pressure. You can decide."

We get inside his apartment, and, without kissing or touching, we move straight to his bedroom. We undress ourselves. The foreplay ritual of taking off each other's clothes has lost all relevance. These last few days, and especially today, were one overextended foreplay.

His pants and briefs are already off when he pushes me onto the silky duvet so that I'm on my knees, my ass toward him. *Should I have uncircumcised, unprotected sex?*

He moves in to touch the opening of my legs with the bare tip of his "wurst," a smart tactic.

"Do you want me to get a condom?" he asks. My heightened arousal consumes my caution. At this moment, I'd risk my life—even my health—to feel his entire being inside me.

"No," I say.

Quickly, smoothly, he slips in and out, easy without a condom. The release and relaxation I feel is immediate. His skin—and foreskin—feel so good.

He then folds my legs over and reclines on the bed as he bounces in and out of me from the side. He then inserts one leg through mine and lifts himself up, so that I'm now lying on my back and he's sitting on my inner thigh while my other crosses over him to wrap around his waist. He picks up in pace, massaging my inner walls with a delightful, fleshy friction that's a welcome relief from that annoying, plastic-y friction.

Unhampered by a rubber, he exits to brush his cock over my clit, but, before I could organism, he raises my legs above me and kneels over my ass. My calves hug his neck as he glides in and out again, steering his hands to play with my clit to my utmost delight. He widens his legs while mine freestyle in the air from uncontrolled pleasure. My arms contort at my sides. I'm not sure if there is a name for such a position; we may have invented it. If you could view our bodies from above, I think they would form a swastika.

"Oh, Nilly. Fuck."

"Sebastian, you are so hot."

He maneuvers my legs completely upright so that all my weight is on my shoulders. With my feet hovering over my face, he sits on my ass as if my body were butter, and he's churning it with his cock.

Blood drains to my head as he looks down on me, staring at my Jewish star, his blue eyes emitting rays that make me feel like I'm floating in pure, white light. My dizziness expands as he churns and churns, until I'm whipped into a frenzy, and I lie there as soft as melted butter.

He remains inside me for a few minutes because we can. Because we want to be one. This is the continuation of paradise, where no famine, no shame, and no disease exist.

CHAPTER FOUR

Sebastian wakes me in the middle of the night and takes me in a spooning position. In the morning, we keep it simple: missionary style. Sex without condoms is so easy and unrestrained. Ironically, it energizes me for the 10 am Hebrew tour of "Jewish Berlin" that will turn heaven into hell.

We meet at the U-Bahn station near the Berlin Zoo. Who knew Berlin had a zoo? I keep discovering so many new facets to the city.

I introduce myself to the tour guide, Oren, and take delight in speaking Hebrew, the Biblical language, in the former land of the Nazis. As we wait for the typically late Israelis, he tells me and a few others how he moved here from Tel Aviv five years ago with his wife to complete his doctorate in Jewish history. His father was a "*yekke*," a German Jew, so he took advantage of the German provision offering Jews with German ancestry an easy path to citizenship.

We look around for last-minute arrivals, and I sense the Israelis from a few feet away by their confident swagger, loud speech, short height, balding heads, and—yes—Jewish noses. Some start asking Oren questions very relevant to the topic at hand.

"Are we ending the tour near the Primark clothing store?"

"What time do the malls close?"

"Can I get a discount to the tour if I buy four tickets?"

Still, they're my people. I feel a great sense of comfort, familiarity, and even relief with these not-so attractive creatures around me. If the beautiful Sebastian were to ever wrong me, I feel like they'd be there for me.

Together, on the S-Bahn, which stands for "*Stadt,*" or "city train," we head to the Grunewald platform where most of Berlin's Jews were deported to Auschwitz via freight trains.

Oren explains how, after reunification in 1990, Germany began a rigorous process of *Vergangenheitsbewältigung* (a long German word that means "reckoning with the past"). In the early 1990s, Deutsche Bahn, the German railway company, acknowledged its role in Jewish deportation by turning the old train tracks into a memorial, flanking the edges with plaques detailing exactly how many, on which date, and to which concentration camps the Jews of Berlin were deported. They culled from meticulous German records; each Jew was required to pay for their one-way ticket to death.

"Between the end of the First World War and the beginning of the Third Reich, during what was known as the Weimar Republic, Jews enjoyed a type of Golden Age in Berlin. While they consisted of less than five percent of the local population, they stood out, as leaders in business, academia, science, and the arts, sometimes to the envy of their gentile neighbors. German Jews were pioneers in the department store industry. They owned cabarets and nightclubs. They owned two-thirds of the private banks. They were heads of media empires. Out of the twenty-nine Nobel Prize laureates to come out of Humboldt University, nine were Jews. In short, all the stereotypes of Jews controlling the world were true."

We all laugh. We're allowed to, as Jews.

"But they didn't control the world enough to stop their slaughter, and these wealthy Jews were really a minority. Most were middle or lower-middle class. When Hitler rose to power, half a million Jews lived in Germany. About 165,000 lived in Berlin, not including thousands of undocumented Jews from Russia and Eastern Europe who escaped the pogroms of the antisemitic czars and Cossacks.

"Many German Jews were proud of their integration into German society and were embarrassed by the more insulated, religious Jews of Russia and Eastern Europe, calling them '*Ostjuden*'—Eastern Jews. About 100,000 German Jews fought in World War I as patriots, about a third received medals of valor, and about 12,000 lost their lives. But Hitler didn't differentiate.

"When he came to power, about 65,000 Berlin Jews saw what was coming and left, usually for a hefty fee. Jewish emigration filled Hitler's coffers. *Kristallnacht* of November 9th and 10th of 1938 convinced Jews who thought Hitler was just a phase that it was time to go. About two-thirds of German Jewry fled in time, but the doors were getting tighter and officially closed in 1941.

"As the plaques show, the organized deportation of German Jewry began in the fall of 1941. One hundred Jews on average per train—full capacity. The numbers dwindled as Germany became more *Judenrein*, but the deportations did not let up even in the spring of 1945 when the Germans were on their way to surrender. Jewish slaughter was a Nazi obsession, and they found ways, which I'll reveal later, to ensure that no Jew was left behind—alive."

Yesterday, Berlin became to me a city of pleasure—of Jewish pleasure. Today, I'm fully reminded of Jewish pain.

At the end of the memorial tracks, blue-and-white Israeli flags hang over the edge, flowing into what looks like a trench. I place a stone on one of the flags, presumably hung there by Israelis, *in memoriam*. My being here is its own flag, a blue-and-white celebration against the gray, dark clouds. Israelis who come here, however annoying they can sometimes be, are lights leading the new way toward tolerance and freedom.

We get back on the S-Bahn to head toward Mitte, near Prenzlauer Berg in the former East. From the Hackescher Markt station, we walk to the site of Berlin's first formal synagogue, built in 1714 to accommodate the Jewish population sown in 1671 with the arrival of fifty wealthy Jewish families expelled from Vienna.

"The regional German prince did not welcome them out of kindness," Oren explains. "Each household paid $90,000 for the right to enter Berlin— through a gate intended for cows and swine. Decades later, when the prince needed more cash, he sold the Jewish community the right to build a synagogue provided it stood there inconspicuously, shorter than any local church. The Alte, or Old Synagogue, as it came to be known, was spared from *Kristallnacht* since its rooms were rented out to the German postal service, but it wasn't spared the Berlin bombing of 1945."

Leftover concrete stones from the foundation now make up a haunted memorial park surrounded by busy office buildings. In the corner is a hunk of a sculpture, "The Block of Women," designed in boxy, communist style, commemorating what became known as the Rosenstrasse protest after the name of the street.

"In February 1943, about 30,000 Jews worked as forced laborers in armament factories across Berlin. But with Hitler's successes in the East, he could replace Jewish labor with less racially inferior people. His dream of a *Judenrein* Berlin could finally come true. So that month, in what was called the Fabrik Aktion—the Factory Operation—trucks went about the city and, without warning, picked up Jews from the factories.

"You could avoid deportation under very certain conditions, such as being married to an Aryan or being a '*Mischling*,' the child of a Jew and Aryan. The Nuremburg Laws of 1935 forbade Aryans from marrying Jews, but mixed couples still existed, mostly Jewish men married to Aryan women. During the Fabrik Aktion, about 1,800 Jewish husbands were imprisoned at the Jewish Welfare Administration located on this street, one of the six pre-deportation assembly camps across Berlin, since the Nazis used Jewish institutions to process Jewish deaths.

"In a little-known act of civil disobedience, women gathered here for a full week in the cold, demanding their husbands' freedom, even as Nazis drove by with machine guns threatening to shoot them. Eventually, the men were released. Propaganda Minister Goebbels wrote in his diaries that the time wasn't right to deport them, and most survived until the end of the war."

Oren points out the imagery of the sculpture—women crying for their husbands, standing in defiance, kneeling, and finally, reuniting with their beloveds. The top half features Jewish symbols: a Star of David, the Menorah, and the Lion of Judah.

Oren reads the German letters carved on the backside: "The power of love defeats the violence of the dictator."

I can't help but wonder if Sebastian would ever fight for me like this, but then Oren says something that saddens me: Aryan women resisted divorce in greater numbers than Aryan men since men risked professional advancement if they kept a Jewish wife.

We walk to a corner pillar plastered with facsimiles of deportation documents listing Jews sent to Auschwitz, detailing their DOBs, places of birth, and street addresses. I recognize one of the street names from Prenzlauer Berg. How eerie to think how many Jews once walked these streets, going about their lives—then their deaths. Written next to their given names, like "Kathi" or "Dorothea," is the Jewish name Hitler "gave" them. In 1939, the Nazis forced all Jews to register with an additional name, "Sara" for women and "Israel" for men, so that they could never be mistaken for a gentile.

"So what happened after the round-up?" Oren asks us. "How could you survive if you were Jewish?"

"You had to bribe someone?" someone guesses.

"Nazis didn't need bribes from Jews," Oren answers. "They just took their property."

"You had to hide," I guess.

"Exactly. Jews who evaded the Fabrik Aktion lived as 'U-boats,' underground Jews. So how could the Nazis find these Jewish 'submarines?'"

"They had to raid houses one by one?" someone suggests.

"Too time consuming."

"Get other people to find them."

"Yes. More like 'hunt' them. But who?"

"Other Jews?" someone asks.

"Exactly. Only Jews truly knew the survival habits and hiding places of other Jews."

Oren opens his binder and shows us a picture of an attractive blonde woman named Stella Goldschlag. She later became known as the "blonde poison," the most notorious and dangerous member of the Gestapo's Jew-catching "*Greifer*" service.

"Stella grew up in an assimilated Jewish family that referred to themselves as 'Germans of Jewish origin.' Stella thought nothing of her Jewish roots and dreamed of becoming a jazz singer, but the rise of Hitler killed that dream. By 1935, she was forced to enter a Jewish high school.

"During the Fabrik Aktion, she hid behind boxes and avoided being rounded up. She waltzed out of the factory gate with her mother, passing for an 'Aryan' because of her blonde curls. No sooner did a Jewish '*Greifer*' catch her at a Berlin café, and eventually victim became victimizer.

"The Gestapo saw in her an asset. Her good looks, charm, familiarity with the Jewish community, and especially her instinct for survival would indeed turn her into a star—but not a jazz star—a star Jew catcher.

"They tortured her and threatened to deport her parents if she did not cooperate, so she did, at first reluctantly, but then with skill and panache. In exchange for her parents' lives, freedom from wearing the yellow Jewish star, and some money and extra food rations, she'd turn in her old friends. She'd hunt Jews in cafés, in the streets. She'd lure them by offering to help. Sometimes, she posed as a damsel in distress."

I'm instinctively disgusted, but then I wonder what I would do if my parents' lives were threatened. Could I blame her for this evil, or should I direct my disgust solely at the Nazis for forcing a Jewess to make such a horrific decision?

"Eventually, her parents were sent to Auschwitz anyway, despite their daughters 'stellar' work 'catching' anywhere between 600 to 3,000 Jews."

Some of us gasp in horror.

"What happened to her?" someone asks.

"She survived the war," Oren says but then goes on to explain how she was convicted of aiding and abetting murder by the East German government and served ten years in prison. During the war, she had given birth to a daughter by one of her various lovers. The girl was raised by a foster family and wanted nothing to do with her mother. Stella divorced and widowed several times throughout her life and lived in denial of her guilt. She was found dead outside her window in 1994, an apparent suicide.

As we continue walking on, I feel a sudden fear that Stella—or other "catchers"—are lying in wait. But then we get to Hackescher Höfe, a series of commercial courtyards brimming with boutique shops, cute cafés, and smiling, cheerful people, and I'm back to civilization.

Oren shows us the famous and controversial "stumbling stones," an urban Holocaust memorial project initiated by a German artist consisting of brass stones embedded into the cobbles, each etched with the names of Jews who once lived at that exact address. Over 50,000 "stones" have been installed all over Europe, with some 7,000 in Berlin alone.

On Grosse Hamburger Strasse down the street, more stories of Jewish death, and not just because of the old Jewish cemetery there dating from 1672. In front of it stood the Jewish Home for the Aging, which the Nazis had converted into the most infamous pre-deportation assembly camp. A memorial plaque put up by the GDR commemorates the 55,000 Jews deported from here to Auschwitz and Theresienstadt.

But contemporary Jewish life is not far off. We pass a thriving Jewish high school named after Moses Mendelssohn to reach our final stop where we look up at the shiny, golden, restored dome of New Synagogue, today a symbol of Jewish revival in Germany. Strangely, it resembles a minaret, and Oren explains how architects at that time often drew from the Moorish style of the Golden Age of Spain to differentiate synagogues from the Gothic and Renaissance churches.

Originally inaugurated in 1866 to much local fanfare, the synagogue was saved from destruction during Kristallnacht by a local police chief who protected it by telling the Nazi Brownshirts that the synagogue was off limits; the Kaiser had pronounced it a preserved historic landmark. The police chief, however, could do nothing to preserve it from a 1943 Royal Air Force raid. Fifty years later, it was re-inaugurated with its famous façade.

"When Germany reunited in 1990, only about 20,000 Jews lived in

Germany. The German government realized that Hitler almost succeeded. So, with the fall of the Iron Curtain, Germany decided to open its doors to some 100,000 Soviet Jews to repopulate the country with the people it had decimated."

I wonder why I never heard about this immigration wave, a much more apt correction to the Holocaust than the influx of refugees from Jew-hating Muslim countries.

"Today, anywhere from 7,000 to 20,000 Israelis live in Berlin, depending on your sources," Oren says. "The influx really began in 2006. That's when Berlin hosted the World Cup, and people realized how cool the city was. Also that year, the Holocaust Memorial opened near Brandenburg Gate. Soon enough, more flight routes opened between Berlin and Tel Aviv, and now Berlin is the top European travel destination for Israelis."

I leave the tour thinking that, for the first time since landing in Germany, I could actually live here as a Jew. And I'd be safe if Sebastian would fight for me, like those women fought for their men. If love—assuming that's what we have—will conquer the violence of the dictator should Germany, God forbid, ever come to that again.

Tonight, I get to see Sebastian play guitar for a German rock band called The Minions at a live music bar in a district called Kreuzberg, apparently one of Berlin's coolest neighborhoods.

I meet him there on my own, learning my way about the city through its very efficient, punctual public transportation system.

With its disco-balled hall for a standing-room-only audience, Lido reminds me of a concert hall where up-and-coming bands get discovered. A DJ warms up the crowd with German rock. I recognize German words like "*Leben*" (life) and "*Liebe*" (love), a nice relief from the German vocabulary of hate and death I learned today.

Sebastian meets me at the bar for a quick, pre-performance beer. He introduces me in English as his "Israeli lady" to friends, colleagues, and acquaintances in the crowd, making me wonder if that means I'm his girlfriend, even though we never discussed our status.

"Is Lukas single?" I whisper to Sebastian after conversing with Lukas, the bassist, about his plans to go back to Israel.

"Yep."

"I was thinking of him for my friend, Dana."

"I'm sure he wouldn't mind an 'Israeli lady,'" he says and pinches my side.

As Sebastian goes backstage, his friend Bernd approaches me. He's cute (but not as cute as Lukas) with spiky brunette hair that adds an inch to his 5'10" height—still taller than the average Israeli. *So many men to choose from!*

"So you're the one from Israel?" Bernd asks from a bar stool.

"Yes," I say, unsure if "the one" means Sebastian has "ones" from other countries.

"How you liking Berlin?"

"I love it so far," I say. "People are really nice and open, and it's just interesting."

I won't get into the Jewish stuff.

"Well, Berlin isn't really Germany," he says. "Go out into the country, it's different. People are much more closed-minded. Berlin is very international. Like Tel Aviv."

"You've been there?"

"Yeah, last year. I work with 3D printers, and my company sent me to check out some companies there. They're big in the field. Spent a night in Jerusalem, too. But I'd only stay in Tel Aviv next time. Jerusalem's way too religious for me."

Maybe that's why Berlin and Tel Aviv have a symbiosis. Berlin is the most un-German city of Germany, the least "Nazi." Tel Aviv is the most un-Jewish city of Israel, the least "Jewish." They're "Denial Central," where German or Jew could live free from the demands of history.

"Did you go anywhere else in Israel?" I ask.

"Ramallah, but that's not in Israel. That's occupied territory."

Here we go.

I've been careful to keep my conversations with Germans apolitical. Even I have enough tact not to immediately bring up what I perceive as Germany's flaws, so why does he feel entitled to bring up his criticism of Israel so quickly? Is he testing my positions for Sebastian's sake? *What did Sebastian tell him about me?*

But I don't really want to go into how Israel is or is not "occupying" Ramallah, which is under Palestinian control, mostly because you can't discuss such things at a bar.

"It's complicated," is all I say.

"It's not really. Israel should just get the fuck out of the settlements."

Is he really doing this to me now, minutes before Sebastian is about to perform?

"Bullshit," I say, completely set off. I won't let him get away with this. "'Settlements' are not the problem. Jihad's the problem. Did you ever read the Koran? There's a lot there about killing Jews. You should know a thing or two about that."

He deserved that.

"There are extremists on both sides," he says. "I hung out with Israelis in Tel Aviv who just want to live their lives. I hung out with Palestinians who just want to live their lives, even though it's harder for them under occupation. Too bad the extremists set the agenda. We know in Germany what happens when extremists set the agenda."

"Oh, right, you think you're the moral leaders of the world because you're not Nazis anymore. You know why you're not Nazis anymore? Because the Americans, British, and Russians kicked your ass. Now there's peace. So maybe Israel needs to just kick the ass of genocidal maniacs."

He steps away from me. "Woah," he says. "You're so aggressive. Don't worry, I won't tell Sebastian he's dating an extremist."

I snarl. "Oh, right. I'm the bad guy now. The extremist. The aggressor. The 'colonialist.' Don't worry. He already knows I'm a Nazi from Ariel. A huge settlement. I eat Palestinian children for breakfast. Now if you don't mind, I'd like to enjoy the show."

I walk away from Bernd, shaking, feeling intellectually violated. Actually, I feel even more violated than when I chanced upon Creepy Guy's erection.

The lead singer introduces The Minions, but I can hardly concentrate on the music. I don't hear a rock song about life and love but the marching band of the Third Reich.

After all the progress I've made seeing Germans in a different light, a human light—a good light—this jerk has taken his people a step back. Bernd hardly knows me, but he already hates me—that hatred I had first suspected Sebastian would feel for me.

After the show, Sebastian finds me in the corner, away from his friends, where I've been texting Ariella to tell her what happened.

"Typical German leftist," were her comforting words.

I kiss Sebastian reluctantly and compliment him perfunctorily. The joy I felt being his "Israeli lady" is gone.

"What's wrong?" he asks, sensing I'm upset.

"Could we go? It's too loud for me here. I'm getting a headache."

He looks concerned. "Ok. I'll just get my stuff."

He says his goodbyes quickly, and we leave.

"Okay, Nilly," Sebastian asks behind the wheel. "What happened?"

"Your friend Bernd."

"Oh, God. Bernd. He's a bit socially awkward. What did he say?"

"I think he's antisemitic."

"Why? Because he's against settlements?"

"You knew that about him? Why didn't you warn me?"

"I thought I did. In any case, I didn't think he'd make an issue of it."

"How does he even let you date me? I mean, he knows I'm from Ariel, right?" I don't look at him but at the people walking the colorful streets of Kreuzberg, which would normally charm me.

"Yeah, and then I showed him a picture of you, and he said he wouldn't boycott you either." I'm such a sucker. I feel better. "I should have told you beforehand, sorry. I thought you knew that's the default German position."

"Well, it's how he said it, so self-righteous, like Jews living in their ancestral land is the same thing as murder. And where and when he said it. I mean, I don't want to talk about politics, especially when I'm at a concert—your concert. I could hardly enjoy your show."

"I'll talk to him about it."

"No, don't."

"Germans like to talk about politics. They like to think they're so informed."

"Is the guy actually your friend?"

It starts to drizzle, and he turns on the wipers, which squeak. "We're childhood friends from Dresden, but he's always been kind of weird. A lot of Germans just don't like to see any type of nationalistic armies. That's what got us in trouble."

"What about Palestinian nationalism? Palestinians murder Jews in cold blood for nationalistic reasons just like the Nazis did."

"But Palestinians don't have an army, so people think they're the underdog," Sebastian says, gently, diplomatically, but I wish he would just take my side and kick Bernd's ass instead of "talk" to him. "Israel's a huge military power. It's strong. Its people live in democracy. So Germans think Israel has to be more responsible."

"You know, at first I thought Jews think about the Holocaust more than Germans do, but now I'm starting to think you guys are more obsessed with it than we are, with your 'Never Again War.' Just because Hitler had a nationalist army doesn't make all nationalist armies immoral. It's called the 'Israel Defense Forces' for a reason because self-defense is moral. We wear uniforms so that we can differentiate between combatants and civilians, not like Palestinians who use civilians as shields and weapons.

"But you and Bernd can't see the truth watching biased news from your comfy sofa in Prenzlauer Berg or Kreuzberg or wherever. You don't have to worry if you'll survive another day without getting run over or stabbed or shot by a terrorist. Well, maybe now you do, thanks to the great Palestinian contribution to humanity: terrorist attacks. So please never insinuate that IDF soldiers are like Nazis. I hate it when Germans do that! It's so twisted!"

Sebastian's exasperated. So am I. "Don't get so worked up," he says. "I didn't say I agree with him. I'm just explaining how people like Bernd think."

"You know, we were the underdogs, once, in part because of your country. Germany created hundreds of thousands of refugees. I mean, with all your ideals of welcoming the underdogs, shouldn't the Arabs have been kind to the Jewish refugees instead of trying to kill them?"

He's silent for a few moments, probably thinking of a comeback. "Nilly, I don't want to argue with you."

"Fine," I say.

We finally park, and I head to his bedroom, still withdrawn.

"I'm going to change," I say. *And not into the sexy lingerie I had planned to wear tonight.*

"Okay, I'll make some tea. Then we can relax on the sofa, maybe finish the movie."

"Okay." I won't argue about what we'll do tonight, either.

I change into a long nightgown and wait for him on the sofa as he brings fresh, homemade ginger tea. The rain hitting the windows calms me, as does the tea. He takes off his jeans by the sofa so that he's in boxers and a T-shirt only. It's a shame Bernd killed my sexual appetite tonight, especially when we could have condom-free sex.

"Don't mind Bernd," he says, sitting next to me. I'm tempted to put my head on his shoulder, but I don't. "He just doesn't know how to talk to a really pretty girl. He's a nerd at the end of the day. Him and his 3D printers."

"Yeah, but some Nazis were nerds." Talk about a safe word warding him off.

"You're still upset. Do you want me to leave?"

"No," I say, not too convincingly. I really don't know what I want.

"You're very sensitive to these political issues."

"I had a hard day, seeing where all the Jews were deported, learning about how the Nazis turned Jews against Jews. You guys were just awful."

"Well, I'm not those 'guys,' and yes, the Nazis were awful." He fiddles with the remote and turns the television on—then off—before turning to me. "I think you need to take out some aggression."

"Probably. What do you suggest?"

"Hurt me?"

"What?"

"Hit me, spank me, choke me, do whatever you want to me."

"You mean cause you pain?"

"Yeah. Use me as your punching bag. Get it all out."

"You mean to pretend you're really an SS officer?"

"Sure."

He reaches for his jeans, pulls off the belt, and hands it to me. I finally smile—mischievously.

"Use it," he demands.

"Are you serious?" Now I even chuckle.

He sits up and takes off his shirt to reveal a perfect Aryan torso ready for a whipping.

"Come on. Give me your best shot."

"You're not serious."

He takes me by the neck with one hand, forcefully. "You bet I am." His fingernails dig into my skin, causing tiny gashes. I have no choice but to whip his arm.

"Is that the best you can do?" he asks and takes off his boxers, which make me want to hit him harder.

This time, my whipping produces red stripes on his chest.

"You like that, *Nazi?*" Now the "safe word" has the opposite effect.

To stop me, he pins my left hand onto the back of the sofa. With the belt in my right hand, I slap it against his chest and over his shoulders, but my pressure is too weak; he is unfazed as his free hand works doggedly to take off my panties.

He grabs the leather strap from my weakening grip and pulls it out of my hands. My strength is no match for his. He kneels over my body and inches his crotch toward my face. He places the whip around my neck to force my mouth closer to his crotch. I'm in a defenseless position as he fucks my mouth. I grab hold of his ass, which only makes matters worse.

He provokes me with, "Take it, settler bitch."

The only way to take it is to bite it.

"Ouch," he says and drops the belt on the sofa. "That hurts."

I grab the belt.

"Good. *Nazi mezuyan. Egmor ot'cha.*" Fucking Nazi, I'll finish you.

I fight back, pushing my shins against his chest, and when he tries to get back at me, I whip him wherever I can with more pressure than before. He's off guard, so I pivot him with my legs until he's lying on the sofa. I've wrested control. I scramble to sit on his upper thighs and maneuver the belt under his neck, which I utilize as an axle. Holding both ends for support, I crawl on top of him and open my legs over his face, making him pleasure me. But he's not licking me as I want. I let go of the belt and turn around with my pussy still on his face. I take off my nightgown and face his "Nazi" cock and grab it like it's a joystick. The direction in which I turn it becomes the direction of his tongue's movements. *That's more like it.*

Not wanting the fight to be over, I put the joystick in neutral and search for the flap of skin that shouldn't be there. I pull it and try to take it off.

"I'm going to get rid of this fucking thing," I say.

"Don't do that."

I don't stop. He deserves the pain, but he fights back by squeezing my ass, hard.

"Suck it," he says.

"No."

"Settler bitch, suck me."

"No way."

His moves his hands from my ass and firmly presses down on my back, forcing me to bend over his cock. He's overpowered me. I'm now a trembling Jew on bended knee as he's spanking my ass, hard. My mouth envelops his uncircumcised cock, taking it in completely. I'm going to lose. My loss is even more pathetic because I don't want to win. I would have folded, just like Stella.

But no! I'm not Stella! I'm "Sara!"

I use my teeth again. He pushes and topples me forward so that my face bangs on the armrest, and I'm on my knees again. He pulls my hair and takes me from behind until I'm in his favorite position—underdog.

"Du jüdische Schampe! Ich mach dich fertig."

Little does he know the German language empowers me to fight back. With all the discipline I can muster, I grab the armrest and pull my body forward, and the physics of our position means he has no choice but to exit. He lies back, surprised and tired by this maneuver.

I eye the belt, grab it quickly, and swirl it like a lasso. The determination in my face alone threatens him into submission as I ride him yet again to victory, now using the belt as a halter around his neck. This night must end with a Jew on top choking a German. And it does.

I feel much better.

CHAPTER FIVE

"Ready for the Christmas market?" Sebastian asks once we wake up.

I went to sleep a victorious Jew and wake up a little Christian girl on Christmas Day about to open her presents.

"Yeah!" I enthuse.

Over morning coffee, Sebastian explains how Christmas markets start with something called "Advent" four weeks before Christmas.

"The first took place in Dresden in 1434. The Striezelmarkt. I'll take you there. I'm sure you'll love them. It's a huge German tradition. For me, they're just a remedy for the winter depression."

We walk down his street and enter a vaulted brick hallway leading into a complex called the KulturBrauerei, once the grounds of a former brewery that today serves as a "brewery of culture," equipped with a movie theater, museums, dance clubs, and vintage, artsy shops.

I feel like I've entered an enchanting Scandinavian town. Little wooden huts form food and drink stands. One hut is shaped like an igloo—another, a Nordic tavern. A huge Christmas tree and merry-go-round dominate the vast, packed courtyard. This feels more like an Israeli *shuk* from the way people rub up against each other as they push through the crowd, uncharacteristic of stiff Germans. I would say it smells like an Israeli Independence Day barbecue, but the meat is pork. Wurst is being grilled on open flames at various stands.

"Let's start with some Glühwein," Sebastian says, describing it as mulled wine cooked with spices like cloves and cardamom, a Christmas market specialty.

"Can't wait!"

We get in line for Glühwein just before an elderly couple arrives.

"Please, go ahead," Sebastian tells the couple, who must be in their mid-seventies.

"No, you were here first," the gentleman replies courteously (in German I understand by context), looking aristocratic in a knitted sweater, turtleneck, and leather gloves. I wonder how such a refined people could have ever been

Nazis. Israelis aren't this polite waiting in line. To them, a spot in front of a packed line is like a winning lottery ticket.

"Germans are so nice," I say to Sebastian.

"Not always. Berliners actually have a reputation for being rude."

"Haven't really encountered that," I say. *Except with Bernd, whom I won't mention anymore.*

Sebastian orders Glühwein for 3 Euro each, a real bargain by Israeli standards. A holiday fair, let alone a free one, would never be so elaborately decorated and illuminated in Israel, which doesn't have the money to invest in such productions. No wonder so many enlightened German Jews converted to Christianity. *How could they not want to partake of this fun?*

As I sip the Glühwein, a truly delicious cure to the winter cold, and watch happy German children ride the colorful carousel, grandparents cheering them on, I'm seized with a sudden case of Christmas envy. *How unfair!* Germans get to enjoy the good life while Jews living in Israel, especially the descendants of Holocaust survivors, still suffer so much financial hardship and war.

We continue along, our glasses half-full.

"Are you hungry?" Sebastian asks. "You should try *Kartoffelpuffer*, another Christmas specialty. Fattening but *ta'im*."

"What's that? Something with potato?" I recognize the word "*Kartoffel*."

"I'll show you." At the *Kartoffelpuffer* stand, a woman dressed in a checkered apron is frying what appear to be *levivot*, the traditional Hanukkah potato pancakes named after "*lev*," or heart, for the shape they sometimes take on.

"*Kartoffel* is potato, and *puffer* is a type of fried pancake." The woman serves three pancakes on a plate to the first customer in line, with a side of applesauce.

"You mean you also have potato pancakes?"

"Why? You have them in Israel?"

"Yeah! It's a huge Hanukkah tradition—that's like our Christmas. We also serve it with applesauce. I wonder if the Jews who lived here adopted it from the Christians, or vice versa."

He shrugs. "What came first, the chicken or the egg?"

I take my first bite with delight; they taste as good as my mother's *levivot*.

"What is Hanukkah exactly?" Sebastian asks as we munch over a tall, outdoor roundtable. "I've heard of it but never really understood it."

"Well, it's a holiday celebrating the victory of a small Jewish army against the Hellenist Greeks who wanted to destroy the Temple in Jerusalem and prevent Jewish freedom of worship." I explain it in modern liberal terms a German should understand. "Legend has it that when the Jews drove out the Greeks, a bottle of oil that was supposed to light the Temple's *menorah* for one day lasted for eight days. That's why we're supposed to eat oily foods. Most Jewish holidays go something like this. 'They tried to kill us. We won. Let's eat.' We also eat fried jelly donuts. They're called *sufganiyot*."

"Wait a minute. We have them, too."

"What?"

"Yeah, they're another Christmas specialty. Actually, a classic Berlin food. Outside of Berlin they're called 'Berliners.' Here they're called *Pfannkuchen*. Let's get some, too."

The German "*sufganiya*" is the fluffiest I've ever tasted.

I'm even more convinced that Hanukkah traditions somehow crossbred with German ones when I look up and notice a Star of David hanging from a decorative cable.

"Is that for Hanukkah?" I ask Sebastian, pointing to the star decor.

"No, I think it's a symbol of the nativity. I think you could use any star. But you know what's cool? Every Hanukkah, some synagogue puts up a huge *menorah*—or what do you call it?"

"A *hanukkiah*. It has eight branches and a stem. The *menorah* has six branches and a stem."

"Yes. That. They put up a huge one by Alexanderplatz and Brandenburg Gate."

"I wonder when Hanukkah is this year," I say, checking on my phone to find out. My "*lev*" warms at what I find. "Did you know the first night of Hanukkah falls exactly on Christmas Eve this year?"

"Really? Cool!"

I don't need to be Christian to fully enjoy this market. I appropriate the German celebration for my own cultural purposes and treat this as a "Hanukkah Markt." There truly is such a thing as a Judeo-Christian tradition, and, tonight, we'll create our own when I cook Shabbat dinner for us.

"I have another surprise for you," Sebastian says as we leave the

KulturBrauerei.

"Uh-oh. Do I have to be naked for this one?"

"No. Actually, the more you wear the better."

We get on a tram and breeze down Danziger Strasse, which turns into Bernauer Strasse, a street that once divided East and West; one stretch of it has been transformed into an outdoor exhibition on the Berlin Wall. We walk eastward a few blocks until he points to the surprise: "Kosher Life."

Ariella would be very proud of him. The grandson of maybe-Nazis is taking me to the local kosher supermarket in Berlin. Maybe he really *is* a *motek neshama*!

I kiss him on the cheek. "*Motek*," I say.

A man with a black hat and a woman with a religious head scarf are pushing a cart through the aisles stacked with iconic Israeli foods, like *Bisli* and *Bamba*, along with brand-name Israeli crackers, cookies, and cakes, and some kosher American brands.

Even though the design of the market is plain and drab, and the kosher foods don't look as appetizing as the Christmas market specialties, the excitement I felt at the KulturBrauerei carries on here.

I have an urge to drop as many traditional Israeli products into the cart as possible—until I check the prices. If I thought Israel was expensive, this place is exorbitant. *A packet of wheat thin crackers costs 4 Euro?*

"We could pick up crackers in my neighborhood market," Sebastian says. "It's much cheaper there. Just get your favorite stuff here."

"Well, I'll at least get kosher meat," I say and then look for the meat section.

There's no kosher butcher counter, so the meat is either refrigerated or frozen. Sebastian takes out a packet of hot dogs and says: "Look, all the kosher wurst you want!"

I laugh and put the hot dogs in the cart for fun, although his humor whets my appetite for a different "hot dog." I intermittently hold Sebastian's hand as I browse, ensuring his comfort. He looks out of place here, like Santa Claus in a synagogue.

I end up buying frozen chicken for soup, ground beef for meatballs, the Middle Eastern spice *hawaj* that my mother likes to use, traditional long-stem white Shabbat candles, and even *challah*! We'll have a lovely Shabbat meal. It better be, considering I ultimately spend 50 Euro on less than ten items.

At Sebastian's neighborhood market called Lidl, I seek out Berlin's infamous "Milky." Each cup of chocolate pudding costs literally 19 cents. *How cheap!* Low-fat milk goes for 60 cents—almost a quarter of the cost of milk in Israel. That seems to be the German-to-Israeli cost ratio of the supermarket staples that fill my cart. I spend 25 Euro on 15 items.

I leave completely sympathizing with the "Milky Generation."

The Shabbat candles from "Kosher Life" turn this weekly Jewish feast into a romantic candlelit dinner. I recite *kiddush* over store-bought Glühwein that Sebastian warmed in a pot, feeling a heartwarming satisfaction from performing this ritual here, on a block where hundreds of Jews must have performed it. He listens intently.

For you sanctified us and made us holy.

I'm glad he can't understand Hebrew. I can imagine how Germans might consider this blessing proclaiming Jews as "the chosen people" totally arrogant—and laughable now. In his quest to co-opt the Jews' "chosenness," Hitler murdered six million of God's supposedly actual "chosen."

I understand how Jews who live in the diaspora, away from Jewish lands, feel the need to take upon Jewish rituals to connect to their faith, history, and nation, but Hitler has proven that these rituals do not grant any kind of metaphysical shield against disaster.

The Jews who left for Mandate Palestine and traded *kiddush* cups for guns were the truly "chosen" ones. Thanks to those pioneers, I'm here, feeling safe, backed by a country that will, at its best, protect me.

"So what does that mean?" Sebastian asks as he gets up to turn on *The Gladiator* soundtrack by one of his favorite composers, Hans Zimmer. The first track he plays is entitled, "Now We Are Free." *How appropriate.*

"*Kiddush* means 'sanctification.' So it's like we separate Saturday from the rest of the week when we work and deal with life's hassles. We also remember how God took the Jewish people out of Egypt and freed us from slavery, and how today we aren't slaves anymore, especially on Shabbat, when we even force ourselves to enjoy life's pleasures, like this Glühwein. Because what's the point of working so hard if you don't enjoy life?" I tear off a piece of *challah*, which is like a loaf-sized, fluffy roll. "Here, try this."

"*Ta'im*," he says. "I guess we also have our Shabbat. Sunday. You'll see how everything is closed. It's pretty holy. And Germans take a lot of vacations. We get like twenty-four vacation days a year."

"No way. That's a lot! I get only twelve."

"Now that's slavery!"

"I know! You guys may observe Shabbat better than we do! And we start our weekend on Friday, which means some people have to work on weekends to keep up with the rest of the world."

"Why do you start on Friday, anyway?" Sebastian asks as he digs into my Israeli salad.

"I think it's because the Muslim 'Shabbat' is on Friday. A lot more Muslims than Christians in Israel."

"Do I have to do anything special for Ismael on a Friday when he comes over here for Christmas."

"Have no idea. Better to ask him."

Every time Sebastian mentions Ismael, I feel like I must compete and prove how much more liberal and tolerant Judaism innately is than Islam.

I'm surprised it's not self-evident to Germans. Jews contributed tremendously to German literature, art, science, and music throughout the ages. Muslim communities, as far as I know, never existed in Germany until the twentieth century, when West Germany welcomed Turkish workers in the 1950s. The sultans never conquered Germanic lands. Today, Muslims outnumber the Jewish population at its peak, yet I have not heard of any famous Muslim-German contribution.

Even the Muslim world considers a Jewish life more valuable than a Muslim one. In 2011, the Islamic terrorist group Hamas traded 1,027 Palestinian prisoners for the captured Israeli soldier Gilad Shalit. According to this racist calculation, one Jew is worth about 1,000 Muslims, so if 130,000 Jews live in Germany against 1,300,000 Muslims, I guess we're about even.

"What are your plans with Ismael?" I ask, genuinely curious.

"Well, he told me he wants to see the city and shop and also go out to bars, which I find strange because he's Muslim, but he told me he drinks alcohol on vacation. I offered him to meet the Syrian refugees I teach, but he wasn't interested. In any case, I want to invite a Syrian family over to my mom's for Christmas, especially because of Dresden's right-wing reputation, and it would be cool because he could translate. I need to ask the state authorities to match a family with us because my students' families are still in Syria, and my mother wants women and children, too."

"Good luck," I say with obvious cynicism, but it's Shabbat, a respite from reality, so I won't question why the "refugee" population consists mostly of military-age males.

"You sound skeptical," he says.

"Let's not get into this," I say. "On Shabbat, you're only supposed to discuss topics that make you happy—not business or current events." I get up to serve him my *hawaj*-spiced meatball stew filled with vegetables. I admit, it smells delicious. "Shabbat is also called, 'a taste of the world to come'—like the after-life on earth, an eternal space of joy and pleasure, with good food, good alcohol, good company, and good sex. Did you know you're actually supposed to have sex on Shabbat? It's a *mitzvah*—a Biblical commandment."

Talk about the superiority of Judaism.

"Really?"

"Oh, yeah," I say, teasingly, as I put down the bowl of stew.

He takes a sip as I pour my own bowl.

"*Ta'im!*" he says.

"And I have dessert," I say.

"More settler chocolate?" he asks.

"I guess you could say that."

Done with the main meal, I go to the bedroom and put on the lingerie I had wanted to wear last night: a hot pink, lacy top that cups my breasts with a matching, silky fabric that falls to my upper thigh. It doesn't come with underwear.

As I walk back into the kitchen, he stares at me in awe.

"Nice chocolate wrapper," he says.

I sit on his lap, and we start kissing.

"Mmm. *Ta'im*," he says as he grabs hold of my inner thigh. "I could do Shabbat," he whispers in my ear as his fingers reach for my melting morsel. "Totally."

CHAPTER SIX

Today, Sebastian has planned a walking tour of the Altstadt, or "Old City" of Dresden, to be followed by a visit to his mother.

From the window of the Audi, I stare at the dense forests flanking the road on our way to the State of Saxony, and all I imagine are Jews running away or hiding within the pine. Even as we leave Berlin, I still see the Holocaust all around me.

"So many forests here," I tell Sebastian, without commentary.

"Well, they're industrial forests," he says. "That's a big industry in Brandenburg. It was a state in East Germany, sometimes called the 'sandbox' because the land is sand-soil, so not so much grows here. But it's not all drab. There are many lakes, and there's a nature reserve with all these canals called Spreewald. We used to go there under the GDR. At first, we'd drive a communal car, but when I was six my father got a 'Trabi,' the East German car. He waited since I was born to get one. They're known to be clunkers, but it was fun. Driving through here makes me feel *Ostalgia*."

"What's that?"

"Nostalgia for '*Ost*,' the East. We had good times. Well, at least when my parents weren't fighting. The only really good memories I have of my father are of him taking me to the opera house in Dresden, which you'll see today. And our Brandenburg outings." He speeds up. "But I don't really miss the Trabi. It couldn't go so fast, and there's no speed limit on the Autobahn."

He turns on the radio to American pop as we glide through stretches of pine until flat, sandy planes surround us, but the green of the grass is muted by the grim clouds. The only "orchards" I see now are those of wind turbines. Their tops twirl to Carly Simon's "You're So Vain."

"They play a lot of American music on the radio," I say.

"Yeah," he says. "It's better than most German pop. The American pop scene is much more developed. I think it would be interesting to work in LA one day. They have a strong music scene there, also for film scores, which I've been dabbling in. Here, I'll play you something." He fiddles with his phone. "I started it when I came back from Tel Aviv. Just for fun."

He asks me to plug his phone into the radio deck, and he hits "play" on a music file. The composition starts out with a curious but cautious piano melody, soon to be joined by strings that unify the piano with percussion and winds. The melody grows more confident, as if it's telling the story of our romance. But toward the end, violins take it for a melancholy turn.

"It's beautiful," I say. "It's too bad you can't be on good terms with your father so that he could hear what kind of gift you have."

"I guess," he says, looking straight at the smooth road ahead, uneasy with talk of his father.

We cross into the State of Saxony in silence; the forests and planes have been replaced by fertile hills. He points to the sign on the road for the "Meissen Manufaktur," the famous porcelain factory where his mother had worked. It reminds me how Germany's history began way before 1933.

I'm astounded by the beauty and intricacy of the Dresden skyline as we drive across a bridge over the Elbe River, so much so that I don't think about its destruction during World War II. But at the end of the bridge, Sebastian points to a building consisting of two brown, block structures that don't belong amidst the majestic domes and towers.

"That's the new synagogue," Sebastian says. "Where the old one used to be."

"Really? Didn't know Dresden had one."

"Yeah. It was rebuilt like fifteen years ago."

"Was it destroyed in the bombing?"

"No. *Kristallnacht." I guess that's worse.*

"Do you know how many Jews live in Dresden?"

"No clue. I don't even think I've ever met a Dresden Jew."

We join ten other tourists in the dry cold for a tour given by a brunette, pale British woman named Stefanie who must be around my age. She came here to study art at Dresden's prestigious art academy four years ago and married a German man, which means I have questions for her that don't relate to Dresden.

We start at the restored *Residenzschloss*, the Baroque castle beautified by August the Strong, the Duke of Saxony from 1694 to 1733, who transformed the historical capital of Saxony into the "Florence of the Elbe."

I had no idea Dresden was known for culture and beauty as much as for bombing and death.

Stefanie explains how, under August's reign, Germany consisted of a series of states, mini-states, principalities, duchies, and free cities loosely united under the Holy Roman Empire of the Germanic Nations. Seven prince-electors from seven royal families, including the Saxon tribe, elected the "Kaiser."

Prince-Elector August was a man of many hobbies: art, architecture, and women. He had hundreds of mistresses, official and unofficial.

"Some of his concubines lived in the palace to your right, today a five-star hotel, connected to the castle by that bridge, so that his one legitimate wife and the people wouldn't see his comings and goings," Stefanie says. "But it wasn't enough for him to be a prince-elector; he wanted to be a king. So when the Polish king died, he bribed his way into the Polish monarchy. One catch: Poland was Catholic, and Saxony was the cradle of Protestantism.

"August, however, wasn't only 'strong' but flexible. He converted and became the Catholic King of Poland in 1697, much to his wife's dismay, so August banished her to another castle where she spent the rest of her days as a local hero. She was a devout Protestant, like many of August's subjects, so the new king was wise enough to allow the Saxons freedom of Protestant worship, such that today Dresden is known as a city of Catholic-Protestant tolerance. The bridge on the other side of the castle, by the way, connects to the Catholic cathedral, another type of 'mistress.'

"Don't think 'Strong' refers to political strength. The appellation was given to August for his physical strength; as a boy, he was known to break copper horseshoes with his bare hands. After unsuccessfully waging war against Sweden for control of the Baltic states, August's 'Game of Thrones' was over. All he had left to do was to 'Make Dresden Great Again.'" Everyone laughs at the popular butt of jokes: America's president-elect. "Because if you can't be politically strong, you can at least appear to be. He revamped his city, his palace, and filled it with beautiful things he bought with money he made from mining the rich Saxon lands, taxes, and Meissen porcelain, Dresden's famous china, invented under his reign."

"Your mother's," I say to Sebastian then turn my attention back to Stefanie, riveted.

"August brought some of the finest Renaissance paintings to their palace, and Dresden became a mecca for craftsmen and jewelers, such that the city became known for *Finearbeit*, precision work. That tradition continued up until the war, with many modern, consumer goods founded or perfected in Dresden: filter cigarettes, coffee and tea filters, contact lenses, typewriters and cameras, and—thanks to August and his womanizing ways—the brassiere, nylon stockings, and the latex condom.

"So during World War II, the people of Dresden thought the city's reputation as the 'Florence of the Elbe' immunized it from bombing. How could the Allies harm this beautiful city, as beautiful as Prague and Paris and Oxford?

"But at that point even the 'Baroque Pearl' became a Nazi war machine. Cigarette factories manufactured bullets instead of cigarettes. The camera industry made lenses for that deadly bulls-eye. Meissen porcelain was good material for airplane parts."

I look at Sebastian, who's listening intently. His mother's former employer was apparently involved in the Nazi war machine, and didn't he say his grandfather worked at a lens-making factory?

We walk toward a Baroque tower extending into stone walls: the entrance to the Zwinger Palace, August's "backyard." Stefanie stops under the tower in front of a sign written in German, translating:

On February 13, the British-American bomber gangs annihilated the old city of Dresden until the Zwinger palace was almost destroyed. In May 1945, the Soviet Army freed the people from the fascist tyranny.

"This sign was put up by the German Democratic Republic, the East German government, who wanted to portray the communists as the saviors of Dresden. Ironically, the Soviets collaborated with English-American 'bomber gangs' to bomb Dresden. At the 1945 Yalta conference, the three Allied Powers decided to make Dresden a target to hasten the Russian advance on the Eastern front.

"The British people once loved visiting Dresden; a community of British ex-pats even made their home here before World War I. My grandmother spent holidays here with her parents. That's probably why I was drawn to the city. But that love was gone during World War II. The British never forgave or forgot the Nazi firebombing of Coventry in 1940, a medieval city in the middle of England with a beautiful church. 600 civilians died. Dresden became revenge for Coventry.

"The bombing of Dresden is still controversial today. Some argue it wasn't necessary—it was clear the Nazis were losing. But one theory has it that the bombing of Dresden was meant to make the Allied victory as decisive as possible. Devastate German morale completely. Hurt the Germans where it hurt most so that they will never launch any more wars of aggression.

"And so, on February 13, on a clear night just before Valentine's Day, 1945, the Royal Air Force made its way to Dresden to give the city a 'Valentine's gift.'

"The first round of planes were small ones, and they dropped white parachute flares to mark the spot. The people watching them from their shelters called them 'Christmas Trees.' With the city marked for destruction, Lancaster bombers took flight carrying tons of explosives. They blew open the roofs, exposed the timbers, and made craters in the city streets, preventing rescue workers from reaching the fires. Sounds cruel, but the British learned this technique from the bombing of Coventry. Then came a quarter of a million incendiary bombs, the sticky bombs, that would keep the fires raging in the wind. Flames reached over 1,000 degrees Celsius. With a pillar of fire above, the inferno had nowhere to go than through the Old City, sucking up the oxygen in the process. The 'perfect firestorm.'

"Most of the people died from asphyxiation, or carbon monoxide poisoning. Shelters weren't equipped with air filters. The only ones with proper bunkers were the Nazi leaders."

Sebastian whispers to me. "That's how my grandfather died. He suffocated."

I nod, wanting to feel sympathy, but I can't. Deep inside I'm glad the Royal Air Force viciously attacked the Nazis. His grandfather suffocated, the way my grandparents' families suffocated in the gas chambers. Measure for measure.

"25,000 Germans were registered as dead, but the number is probably closer to 40,000 since Dresden absorbed many refugees from other parts of the country who thought they'd be safe here," I let Stefanie's information distract me from feeling the sympathy I don't want to feel. "But as the sign says, the Old City of Dresden, and this here Zwinger Palace, were almost destroyed—but not to worry, I'm not going to show you ruins. Most of Dresden was rebuilt by the unified German government, but the Russians restored this here Zwinger where August received court, held equestrian tournaments, and, of course, partied."

We step inside a courtyard that must be the size of a football field. Normally, I don't care for Baroque—this dramatic, sweeping, symmetrical style is too kitschy for me—but I'm overtaken and stimulated by the architectural splendor, sculptural flourishes, and engineering brilliance of the buildings, gates, and towers surrounding us.

Jews, never into the "graven image," hardly ever produced such flowery, ornate architecture. Modern Israeli architecture is usually characterized by sheer efficiency, the hallmark of Tel Aviv's Bauhaus. Israel's most glorious structures could be attributed to the Romans and Ottomans, like the amphitheater in Caesarea or the Dome of the Rock in Jerusalem.

Stefanie shows us pictures of the Zwinger after the bombing. I don't know if I'm a horrible person for feeling more sympathy for these beautiful buildings than for Sebastian's grandfather.

We exit toward Theaterplatz, once called Adolf-Hitler-Platz, whose centerpiece is the Semper Opera, the only other structure the Soviets heavily invested in and re-opened.

"This is where your father took you," I say as Sebastian looks at it wistfully. I imagine him as a beautiful, blonde boy entering the Neoclassical, Rococo, and Baroque façade with wonder, as if it were a magic castle.

Stefanie explains how the opera house was named after the architect Gottfried Semper, a renowned architect at the time and a liberal Democrat, who built Dresden's synagogue in 1840—about 100 years before *Kristallnacht*. She shows us a picture of the synagogue, built in Moorish style.

"Did you know that?" I ask Sebastian, fascinated by how one of his favorite places in Dresden was built by the architect of the city's synagogue.

"I think I learned it but forgot."

"Was there a big Jewish community in Dresden?" I ask Stefanie.

"Large enough to justify the construction of a synagogue. In 1933, about 6,000 Jews lived in the city. By 1945, that dwindled to just over a hundred who stayed alive because they had an 'Aryan' spouse or parent. Still, even these Jews were ordered to report for deportation the week of the bombing. The bombing probably saved them."

Now I feel less bad for my lack of sympathy.

"An artist in the city, Otto Griebel, not a Nazi fan, witnessed the Semper synagogue burning to the ground not far from here, on the banks of the Elbe. He recorded how a local curmudgeon stared at the fire and prophesied: 'This fire will return. It will follow a large curve and then return to us.' And so, in 1945, Semper's opera, completed just a year after the synagogue, displayed new architectural flourishes: natural space and light."

She shows us a picture of the grand opera house in ruins. People murmur in pity, including me.

We continue alongside the Catholic cathedral and up a decorative flight of stairs to the Brühl Terrace—nicknamed the "Balcony of Europe"—for a view of the Elbe River, ashen against the clouds, and its historic fleet of paddle steamers. We circle back down stone steps and push our way through a crowded outdoor corridor lined with Christmas food and souvenir stands. At the end of the "tourist trap," we reach Dresden's most iconic building: the Frauenkirche, "Church of the Lady," an imposing, elegant, domed Protestant church built by the people of Dresden in defiance of August's conversion to Catholicism.

"When I was a kid, this was all rubble with plants growing out of it," Sebastian tells me. "It used to be called a *Denkmal*, a memorial."

His personal commentary makes the tour all the more intriguing, and difficult. Because I care for him, he makes me want to care more for the people of Dresden when I still want to care more for my people.

Next, we stop at a certified Meissen porcelain shop identified by an oval sign of two crossing swords, one of the first trademarks in the world, designed to protect August's precious porcelain against fakes. Sebastian and I window shop for plate sets we could never afford. A dinner plate intricately hand-painted with pink flowers costs over 500 Euro.

"My mom painted plates," Sebastian tells me, smiling. "So just let me know what you like, and I'll get you a discount."

"*Motek*," I say.

Through the window, I see a heart-shaped pendant painted with a lavender butterfly. It's priced at 175 Euro, not bad comparatively. "That's pretty."

"Hmm," is all he says. I don't get my hopes up that he'll get it for me. In any case, I'm not sure how I would feel accepting a gift made from material that went into Nazi warplanes. I might have to apply my mother's boycott on *some* products.

Stefanie further builds the plot of Dresden with the Meissen legend: "An alchemist named Friedrich Böttger offered August his services turning base metals into gold. Up for the gamble, August gave him a special workshop—more like a jail cell—in the town of Meissen, right outside of Dresden. Böttger kept stalling and tried to escape. Finally, with some help from a court scientist, he experimented with the clay from the Saxon hills, and eventually they came up with the formula for 'White Gold,' the finest porcelain in Europe at the time."

Its strength is demonstrated through a huge mural just ahead of us made from 23,000 Meissen porcelain tiles: the "Procession of Princes," depicting the dukes of Saxony since the twelfth century. Only 300 tiles were damaged during the firebombing.

Stefanie makes her closing remarks where we started.

"Dresden is the story of beauty and destruction, but it could also be the story of hope. The golden cross of the Frauenkirche, which re-opened in 2005, was designed by the son of a Royal Air Force bomber pilot. Coventry and Dresden are now sister cities. Rubble from the bombing of the church at Coventry has been sculpted into a decorative cross inside the Church. And now for a personal story."

I'm more intrigued than ever.

"My grandfather fought in the Royal Air Force. While he was not part of the Dresden bombers, he and the Germans were bitter enemies. And here I am now, married to a German man. So Dresden was once an example of what happens when people hate, but today it's an example of what can happen when people love."

I take Sebastian's hand. *Could this be our ending, too?*

I give Stefanie a generous tip.

"She was great," I say to Sebastian. "I love Dresden already."

"Yes, good tour." He nods. "It was a good refresher for me." I sense discomfort, maybe because the tour forced him to think about his grandfather. "Come. I'll take you to the Striezelmarkt, my favorite."

The Striezlmarkt at the Altmarkt, the old market square, is even more elaborate than the one at the KulturBrauerei. A dominating Ferris wheel makes it feel like an amusement park. Stylized medieval German font advertises an array of traditional German foods over wooden huts decorated with carvings of elves, Santa Claus, and other Christmas icons. German folk songs coming from a theater set up in the middle of the square add to the merriment.

We order Glühwein, of course, and Sebastian introduces me to *Spätzle*, a German type of egg noodle and cheese, while Sebastian orders a *Rotwurst*, which looks delicious. As we drink and eat, I don't want to ruin the enchanting Dresden festivities with the questions running through my mind, but one glass of Glühwein makes me carefree enough to ask: "So how do the people of Dresden view the whole bombing?"

"Honestly, most people realize that the Nazis started the war, but they also feel very victimized. There's a moment of silence every year on February 13, but we don't go around thinking of the bombing all the time. You can't live like that. My mother said her mother didn't know anything about the Holocaust, the death camps. Whether Dresden had to be bombed like that, like Stefanie said, it's a debate.

"But I think the Allies definitely taught Germany a lesson, if that's what they wanted. Dresden was turned into chalk, and then the Soviets took power. Dresden suffered a lot. Did we deserve it? I don't know."

"And your grandfather?" I ask, leaving the question open. He stops drinking the Glühwein.

"I never met him, so I hardly think about him, and when I do, I just feel...nothing. I don't really feel like I'm allowed to mourn for him. A lot of people died. It was a human tragedy. War is a human tragedy." He sighs in exasperation over the topic. "Maybe that's why I'm into conflict resolution. I probably get it from my mother. She's a pacifist. I mean, she lost her father, so that was very personal. She doesn't want to see any more fighting. I think in Dresden a lot of people go by the 'Never Again War' motto you don't like. But you also have right-wing protests here. The Pegida movement meets at Theaterplatz every Monday night. Hopefully they won't turn it into Adolf-Hitler-Platz again. People in Dresden are pretty liberal, though. The racists and neo-Nazis come from other parts of Saxony."

I'm upset that I brought this up because I want a "Berliner" for dessert, and sweetness doesn't go well with this conversation.

"So how does your mom feel about you dating an Israeli girl?" I ask. "Should I be nervous?"

"Nah. My mom's cool. She doesn't judge people based on their nationality or religion." I'm not exactly comforted.

"Was Meissen porcelain really used to make Nazi warplanes?" I ask.

"I haven't heard that. But we could ask her. Let's go. She's waiting for us."

His mother and stepfather live in a one-story house on a quiet, suburban block with quaint, private homes embellished by well-kept gardens. Sebastian parks in the driveway; we'll take a bus back to Berlin.

His mother opens the door, looking even statelier than I've seen in pictures, with her blonde, coiffed hair (most likely dyed to cover the gray) and an upright, lean body. As we shake hands, her fingers are so dainty I'm afraid I'll break them. Sebastian must have inherited his fluorescent blue bulbs from her. Her regality makes me more uncomfortable because here I am, this wild Jewish girl from wild Tel Aviv who knows little of formality.

"This is my mother, Klara," Sebastian says in German. His mother speaks very little English, which may work in my favor. Children of the GDR learned Russian instead of English as a second language.

"Mama, this is Nilly."

"Nice to meet you," she says as she lets us in.

"*Ich freue mich Ihnen zu kennlernen,*" I say, the German equivalent I've memorized.

His stepfather looms behind, a burly man with a mustache stretching to his round cheeks, providing a foil for Klara's gracefulness.

"And this is Alex, my father," Sebastian says as I shake Alex's large, strong hands. I repeat the German phrase.

The living room is decorated with about a dozen porcelain plates fastened to the wall, painted with pretty pictures of birds and flowers. This isn't a living room, but a museum. I'm afraid I'll bump into a plate and break one.

"My mother painted some of those," Sebastian says, motioning to the plates.

"Beautiful," I say. "*Finearbeit* runs in the family."

"Have a seat," Klara says in simple German I actually understand, pointing to the sofa. "I'll bring some tea."

Her husband comes out of the kitchen carrying a silver tray with a teapot, cups and saucers, sugar, and a plate of cookies.

"Meissen porcelain tea cups," Sebastian says as Klara sets them in front of us.

Alex lifts a saucer and shows me the back. "You see, the logo," he says. "Two swords."

"Very cool," I remark.

"Painted by hand," Klara says, via translation.

With Sebastian and Alex's help, Klara explains how she worked at the "House of Meissen" for thirty-seven years before retiring. She took up an apprenticeship at the manufacturer at age twenty-three and learned how to copy and adapt graphic images dating back even from the time of August the Strong.

Over 700,000 molds exist to create the intricate, small parts assembled by Meissen-trained sculptors. Klara points to the ornate teapot lid. One mold, for example, is dedicated solely to the flower forming its tip. Since the molds survived the bombing, pieces from the eighteenth century could be recreated with contemporary Dresden *Finearbeit*.

"That's amazing!" I say, meaning it.

She brings out several plates from different stages of production. Once they come out of the oven and cool from the first firing, staff artists can paint the designs in blue or green, the only colors to turn brilliant during the second firing when pieces shrink by 16 percent. Other colors are applied after the second or third firing, with some pieces requiring weeks to paint.

I realize another reason I'm attracted to Sebastian: He comes from an artistic family and a city that values architecture and design. But now I'd like to get to the less pretty parts of Meissen's history.

I remind Sebastian in a low voice to ask her about Meissen's role during the Third Reich. I'd rather the question come from him, not me. My fingers quiver holding the teacup while he speaks in German I can't understand. The only word that registers in her response is "Hitler."

"She says she doesn't think Meissen porcelain was used for warplanes," Sebastian says to me. "But Hitler loved Meissen porcelain and had plates made for him and the Nazi party. Some are on display at the Meissen museum."

I grimace, sad over this brown stain in the "White Gold."

Klara speaks some more, and Sebastian translates. "She also said under the GDR, the East German government took over the company, and Meissen made pieces dedicated to Marx and Engels. Before that, it was owned by the State of Saxony, like it is today."

"Wow," I say to Sebastian, gentle with my judgment. "It's been through a lot."

Sebastian and Klara nod.

"So you are architect?" she asks in English, changing the subject.

"Yes."

"You have interest here in Dresden, yes?"

"You mean is Dresden interesting to me? Very."

She tells me about museums I should visit next, repeating Stefanie's recommendations: The New Green Vault housing the treasures from August's court, the Gallery for Old Masters housing Rafael's famous "Sistine Madonna," and the Zwinger Palace's Porcelain Museum. She even suggests I see the new synagogue, the only hint to my "difference." *I really should come back.*

But the art of Dresden still doesn't interest me as much as the secrets held in the museum of this household. What did Klara's mother teach her about the war? What did Meissen really do during the war? What does she think about her son dating an Israeli? These gruff, hard questions would feel as severe as hammers smashing the fine plates on the wall.

"Well, Mama," Sebastian says. "We better head back. We have a long way."

I leave the "Schröder Museum" both relieved and disappointed. Little of consequence has been shared between us. We were as delicate and uncracked as Meissen porcelain.

CHAPTER SEVEN

I hardly talk on the bus ride back, and not because I don't want to ask more questions. I'm pensive; it's our last night together. I ask to listen to his film score and some of his other tracks to pass the time. I feel him through his musical talent, and it soothes me.

Sebastian is an unearthed Saxon mine, filled with secrets and treasures. When I dig into him, I dig into myself, too: my own opinions, values, and even prejudices.

Once I stopped being creeped out by Berlin's Holocaust ghosts, I began to love it as the cosmopolitan, sexy city it is—even in the cold, which feels like a metaphysical air conditioner cooling my overheated life in Israel. Berlin's an idyll of beautiful people, cultural richness, historical depth, smooth transportation, and even Jewish life. And no terror attacks.

But the one famous Berlin feature I haven't experienced yet is its nightlife, so when Sebastian offers to spend our last night partying, I don't hesitate. After a day of so much repression amidst delicate beauty—new, old, and destroyed—we need a hardcore nightclub to return us to our primitive selves.

We get to his apartment at about 8 pm and plop on the bed, exhausted. We take a half-hour disco nap in dark silence. Finally, he squeezes my neck.

"You up?"

"Yeah."

"So, Ritter Butzke?"

"What's that?"

"A popular club. Mostly electro. Reminds me of Jimmy Who. I think you'll like it."

"Yeah. Maybe I'll just pack first. Get organized for tomorrow."

"Good idea. Then we'll have some Club-Mate."

"What's that?'

"An all-natural energy drink. Kind of like an iced tea. A Berlin tradition."

Another Berlin delicacy to try. *The fun never ends!*

After packing with absolutely no enthusiasm, I get dolled up, gothic style. I put on tight black jeans, a lacy black top, and black boots and apply lots of black eyeliner and mascara. In Israel, I party at nightclubs every so often, an opportunity to look and sometimes act like a slut. Tonight will be no different.

Sebastian must want me tonight. He looks so handsome in a red T-shirt and designer jeans that flatter his designer body. Actually, he has to want me forever.

At a Späti near his house, he buys two Club-Mates and a vile of vodka. He instructs me to throw back a few sips of the Mate then fills the void with vodka. The pauper's cocktail tastes like medicine, but it's way tastier than the standard, boring Red Bull-vodka combo. After a few more sips, I feel like I'm drinking a magical elixir.

I'm already tipsy when we get to Ritter Butzke where hundreds of people are standing in line in the cold. Umbrellas pop open to the rain. Fortunately, Sebastian has connections, and we're on the guest list. We waltz right in.

As soon as we enter, I feel that familiar liberating, loose, pick-up energy. We check in our coats, go to the bathroom at grungy, graffitied stalls, and move straight into the main hall pumping out electro from a top-notch sound system. The beats penetrate my heart.

We order another delicacy: *Schorle*, or German fruit soda, mixed with vodka.

On the dance floor, a few sips away from full intoxication, I put my arms around Sebastian and pull him closer to me. Yes, I want us to be tied by our primal attraction, not our horrific histories. The only firestorm I want to consume me here is the firestorm of desire.

Done with the *Schorle* mix, we begin to grope each other. It's so crowded that no one could notice that his hand is rubbing my crotch over my jeans, and even if people could, they wouldn't care. My hand moves over his crotch in kind.

I'm frustrated. I want to feel his skin. Even his foreskin. I apply more pressure so that he knows it.

"Come," he says, as we go to an outdoor corridor leading to more dance halls. I'm so hot for him that I don't feel the cold. We enter a smaller, emptier hall for house music and head up a staircase to a balcony where a few couples are making out on some tattered sofas.

With the privacy the balcony affords us, he pushes me against the wall.

This time, as we kiss, he sticks his hand inside my bra to play with my nipples. I insert my hand inside his pants, feeling for his cock. I find it and grab hold of the entire shaft. It's as hard as a metal pole I want to dance upon. I hold on tight. It's my anchor—to Berlin.

"I don't want to leave you," I say.

"I don't want you to leave," he says, but I think he's referring to my hand.

I can't let go. I don't care how different we are. I don't care if his grandfather was a Nazi. I don't care if his mother is a left-wing fascist.

"I like it so much here," I say, still holding on. "I like you so much."

"I like you so much, too," he says and kisses me passionately, making me believe his words are sincere.

"Don't make me leave!" I say, not caring how needy and pathetic I sound. *Nichnas ya'in yotzeh sod*, the Hebrew version of *in vino veritas*.

He answers by dipping his hands into my panties so that we're standing there with our hands in each other's jeans. I whimper.

"You're so wet," he says. "Let's get out of here."

On his bed, he takes me in three stages: First, he drops warning markers with his mouth on my clit. Second, he goes in with the cluster bombs of his cock, attacking me in and out. Third, his fingers serve as sticky bombs inflaming my clit while he's thrusting—until I'm completely, utterly ruined.

He wakes me at around 11 am by finishing me off again with his fingers, but I go back to sleep and dream about what I'm too hungover to do to him.

Sadly, I wake up at 1 pm. The Berlin dream is almost over. My flight's in nine hours.

I don't want to go back to my lonely bed. I don't want to wake up again, designing boring, cookie-cutter buildings, no matter how they secure my country. The architecture here is so much more diverse, from the gothic Churches to the Baroque palaces to the reconstructed synagogues. Modern Germany is still rebuilding, just like Israel is, struggling to preserve its historical landmarks while adhering to the progress of modernity.

Sebastian has already planned our farewell "brunch": cheese fondue. I don't even know how he has the energy to cook, but he's superhuman.

Holding a cup of coffee he prepared for me, I engage in my new favorite pastime: watching him prepare food. I'm enamored by the grace of his muscles as he assembles the fondue set, cuts up vegetables, and puts frozen rolls in the oven so they could expand into warm, fluffy balls.

Now I'll return to slouchy, hairy Israeli men. Okay, so I'm sounding like an antisemite again, but I've come to the sad realization that, to me, the average German man is more handsome than the average Israeli.

But now my attraction is not just about Sebastian's superior looks. He's been sweet and giving and interesting, sensitive to my Jewish background, even taking me to Kosher Life—an allusion to the life we could lead together? So he still doesn't support the settlements, but he supported me so kindly throughout this trip. *Must I be politically aligned with a romantic partner?*

We take to his sofa where he places the fondue set. When the cheese melts, he dips in a breadstick for me to taste. Creamy and delicious, like him. But my stomach starts to ache, as if the cheese is coagulating in my intestines, when I think about bringing up our future.

Dana advised me not to bring it up because men don't like pressure, but Ariella encouraged me to, warning me not to waste my time with a man with whom I probably have no future. Weighing their contradicting advice worsens my nausea.

I lean my head on his lap and look up at him, frowning. I feel very hot. *Is the heater on too strong?*

"What's wrong?" he asks.

"I'm sad I'm leaving."

"I'm sad you're leaving." He begins to play with my waves, now one of his favorite pastimes.

I sigh heavily and put my hands on my stomach. Maybe I shouldn't have eaten the fondue.

"Will I ever see you again?" I can't help but sound desperate.

My stomach makes funny noises during the seven seconds he takes to respond.

"I'm sure we will." He doesn't sound convincing. "Either I'll come back to Tel Aviv or you'll come back here. My schedule from Christmas through January is pretty hectic, with tours and sessions. I'm playing at a ski resort in Switzerland over New Year's. I'm going to Thailand in February. I always try to escape one month during the winter. Maybe March?"

The dream is over. It should have continued with an invitation to Thailand.

"Who are you going to Thailand with?" I ask, feeling possessive.

"For now, on my own. A friend might join."

I literally feel like throwing up. Maybe he'll meet another "Israeli lady" in Thailand.

"March is too long." *There I go, sounding desperate again.*

"I know." He bends his head to kiss me on the forehead. "But we'll text and stuff."

"So we'll have a *textual* relationship?" I'm not trying to be funny. The thought depresses me.

"And Skype," he says.

"Well," I stammer. "Um."

"What?"

The only cure to my nausea is to ask. I can't hold back, not again. "Do you think there's even a future for us? I mean, we live so far apart."

The cheese has fully hardened inside. I feel very heavy.

He thinks again for a few minutes. "Good question. I really like Israel. I do. I just can't see myself living there. My work is here. My language. My music. And I can't be responsible for you leaving your land and your people." *Great. Now he's using Zionism as a tool to keep us apart.* "Your family's there. Your career."

"I wouldn't mind living in Berlin." I can't believe I said that. I didn't plan to. I never seriously considered it, mostly because Berlin is taboo in my family. "Are you looking to settle down anytime soon?"

"Don't you know that Berlin men have Peter Pan syndrome? We want to be little boys forever."

"Actually, I didn't. Do you have it?"

"I would like to have a family one day. Not sure exactly when. I want to get some hits under my belt so that I could support a family if and when I decide to have one. It would be nice to live DINK for a while."

"DINK? What's that?"

"Double-Income-No-Kids."

"Oh."

"My mother would love grandchildren." He chuckles. "And I don't think she'd want a grandson without a foreskin. Do you have to—you know—chop-chop?"

Now he's using Judaism to keep us apart.

My instinct is: *Of course I have to!* But I'm angered how a piece of skin must be a deal-breaker. Why is this ritual so important, so sacred, an absolute must? Had I not grown up with it, I'd probably think this whole "chop-chop" thing is weird. If I circumcise my son—and I can't believe I'm even questioning it—I don't know if I'd be doing it for me, my son, my mother, my family, or my larger family: the Jewish people, differentiated and even persecuted over the millennia because of "chop-chop."

"If I want my mother to help change diapers, he'll have to be foreskinless," I say.

"It still seems a bit cruel to me. Unnecessary. But I guess this just goes to show how different we are—our cultures, our backgrounds, upbringings. If I'm really honest, I'm not sure how easy it will be."

I can't protest. He simply has more courage to state the obvious. The cheese is starting to melt inside.

"You're probably right," I say.

"But we'll see what happens. Let's not make any predictions."

"Okay."

We look at each other, and he goes from playing with my hair to caressing my arm. My stomach has settled enough to accept a kiss, which leads to farewell sex on the couch, but the pregnancy-free stage is over.

As I place a rubber over his foreskin, I feel like I'm placing the filter of reality over the dream that was Berlin and Sebastian. For the first time, sex with him is mediocre.

PART THREE

JERUSALEM

CHAPTER ONE

I step off the El Al plane in the middle of the night feeling no sentimentality toward the country, and not just because I'm exhausted.

Actually, those fuzzy Zionist feelings—in which we Jews feel compelled to kiss the Holy Land, our homeland, the modern Jewish miracle—faded years ago.

Have Sebastian, Berlin, and Germany corrupted me so much that I'm not a Zionist anymore?

What does a "Jewish state" mean, anyway? A Jewish political refuge? A state with a Jewish majority? A state governed by Jewish laws and traditions? A state in which the national holidays are the innumerable Jewish holidays that subsume our vacation time? A state with special, sanctioned control over Jewish lives, such that its government is the only one in the world allowed to expel Jews from their homes with impunity?

Sometimes the "Jewish state" is just so overbearing. I'd believe in it more passionately if its definition simply were: "A state that functions incredibly well, that aims to minimize undue hassle and hardship for its people so that they can realize their dreams." A state that feels like...Berlin.

When I wake up late on Monday morning (having taken the morning off), Sebastian and I rekindle our "textual relationship" with small talk replete with niceties and emoticons offering no real fulfillment. We set no Skype date. He sings no more songs.

Before landing, I made plans to meet Ariella for a debriefing over brunch. I knew I would need Ariella's skepticism, not Dana's permission.

At Landver near my house, the place where I unsuccessfully tried to leave Sebastian, I rehash with her my last conversation with him.

"Well, men are more practical with these things," Ariella says over a shared omelet brunch served with rolls, cheeses, and various dips. "They don't get caught up in fairy tales, and the sad thing is, I believe that if a man really wants a woman, he'll move mountains to make it happen."

I can't argue, the way I couldn't argue with Sebastian when he stated the obvious yesterday. "You're right. Maybe I should just chalk it up to a great experience."

"Better to have loved and lost than to have never loved at all."

"Or better to have had great sex," I say, inducing a smile I really need. "But it's like the great high I had from being with him now has a matching low."

"That's why we need to get married. So that we know he's always there."

"Yeah, but there are marriages where he's not always there."

"True. That's why we need a *motek neshama*."

"So what should I do?" I ask, frustrated.

"Maybe just let some time pass. Process it all. Don't make any decisions now. Just get back into your routine."

"It's the routine that scares me."

I drive to work without any enthusiasm. I wonder if I miss Sebastian, and also Berlin, because I'm just not happy at my job. Even sitting in on the design committee for the Ma'ale Adumim housing project hasn't satisfied me. Maybe, if I were creatively fulfilled, building the homes I want to build in my own style, I wouldn't find fulfillment in the people whose ancestors participated in Jewish genocide. Maybe, if I developed a new dream, I'd dream less of Sebastian.

Spontaneously, I walk into Zimmerman's office and tell him how I no longer want to be a mere "fly on the wall" at the design committee. I want to go in on new projects from the untouched ground up.

"Why is this important to you?" he asks.

"I have some ideas. I want to test them."

"Like what?"

"Well, I wonder if we could build in a way that preserves the beauty of the landscape, that won't require us to flatten mountains or hills."

"Kind of like the Arabs?"

"Well, yeah."

He looks disappointed, threatened even. "That's all very nice and artistic, but that's not what our firm does. That would require completely different designs, and the clients wouldn't go for it. We're given a specific number of units for each site. Especially with the housing crisis, the government's allowing more than ever. Flat land gets us at least two extra floors. That's a few extra million dollars. Anyway, don't you want as many Jews as possible to live beyond the Green Line?"

He's referring to Judea and Samaria. After the 1948 War of Independence, a UN official delineated the 1949 armistice line on a map using a green marker, hence the "Green Line" dividing the territories that almost two decades later all came under Israel's control. Sometimes I like to think it refers to the verdancy of the Israeli side.

"Actually, I don't," I say. "We're not creating cattle cars. We're creating homes."

Now I know what else bothers me about the "Jewish state": Our homes have become mere commodities and political tools.

I leave his office convinced that, once I get my license at the end of the month, I won't stay on board at Zimmerman and Associates. For the rest of the afternoon, I check out classifieds online, easing the void of Sebastian by taking control of one area of my life that can more easily bend to my will.

Out of curiosity, I even check out jobs in Berlin, wondering if any Israeli real estate development company there is seeking architects. With all of its rebuilding, Berlin could be an architect's paradise. I submit my Hebrew resume to one company on a lark.

In the middle, I get a text message from Sebastian. "Hey, Silly, how's your day going?"

"Getting back into the swing of things, SS." I'm sure to add a smiley emoticon. "And you?"

He takes at least an hour to answer. Maybe he's annoyed. Maybe I really should stop making Holocaust jokes once and for all.

"Session work with a new artist this week," he writes back. "Berlin's emptying out for Xmas. Ismael lands on Thursday. He'll get the sofa for two nights."

"I miss that sofa!" *It's ours! Why can't Ismael stay in a hotel?*

"I miss you being on it..."

I'd appreciate and believe his longing more if he didn't wait about an hour to respond to my messages. I hate feeling attached to my phone like this.

After a forced delay in kind during which I drive home, I ask: "And are you hosting a Syrian family for Christmas in the end?"

"No. The authorities couldn't find one for us, so it's just Ismael and my family. What are you doing for Hanukkah?"

Would Muslim families even want to celebrate Christmas? I feel like asking, but the intellectual condom is back on.

"I'll light the *hanukkiah* with my family and eat *Kartoffelpuffer*," I respond from my sofa while eating a microwaved pasta dinner, missing his gnocchi, his coffee, and that yummy Gruyère cheese.

But the next message doesn't come from Sebastian.

"Did you hear? Terror attack in Berlin!" Dana writes to me.

"What???"

I check the news online: "Truck crashes into Christmas market, terrorism suspected."

Wow. Wow. Wow. I expected a terror attack to hit Berlin, but not so soon, not when I was just there, at those magical Christmas markets, envious of Berlin for never having to go through what we do.

I keep reading.

A lorry purposefully drove into Berlin's largest Christmas market, near the Kaiser Wilhelm Memorial Church in west Berlin, bulldozing over throngs of people. Reports start with four casualties, but numbers go up as I refresh the pages. The German media still won't definitively call it a terrorist attack, let alone an Islamic terrorist attack.

I hate myself for feeling glad to have a legitimate excuse to call Sebastian.

"Oh, my God!" I say, calling him from WhatsApp. "I just heard about the terrorist attack. You okay?"

"Yeah. Just heard, too. Got a call from my mom. I'm okay. I'm home."

"Oh, my God, to think I was just there at a Christmas market. Guess it's Germany's turn..." *That's the most politically incorrect I'll be.*

"Yes. After the France attack, it was just a matter of time."

You mean not after Israel's attacks? A snarky response I restrain. He must believe terrorist attacks against Israel are an act of war against the "Occupation," disconnected to jihadi attacks in Europe.

"Ah, shit," he says, cutting the conversation short. "I'm getting a lot of calls. I better let people know I'm okay."

"All right. Take care of yourself."

"I will. Miss you!"

"Miss you, too."

I remember those days, immediately after terrorist attacks, when I'd reach out to people who might have been in the vicinity of the attack to make sure they were okay. But ever since the last terror wave, I just hope for the best, relying on Facebook status updates (or that new "Marked As Safe" Facebook feature) to find out if my friends and family are alive.

It really is Germany's turn, like Ima predicted, not that I'm happy about that. It should be no one's turn, not even the former Nazi country. Surprisingly, I feel as sad as I would feel had the attack occurred in Israel. I've grown to love Berlin, and I hurt for the city.

By morning, the perpetrator is determined to be a migrant who got into Germany posing as a refugee and who the German authorities once detained but then let go. Among the twelve dead are the Polish driver (whose truck was apparently hijacked) and an Israeli lady on vacation in Berlin with her husband, who is now wounded in the hospital. I guess I was wrong when I told Ima that Jews are safer on German soil than in Israel.

Suddenly, I lose all desire to move to Berlin. Germany imported the terrorism I so wanted to escape.

Finally, the German media designates the attack as an act of terror but still has not pinpointed the motivation. *God, these Germans are so stupid! Can't they connect the dots? Who else would take a truck and ram it into innocent men, women, and children? Hindu immigrants? Buddhists? Their Russian Jews?*

I read some German op-eds via Google translate and gather that most major German pundits are more worried about the rise of the German right in the wake of the attack than the rise in Islamic terror. Some excuse the terrorist attack as an act of insanity by an emotionally disturbed, frustrated immigrant. Chancellor Merkel makes a plea to crack down on terror while preserving compassion for the refugees.

Truth is, she doesn't sound much different than some Israeli politicians who vow to crack down on Palestinian terror while buying into their excuse for it: frustration over the "Occupation." Despite Israel's bravado as a leader in the "war against terror," I hope Germany doesn't look to Israel for an example. We Israelis have become habituated to these attacks, which seem to have no end in sight.

In more news, the United Nations is planning to meet this week—but not to discuss the terrorist attack in Germany. A new Israel-bashing resolution is on the docket to declare Jewish settlements, naturally including Ariel and East Jerusalem, illegal under international law.

In the past, the United States has traditionally vetoed UN resolutions that single out Israeli settlements (i.e. Jews) for censure, but going against decades of policy, the United States, under lame-duck President Obama, allows the resolution to pass on December 23. The German foreign minister applauds the vote, one step toward making the cradle of Judaism *Judenrein*. He might as well have shouted over a loudspeaker, "The Jews are our misfortune."

What did Germans learn from the Holocaust? To bend over backward to welcome Muslims into their country and homes only to deprive Jews of property rights in their ancestral homeland?

I never thought I'd be overjoyed that Trump, who apparently tried to scuttle the anti-Israel vote, will soon take office, another reason to minimize communication with Sebastian, at least directly. Germans seem to hate him.

While I usually don't write political posts on Facebook, I update my status, expecting Sebastian to read it but not to "like" it, and I don't mean by clicking "like."

Do you know anyone who wants to build a home in Judea and Samaria? I'm offering my freelance services as an architect to build your dream home on this sacred ground, now more than ever!

I haven't heard from Sebastian since the attack, from when I resolved not to initiate any more texts with him. I don't want to be his "text pal." It will take more than 200 characters on a small screen to discuss the entire worldviews standing between us.

On Christmas Eve, which also happens to be the first night of Hanukkah, Sebastian breaks our texting hiatus by sending me a picture of him, his mother, and Ismael standing in front of a small Christmas tree. Ismael, handsome in a sturdy sweater, has his arms around fragile Klara as if he's about to crush her, but she appears comfortable, pleased.

"Merry Christmas from all of us," he writes.

"Merry Christmas and Happy Hanukkah," is all I write back, attaching a picture of me standing in front of the *hanukkiah* set on my parents' windowsill.

I can't help but think how the Hanukkah-Christmas overlap is symbolic. We are one now, Germans and Jews, united not by a tragic past but in the battle for the freedom of the future. I'm even more convinced now that my attraction to Sebastian wasn't only physical but metaphysical. We are bound in this mystical matrix of good and evil. *Can't Sebastian see that?*

Our texting hiatus resumes during the period between Christmas and New Year's, which are like Germany's "High Holidays," involving family dinners, outings, and vacations.

Dana begs me to go out with her on New Year's, but I don't care to celebrate it. Rosh Hashanah is our "New Year's." While I don't observe the Jewish New Year according to Jewish law, I take advantage of our "High Holidays" between Rosh Hashanah and Yom Kippur, the Day of Atonement, as a period for sober reflection—not drunken parties. Maybe this is why the Jewish people are more spiritual than Germans, to a fault; otherwise, Jews might have prevented the brutes from murdering them.

"I'm afraid I'll just think of Sebastian, wishing he was my New Year's kiss," I tell Dana.

"Well, the best way to get over someone is to get under someone else," she says adamantly. "Maybe you'll meet another German guy. I've noticed a lot more German tourists in Israel since you left."

"Do I really need to hunt another 'Nazi?'"

"Absolutely. Let's go 'Nazi hunting!'"

I crack up, realizing I could use a night out with Dana.

We meet on Rothschild and, rather than barhop, I teach her the "Späti" method. We purchase an energy drink—since Israel doesn't sell Club-Mates— empty out the bottle by taking a few sips, pour in vodka from a flask, and drink as we walk up and down Rothschild. Eventually, we end up at Jimmy Who.

In line, I go "Nazi hunting," keeping my eye out for more "Aryan-looking" men. Once we enter, I spot one, although he's not pure "Aryan" at 5'9" with light brown hair and gray eyes. I can tell, mostly from his perfectly straight nose and reserved demeanor, that he might be of "Nazi" descent.

I ask straight out, the Späti mix kicking in, "Where you from?"

"Germany."

Bullseye!

"I was just there!" I say, enthused.

"I'm from Hamburg," he says.

"Oh. I was in Berlin and loooved it!"

"Cool. I go there about once a year," he says in a cold, sturdy German accent, hardly smiling.

"How's Hamburg?" I ask with a full smile.

"It's very nice," he says with a forced smile. *What, am I ugly?*

"What brings you here?" I ask.

"I had friends who came here and told me I should come."

"You like it so far?"

"Well, we just got here today." He takes a sip of beer. *Yes, drink more.* So far, he's not a "Nazi" worth "getting under." Still, with my drunken charm, I put my arm on his shoulder and say, seductively, "Well, you just need more reasons to like it..."

He neither resists nor surrenders. He might as well be a piece of furniture.

I'm sober enough to maintain my dignity and walk away. Meanwhile, Dana has found her own "get under" option, someone she once dated—or fucked—two years ago. I'm left on the dance floor alone, five minutes away from the New Year's countdown, in the exact same spot where Sebastian and I had dirty-danced back in November.

Ten.

Nine.

A moderately handsome Israeli comes up to me with a tame, "Hi." *Eight.* "Hi," I say back. *Seven.* He puts his hands on my hips. *Six.* I put my arms on his shoulders. *Five.* He tightens his hands over my waist. *Four.* I feel dizzy. *Three.* He leans in. *Two.* I loosen my lips. *One.* He goes in for the kiss.

Everyone cheers, but I want to gag. His kiss is slobbery and unenjoyable. I miss Sebastian more than ever.

I move to the side and check my phone, wishing for a text from him, but nothing. My drunkenness gives way to courage—or stupidity—and I send him a picture of me puckering up.

"Happy New Year's from Jimmy Who!" I write.

Come the next hungover morning, he still hasn't responded.

I probably looked so dumb. Or he probably met a girl in Switzerland, a German-speaking girl without Jewish baggage—a leftist who hates Trump. Or maybe Ismael said something to convince him to cut ties with me. Or maybe his mother did. Or maybe, as Dana assures me, he's just very busy.

I wonder if German-Israeli relationships are doomed from the start. Our respective fucked-up-ness rules out long-term romantic relationships. Germans must date fellow Germans and not people who constantly judge them for their nation's past crimes against the Jewish people. Jews must date fellow Jews and not people who can't truly empathize with Jewish victimhood because their nation once perpetrated it.

"I am in pain," I break down to Ariella over the phone. "I admit. It hurts."

"Maybe you just need to make a clean break. You can't keep going back and forth with him like this."

"You're probably right. But how?"

"Write him an email. You can't do this over text."

Both Ariella and Dana approve this message, which I send on January 4.

> *Dear Sebastian,*
> *I hope you had a wonderful New Year's in Switzerland.*
> *You know I had such an amazing time with you here and in Berlin, but I was thinking, without plans to see each other, it's better we part ways. It's very difficult for me to move on and to be free to meet other men when I'm in touch with you every so often or wonder if there is a future between us.*
> *I'm sure you can understand.*
> *Know that you are very special to me and always will be.*
> *Yours,*
> *Nilly*

January 5, 6, and 7 go by, and still no reply. Who knows if he has even read it, but he must have. Just to be sure, I send him a text with a smiley emoticon: "I sent you an email."

If he doesn't respond by January 8, then he never will.

That's when a major truck attack occurs not in Berlin but in Jerusalem. It's captured on CCTV for the world to see. The same kind of lorry that rammed into the Berlin Christmas market drives over IDF soldiers standing in formation at a Jerusalem memorial park, knocking them over as if they're bowling pins, crushing a few under the weight of the wheels. The sadistic driver then attempts a strike by running them over again, in reverse!

Israelis are not as slow as Germans in labeling this a terrorist attack. Bibi and some other politicians lay blame on the Islamic State, probably hoping to court solidarity from the Europeans.

Will Germans finally see that attacks like these are neither protests against political policies nor acts of insanity but a continuation of that same Nazi obsession: the murder of Jews and free people everywhere in the quest for world domination?

But the attack doesn't induce Sebastian to reach out as I did after the Christmas attack. I'm annoyed with myself for waiting for a German to send condolences over dead Jews. I cry myself to sleep, in sorrow over the state of my country and the state of my love life. Sebastian has inflicted *Kristallnacht* on my heart, pillaging and shattering it.

But the next day, I'm given a sign of life—and hope. A photograph of the Brandenburg Gate illuminated with the flag of Israel goes viral on social media. I repost it.

It's the first post of mine that Sebastian "likes."

CHAPTER TWO

The next day, I shut my cell phone off at work. I must unplug. I can't wonder anymore if Sebastian will respond with a proper message. I can't reread our messages, looking for clues into his alienating behavior. I can't spy on him anymore on Facebook.

I open a Facebook chat with Ariella: "Should I unfriend Sebastian on FB?"

"Do whatever makes you feel better, *metuka*," she writes back.

"I think it will."

But Dana doesn't give me permission.

"I don't want you to give him the satisfaction," she writes. "He'll know you care."

"But I do care, and I don't care if he knows that. I think I need to go cold turkey."

"He ghosted you, darling." Dana then attaches a link to an article about the phenomenon, in which a man goes AWOL after either a date or relationship. The writer advises women not to take "ghosting" personally. It's a reflection of the man's issues, not the woman's.

"I talked to my cousin Anat in Haifa about you and Sebastian," Dana writes me a bit later. "She was like, 'Good luck with German men.' She said they're tough nuts to crack. You should talk to her!"

"That would be great! Can you introduce us?"

"Sure!"

On Facebook, I trade Sebastian for a new Facebook friend: Dana's cousin, Anat. We agree to meet up next week when she plans to be in Tel Aviv.

At home after work, I turn on my phone. I admit I'm hopeful when I see an incoming text, but it's from my mother.

"Call me," it says. She usually doesn't send me text messages. *This can't be good.*

"Why did you go to Germany?" she asks me, her voice tinged with anger.

"What?"

"I tried calling you today, but it went to voicemail, so I called you at work. Safta got pneumonia again. She's back in the hospital. I wanted to tell you so that you could visit her. This time her lungs are worse. I spoke to the receptionist and told her it was nice that the firm sent you to Berlin. She said they didn't send you. Berlin had nothing to do with work. You lied to me!"

I'm angry I can't defend Sebastian to my mother, that I can't say that I went there for an amazing German man who's good to me—and who loves Jews and who wants to convert—which is what she'd need to hear to accept him. *Maybe she's right. Maybe I should've stayed far away from Berlin.*

"I just wanted to go for fun, okay. Berlin's a cool place. I knew I needed an excuse with you."

"There was a guy, wasn't there?"

"No."

"There was. You're not the same. You're depressed. He hurt you, didn't he? That German. No wonder."

Instead of dousing the fire of the *Kristallnacht* of my heart, she's added fuel.

"You know what," I lash out, loud and firm. "Yes—there was a guy, and you know what? I'm almost thirty-two-years old. It's my life! I do not have to explain my life to you all the time. I'm not in high school. I don't have to report to you or apologize to you for anything. Can't you just let me be? If I want to date a German, I'll date a German. If I want to marry a German, I'll marry a fucking German. I can't live my life how you want me to live it!"

"Go ahead. Be as miserable as you are now."

"I really don't want to talk to you right now. I'm not talking about my life with you. Ever! You'll just ruin it! Leave me alone. I'll visit Safta in an hour. Please don't be there."

I've never cursed at or hung up on my mother. Germany has made me a hateful person. I hate another Jew—my mother, no less! I hate Sebastian. I hate Germans. I hate Arabs. I hate the world. The only people I love are my good friends—and my nephew and niece.

Actually, I feel relieved telling my mother off. I should've told her off sooner. Maybe had I approached Berlin and Sebastian without the suspicion and resentment she ingrained in me, I would have enjoyed him and the city more freely, lovingly. I wouldn't have placed so many conditions on what we can and can't, should and shouldn't be.

I call my brother Arik to find out where Safta's convalescing. Unexpectedly,

I tell him briefly about my argument with Ima and the basic details of my relationship with Sebastian. I hardly ever discuss my love life with my brother, except when he wants to set me up, but I need a family ally with whom to confide.

"Nilly, you're right," he says. "You're thirty-one-years old. Ima can get like that. I mean, she's 'old school.' I work a lot with German clients. It's not the same generation. She can't see that. Don't pay attention to her. It's your life. I just want you to find a guy that makes you happy. I know it's not easy. At this point, I wouldn't worry if he's Jewish or not. Anyway, your kids will automatically be Jewish." He pauses. "Just next time, don't flake on a guy, okay? It wasn't nice when you flaked on Aviram."

"He told you about that?"

"Yeah."

"Oh, shit. You're right." I forgot that I once "ghosted" a guy. "Thanks, Arik. I guess it's too late to send him my regards?"

"Probably. Anyway, he has a girlfriend now."

"Oh, good for him," I say, although I'm a bit jealous he found someone while my heart is in pieces.

At least Sebastian brought me closer to my brother.

In the hospital room, Safta's hooked up to IVs and a respiratory tube. Wearing a hygienic mask, I hold her hand, but it's not warm as usual. I'm not even sure she knows who I am. Her eyes, barely open, don't light up like they used to. The doctors say she may only have a few weeks to live.

Where I had once silently asked Safta for permission to date Sebastian, now I silently ask, almost plead, in tears:

Safta, I want to honor you. I want to honor my mother, too, as I'm commanded by the Torah. I don't want to disgrace your memory or minimize the pain and loss you have endured, but please—please—give me permission to live my own life, as I wish to live it, honestly and truly. Because if the Holocaust holds me back from living today, then aren't I also, somehow, dead? Let me honor Ima and Aba by letting me discover and be the most authentic woman they, as God's agents, have created. And let me honor you by finding my happiness in this life.

Her hands warm up, and her eyes open wider. She attempts a smile. She's given me permission.

CHAPTER THREE

On Friday, January 20, I meet Anat for breakfast at Cafe Puaa, one of Jaffa's oldest, hippest cafes with an eclectic interior that appears as if some hipster made creative use of household items he inherited from his Sephardic grandparents. The furniture, apparently taken from the flea market nearby, is all for sale. It's uncharacteristically cold today; I come with my Berlin winter jacket.

Anat's an attractive woman with a streaked, cute, curly bob that must be alluring to German men. With pointed, black glasses and a blazer over jeans, she has an intellectual, no-nonsense look.

From our friendly and attentive waitress, we order two cappuccinos and, to share, the *sabich* breakfast, an Iraqi-inspired dish consisting of fried eggplant, hardboiled eggs, *tehina*, and fresh herbs served with a flat, focaccia-like Iraqi pita.

Once our coffee arrives, Anat tells me how she first moved to Berlin for her MBA. She redeemed Austrian citizenship from her mother's side to live and study in Germany. Once she graduated, she found a job as a sales executive for an Israeli company that sells Berlin real estate to Israelis. The company sounds familiar from my internet browsing.

The *sabich* comes, and as we assemble and eat this Iraqi-fusion pita wrap, she tells me how she met Karl, her first German boyfriend, at university. At first, they just studied together in the library and at cafés. She found him attractive and subtly flirted with him, but he hardly flirted back. She assumed he wasn't interested. Then, one day, over a beer after one of their study sessions, he kissed her. From then on, they were a couple.

"Your family didn't mind that you were dating a German?"

"My family's very secular and open-minded. Even my grandmother, whose family fled Austria before the Nazis came into power, didn't mind. She liked that we could speak German together. And Karl doesn't really consider himself German. More like a 'citizen of the world.' He came to a Passover Seder in Berlin with my Israeli friends. He also came to Israel for the first time with me."

"He liked it?"

"Loved it!"

"He didn't have issues with Israeli politics?"

"Not really. Neither of us is so political, but I had to calm him down before he came to Israel. He thought he'd be entering a war zone because that's what he saw on German news. He was surprised to see how modern and relatively peaceful it is."

"So it never bothered him that you're Israeli?"

"Not at all. Actually, his parents visited Israel once and liked it. I find most Berliners are cool with Israel."

"So why did you break up?"

"Well, he wasn't sure if he ever wanted to get married or even have kids. His idea of a committed relationship was: 'DINK.' You know what that is?"

I snicker. "Double-Income-No-Kids?"

"Exactly." We laugh in commiseration. "And I wanted to start a family one day, either here or in Germany."

She dated dozens of German men after she and Karl broke up, one seriously, but he, too, was a Berlin "Peter Pan." She moved back to Israel last year.

"I love Berlin, but at the end of the day, Israel's much more my speed," she says. "I guess you could say this is home. Germans have a lot of walls up. Maybe it has something to do with German society, which is so ordered. They can't express themselves like we do. I missed that Israeli openness, that honesty."

"You okay dating Israeli men again?" I feel like I'm grilling her, but she's sharing her experiences generously. We've developed a good rapport rather quickly, which seems an easier feat with Israelis than with Germans.

"I should be, considering I'm seriously dating an Israeli guy now. He's divorced, and his ex-wife lives in the U.S. with his son, but he's very eager to have it better this time. Met him online. I'm thirty-three, so I knew I'd have to be open to a man with children. It was just really easy to connect with him. Same language, same mentality. And he's good to me.

"At first, I liked German men a lot—they're super sexy and smart, and they love to travel, and I find a lot of them are good cooks. And because they're in no rush to get married, they don't judge you for your age."

I sympathize. "Yes!"

"Here, a lot of guys eat at their mom's. Overall, though, they're close with their families and want their own. The Germans I met aren't as close with their families, and for some reason, most of the German guys I dated never had good relationships with their dads."

"Wow, that's just like the German guy I dated, Sebastian."

After my last bite of the *sabich*, I segue into my Sebastian tale, up until his "ghosting."

"Typical," Anat says, sipping her last bits of cappuccino. "I can't tell you how many times German men 'ghosted' me. Or they were really passive. Or very inconsistent with their communications. Like, I'd go out on a date that I thought went well because we talked and made out, only to hear from him a week or two later, and he wouldn't apologize or think anything was weird about it. A lot of times, they'd just come back from vacation. They have a lot of vacation days. It's like they have all the time in the world. They don't have to seize the moment like we Israelis do because we never know if we'll die tomorrow.

"I also noticed they can postpone sex. It doesn't seem like a need for them. Israelis will always want to come up 'for coffee' on the first date." I laugh. *She knows the code.* "Sometimes, I met German guys on Tinder—Tinder!—and they wouldn't even kiss me on the first date even if I knew they were attracted to me because they told me I was *schön*, pretty. And when they did get sexual, it was, like, overly sexual. Nothing's just, well, normal. No middle ground. This one guy was so kinky, we made out at night in a playground in a shed at the top of a slide, and he made me squirt."

"Squirt? What's that?"

"Female ejaculation..." She winks. "I recommend it."

"Well, I didn't squirt, but we had amazing sex! A lot of kinky sex, now that I think about it, usually after political arguments. Maybe that's how he handled it."

"Maybe," Anat muses. "It's like there's a disconnect between their mind, heart, and body."

"But I would think that since he's a musician, he'd be more in tune with his emotions. You know, as an artist."

"Nilly, do you know any really famous German musicians today? The days of Beethoven and Bach are gone. But even their music was very mathematical. You should listen to their pop music, *Schlager*—or rather, don't. It's this awful, soulless, synthesized shit stuck in the 1990s. They're not known for their actors or comedians, either. Don't you know that famous joke by Robin Williams?"

"No."

"Someone asked him why Germans don't have a good sense of humor. And he said something like, 'Because you killed all the funny people.'" I crack up; that's actually very funny, in a dark sort of way. "You know what they're good at?"

"What?" I ask.

"Logistics. In the start-up world, they dominate apps involving organization."

"That's hilarious."

Too bad I didn't get this primer on the German mentality before my Berlin trip.

We order a *kadaif* to share, a Middle Eastern dish of shredded *phyllo* dough served with sweet cheese and berry sauce. The waitress also serves us, as a complimentary digestif, two shots of the café's homemade Arak anise liquor made with date syrup.

"*Todah!*" we enthuse.

"They'd never give you a free drink in Germany," Anat says.

Tel Aviv restaurant service has become superb, and I'm refreshed by the warmth of my country.

"So Sebastian might write to me a month from now?" I ask, my despair tempered by the deliciousness of the *kadaif*. "When his brain catches up with his heart?"

"Or vice versa. Well, I can't predict the future, especially not with German men. Could be he's super busy with work. In Germany, I found they'll often put work before love. You know how many times I dated a German guy, invited him up, and he said 'no' because he had work the next day? Or this one guy had to put up curtains in his apartment."

"Curtains?"

"Yeah. Crazy. It's hard for them to ruffle their routine." She laughs. "Maybe that's why they wouldn't go out of their way to save Jewish lives."

"I thought Germans were supposed to be super nice now because of their Holocaust guilt."

"Well, there's a difference between being nice and being emotionally available. Don't think their guilt will make them treat you better as a girlfriend.

You have German jerks and Israeli jerks; the German jerks just come in nicer packaging."

"Does this emotional unavailability have something to do with the Holocaust?"

"Good question. Not sure if it's because of the Holocaust or vice versa. Someone should write a PhD on the subject. But there's this—I guess you could call it—lack of empathy. Once, my phone was pickpocketed during a date, and the guy was like, 'Shit like that happens.' Or I slept over at a guy's house once, and I spilled orange juice on me, and he went to mop the floor first."

I sigh. "In the end, Sebastian didn't have empathy for my Jewish heart. So just forget about him?"

"Yeah! What else can you do? Get on with your life! Whether he's German or not, the fact that he treated you this way and made you feel bad is enough of a reason to kick him to the curb. You're here now. You're home. Now let's make a toast to your fresh start."

We raise our Arak.

"To a fresh start!"

CHAPTER FOUR

On January 26, my birthday, I decide to give myself a birthday gift: someone to get under.

The reserves of sexual satisfaction that Sebastian gave me are running out, and I've stopped fantasizing about the "German"—that's what he's become to me again. This time, I won't be a sexual racist. I won't "Nazi hunt." I'll hunt, or be hunted by, whoever catches my fancy.

I meet Dana, Ariella, and a few other friends at a new hot spot called Sputnik not far from Kuli Alma, but it, too, has that common Tel Aviv casual-cool design formula: an outdoor courtyard bar decorated with free-flowing plants and vines haphazardly beautifying an industrial setting. A maze of indoor rooms decorated with funky posters leads to a basement dance bar, where I end up plastered by 2 am.

On the dance floor, dancing to electro, I notice an Israeli cutie. At Sebastian's height, he has thick, brown hair, full lips, and an athletic build.

"Hi!" I say to him, confident from the booze and the extra year of experience I officially gained today.

"Hi!" he says, smiling, pleased to see me.

We start dancing. "What's your name?" he asks.

"Nilly. What's yours?"

"Motti."

I put my arms on his shoulders and relish in their broadness before I move my hands curiously down to his hard pecs, proof Israeli men can have really hot bodies, too.

"Are you an athlete?" I didn't think Israelis could have such bodies unless they're athletes.

"No, I just work out a lot."

He puts his hands on my hips; I like their touch. He certainly is a worthy candidate to "get under."

"Today's my birthday!" I say.

"Well, Happy Birthday! You here with friends?"

"Yeah." I don't look around too hard for them, but I spot Dana. She gives me an encouraging wink and mouths the word "*chatich*" for "hottie."

"What do you do?" I ask.

"I'm in law school."

"Oh, so you must be young. How old are you?"

"Twenty-four."

Too young to marry, but not too young to get under.

"And you?"

"Just turned thirty-two. You like older women?"

"Yes." He pulls me closer to him, making me feel like a "cougar" for the first time in my life.

"What do you do?" he asks.

"I'm an architect."

"Nice," he says, not really interested. He moves in straight for the kiss. *Wow!* It feels so good to have these delectable Jewish lips on mine. Our kissing evolves into a make-out session in the corner where we feel each other up—and down—over our clothes. Little does this young man know that he's given me hope in the physical beauty of my race. I'm ready to unwrap my birthday gift.

"Where do you live?" he asks.

"Tel Aviv. You?"

"Rishon Letsion." A boring Tel Aviv suburb.

"You live alone?"

I don't mind the question. "Yes."

"Then let's go."

We take a cab to my apartment, and I unwrap him on my bed until he's lying naked in front of me.

I face his circumcised penis: a shiny jewel ready for me to polish. It's so clean, smooth, uncomplicated. I begin to rub my hand over it, then, with delight, put my mouth over it, savoring the taste of holiness.

"Do you have a condom?" I ask, ready to get under this circumcised non-Nazi.

"Hold on. In my jeans."

He goes to his pants for another gift to unwrap—if you could call a condom a gift.

He puts on the condom, and I lie down so that he takes me missionary style. The harder he thrusts in and out, the harder I get over Sebastian. I'm finally under someone else.

I stop thinking about Sebastian and think about Motti instead. Well, at least his body. He comes over a few days later, and we have condomized, circumcised sex again. In the end, it didn't take any discussion or philosophy to exorcise Sebastian from my mind and body—just simple flesh. The Jewish god has defeated the German god.

On Saturday night, we go for drinks, to which he graciously treats me even though he's on a student budget. But I realize, after chatting with him over wine, his mind isn't as erect as his body. We're in different stages of life. He lives with his parents to support himself through his last year of law school, which he hates. He chose law because it seemed like a practical choice. He'd rather be an athlete of some kind, maybe a personal trainer, which wouldn't earn him a living in Israel. I suggest he consider sports law, which got him thinking.

After one more round of sex, I realize he has served his purpose. My mind and body are satiated enough to focus on a new project. Last week, through Facebook friends, I was introduced to a couple interested in my freelance architecture services.

Keren and Amit live in Sde Boaz, an "illegal" but growing outpost in the Gush Etsion settlement bloc situated in the Judean Hills near Jerusalem. Most of Gush Etsion was purchased by Jews before the 1948 War of Independence during which the Jordanians massacred 127 Jewish residents after besieging them in the synagogue. Once Israel reconquered the territory during the Six-Day War, descendants of the Jewish victims and survivors returned to resettle the land. Today, it is home to some 70,000 Jewish residents.

After watching the Gaza pullout from their television set in Tel Aviv, Keren and Amit, heartbroken, felt the need to live connected to the land and to prevent more expulsions in the future. Sde Boaz was the perfect fit.

It was founded as a mixed religious-secular, ecological community built on "land under survey," in other words, ownerless land. Any legitimate owner would have claimed it by now, but if an individual were to step forward with a reasonable claim, the matter would go to court, as it usually does in such circumstances. The secular couple spent eight years on a waiting list until a caravan became available. In the meantime, they saved up enough money to build their own home. Now, they're ready. Keren, thirty-five, is expecting her first child.

The prospect of meeting Keren and Amit in Sde Boaz fills me with the anticipation I once reserved for Sebastian's texts and emails.

I drive up there on Friday, chugging up the unpaved road leading to Sde Boaz. I roll down the windows to take in this cool Holy Land air, fresh from overnight rain, feeling like it's an elixir cleansing out toxins from my mind, body, and soul. I park my car near a home made of stone. My Berlin jacket has come in handy again.

Sde Boaz smells like ruffled dirt; the ground is breaking up to give way to the plants and trees in search of spring—and to the foundations of new homes. Sde Boaz looks more like a small village than an "illegal" settlement, with one-story homes built alongside caravans. It was built without fences— on purpose. Residents pride themselves on co-existence with their Arab neighbors.

I take in the panoramic view of the patchwork of Jewish and Arab towns I don't know by name. This view is not unfamiliar to me. Ariel also overlooks interconnected Jewish and Arab settlements. How does the song go from the "Battle of the Bands?" *We're here together, we have no choice/An eternal city, the birthplace of hope.* The words apply to what I see in front of me.

"Come, I'll show you around," says Amit after greeting me. He and his wife both go against Jewish stereotypes, standing tall and physically robust, connected to the earth, their bodies. Amit has strong arms that bespeak of outdoor labor, and Keren has long, wavy, dirty blonde hair that reaches just above her bulging belly. Amit is an engineer; Keren is a graphic designer who works from her caravan.

We pass a wet playground full of happy children who don't mind getting muddy.

"We've really matured as a community," Keren says. "We started out with a few young couples, but now we have about twenty-five families and many more kids. We have a kindergarten—in a caravan—but that will change soon. They play outside a lot anyway."

What a contrast—from being with the grandson of probable Nazis in the capital that spawned Jewish destruction, and whose peer group resents Jewish presence on this land, to being with idealists near the capital of Israel spawning Jewish lives and families, and whose peer group believes in Jewish rights to live here as they wish. Maybe Sde Boaz doesn't make Glühwein, but it makes its own wine from vineyards they've planted.

As we walk along the dirt paths beautified by flowers and herbs the residents lovingly planted, they introduce me in passing to some of their cheerful neighbors and then take me to the outskirts where some of the early founders dug up a *mikveh* from the Second Temple period.

"Jewish archeology and agriculture are everywhere," Amit says.

They show me the community's farm patches and orchards growing herbs, tomatoes, cucumbers, oranges, figs, and pomegranates. They even have a wheat field, as in biblical times.

Amit explains how the *yishuv*, community, was named the "Field of Boaz" after the biblical character Boaz who owned wheat fields near Bethlehem, not far from here. His story is told in the *Book of Ruth*, whose namesake was a Moabite princess who clung to her Hebrew mother-in-law, Naomi, after Naomi's sons had died. Impressed with her dedication, Boaz treats Ruth favorably as she gleans leftover produce in his fields during a famine. Naomi encourages Ruth to court and eventually marry Boaz, who is a relative of Naomi's late husband, so that Boaz, as a family member, could redeem their family property and ensure it remains a family inheritance.

While the story revolves around archaic property laws, it is often romanticized as a love story between Ruth and Boaz, who turned out to be a *motek neshama*. For her loyalty, Ruth, one of the most celebrated converts to Judaism, merits becoming the great grandmother of the first King of Israel, David. I would like to connect Ruth's story somehow to Sebastian, but the crisp, idealistic air stops me from thinking of him.

We inspect the small plot of land of their future home, and my vision comes quickly, clearly. I tell them how I see a cabin made of wood and Jerusalem stone except for the playroom, for which I'd like to experiment with more versatile materials, like plastics, so that the children feel safe and free to make a mess as they play and create. The house would be surrounded by open space on all sides, with the natural dents in the ground creatively adapted toward recreational nooks.

I ask to borrow a ladder so that I can understand the viewpoint from an upper floor. I offer to investigate new roofing technology so that we can move away from the sloped, terracotta roofs very common to homes in the region, in part to allow the roof to serve as a terrace. I envision the second floor windows opening only to the sky, the Judean Hills, and the landscaped terraces—not to people—so that the house comes equipped with a tower against human folly.

Keren and Amit had interviewed four other architects and hire me on the spot.

On Sunday, I announce my resignation from Zimmerman and Associates, effective February 26. Unemployment and social benefits will support me as I build my private practice.

I get started on the plan and blueprints every evening at home. I hardly have time to date, but once in a while, I check out dating websites. The men are nowhere nearly as good looking as Sebastian, but I focus on more than just appearances. These men are unique people with personalities, ambitions, and interests, not any stereotype I've created for myself.

Over drinks, I enthusiastically tell Elad, a civil engineer, about my new project in Sde Boaz. He's not a settlement enthusiast, but ever since Hamas kept launching rockets into Tel Aviv after the Gush Katif pullout, he believes Israel would be foolish to relinquish land unilaterally. While I enjoy our conversation, in which he offers engineering tips, I still have no desire to touch him. Rejecting Sebastian doesn't mean I must give up sexual attraction as a criterion for a romantic partner.

A programmer for a start-up dealing with online sports gaming, Noam lived in Berlin for a year. Over Becks, we laugh together at German idiosyncrasies. I like getting an Israeli man's perspective on German women; apparently, they are refreshed by the fiery Israeli men who take charge. We end our date as "Facebook friends."

Yuval, a businessman, thinks most settlements drain the Israeli economy except for Ariel, but I don't care much for his political opinions. I'm very sexually attracted to him, so, after a respectful political debate, I let him come up for "coffee." I accept that, alongside settlements, a male body I like to touch is another value of mine.

On my last day of work, my colleagues throw me a goodbye party at lunch, and I leave the office feeling empowered and optimistic. Finally, I'm happy.

I wonder if Sebastian can somehow pick up telepathically that I'm happy without him. When I get home and open my emails, I see his name.

By now, I'm amused. Still, I wait a day before reading his email, proof it means something to me, no matter whom I "got under."

> *Dear Nilly,*
> *First, I have to apologize for not getting back to you. I had really bad internet access in Switzerland, and then so much happened. Too much to explain here.*
> *I'm in Thailand, and I've been unplugged for a while. I've had some time to think and write back with a clear head.*
> *I've been invited to lead a music workshop at a school in East Jerusalem in March. The NGO is paying for my flight and putting me up in Jerusalem for two nights. I'd like to extend my trip to spend some time in Tel Aviv.*
> *Could we meet?*
> *Sebastian*

I cry, not because I'm happy he wants to see me, not because he's coming to Israel mostly for a work opportunity, and not because this message is a little too late. I cry in relief that the narrative I built in my head was false. I was not a Jewess he just used and abused for a week. What we had was real.

I immediately forward it to Anat. "Took him about two months!" I write.

"Standard," she replies.

I'm tempted to ghost him in return. *Let him know how it feels.*

As a compromise, I take my time to respond. This time, I'll have all the time in the world.

I write several drafts.

"Asshole." *Deleted.*

"What's wrong with you unemotional Germans?" *Deleted.*

"Dear Sebastian, Thanks for writing, but I'm really not interested in seeing you at this point. I find it rather rude that you took this long to respond to me. Your excuses are lame." *Deleted.*

"Dear Sebastian, No worries. It happens. Sure, let's meet up when you're here!" *Deleted.*

After consulting with Anat, Ariella, and Dana, I decide to go with my heart and keep it simple, curt, businesslike.

> *Dear Sebastian,*
> *Why don't you let me know when you'll be here, and we'll see?*
> *Nilly*

He writes back.

Dear Nilly,
I'll be in Israel from March 9 to March 16. I'll text you before to make a plan.
Sebastian

I check the calendar. He's landing on Purim, the holiday of Jewish salvation, of surprises and the unexpected, and of reversals of fortune.

The *Book of Esther*, on which Purim is based, tells the story of the erratic, hedonistic King Ahasuerus of ancient Persia who appoints the Jew-hating Haman as vizier to rule over his vast empire through tyranny.

But not long before, the king had made another appointment: Esther, Queen of Persia. She was among the kingdom's virgins forced to participate in the compulsory contest for the crown that Ahasuerus held after he banished his former Queen Vashti for refusing to appear with him at his royal carnival.

Unbeknownst to Ahasuerus, Esther is a Jew whose cousin Mordecai is a palace courtier. It was Mordecai who guided Esther toward victory, advising her to keep her Jewish identity secret.

When Haman, a scion of the rapacious nation of Amalek, orders all subjects to bow down to him, Mordecai refuses, but rather than do away with only Mordecai, Haman plans to do away with all Jews of the kingdom—men, women, and children—and to plunder their possessions through state-sponsored pogroms.

Ahasuerus does not know that Haman has also damned his beloved wife, Esther.

At the urging of Mordecai, Esther decides she must approach the king unannounced—no matter that it's a criminal offense worthy of execution—to convince him to repeal the decree. Upon her unexpected approach, King Ahasuerus grants her a royal pardon by extending to her the royal scepter and agrees to attend the wine banquet she prepared for him and Haman.

At the banquet, Esther succeeds in shaking Ahasuerus' trust in Haman by suggesting that Haman's ambitions extended far beyond being vizier. That night, sleep eludes Ahasuerus, and he asks for the royal chronicles to be read to him. He quickly discovers that Mordecai had once saved him from an assassination plot.

Ahasuerus realizes he promoted the wrong man and quickly seeks to reward Mordecai retroactively by having Haman, of all people, parade

Mordecai on a royal steed throughout the city. The downfall of Haman the Evil has begun.

At the next banquet, Esther knows the time is now ripe to reveal her Jewish identity and to plead for the lives of her people. Ahasuerus hears her cry and realizes that she and Mordecai are his trustworthy allies. He has Haman hanged.

At Mordecai's direction, the royal court issues a counter-decree against Haman's "Final Solution," allowing the Jews to defend their lives. The Jews of Persia win the physical and moral war, and the kingdom celebrates its victory over tyranny. Mordecai and Esther install Purim as a holiday of "joy and gladness, light and honor."

I check the date Sebastian wrote to me. February 26. *Rosh Chodesh*, the first day of Adar, the Jewish month whose theme is merriment. I allow myself to be superstitious and take this as a good omen.

CHAPTER FIVE

I debate with Ariella and Dana whether to meet Sebastian at a café, like colleagues, or at the beach, per his request. We conclude that the depth and openness of the ocean might inspire us to be deep and open. The ocean is where Sebastian and I met; it is now where we might officially part.

My heart rate skyrockets as I park my car and approach the "Späti," our meeting point.

It's Sunday, March 10, and most of the country is off for Purim, but the beach shouldn't be too busy, and not only because the weather is mild. Purim is a costume holiday in which Jews are commanded to get drunk, in commemoration of the identity games played amidst the wine feasts of the ancient Persian palace. Today, people are either getting over their hangovers or dressing up rather than dressing down to their swimsuits.

I'm wearing a long-sleeve pink tunic over gray leggings. My face is colored only with lip gloss. In meeting Sebastian, I'd like to be my natural self.

There he is, standing in front of the Späti in a light jacket and jeans, objectively handsome. His hair is a bit longer and blonder, wavy and luscious. I want to pet him like I would a beautiful cat or hold him like I would a beautiful baby. Except now I know that the cat scratches and that the baby spits up.

I approach him and look straight into those eyes. They appear more blue-green than I remember, a reflection, possibly, of the Tel Aviv waters.

He opens his arms to embrace me. I neither resist nor indulge.

"You look great," he says. "I can't believe I'm here with you again."

"Me neither." My tone is emotionless. My joy and anger at seeing him cancel each other out.

"I'll get two Goldstars, yeah?" he asks.

"Sure." I appreciate the gesture, even though repentance involves more than just offering Israeli beer.

He opens the bottles for a toast. "Happy Purim!" he says.

"Happy Purim," I say back, surprised he'd mention the holiday, but repentance doesn't involve wishing me a "Happy Purim," either.

"You know the story of Purim?" I ask.

"Sure. I actually read it on the plane in German."

"Really?" *Shit.* He's already softened me. *Something has definitely changed.*

"Let's just say, it's not so unfamiliar." He winks then looks at the children around us: princesses, goblins, and various animals. "Looks like fun. Did you dress up?"

"As a cowgirl," I respond curtly, not in the mood for small talk or for the sexual innuendo this costume might conjure. A "cowgirl" costume was simply an easy one to pull off, hinting at my new professional adventure in the "Wild West Bank." In costume, I went out with Ariella for the traditional reading of the *Book of Esther* at a synagogue geared toward internationals living in Tel Aviv. Afterwards, we went barhopping along Dizengoff Street, but I kept the night sober in anticipation of today, which feels to me as momentous as Esther's feast with Ahasuerus and Haman.

"Did you dress up?" I ask in kind.

"Nah. Just put on a silly hat and met with a friend for drinks in Tel Aviv." How odd that we were roaming the streets of Tel Aviv at the same time.

"You have a friend here?" I ask. *Another girl?*

"Yeah, I'll tell you about him. But come, let's catch the sunset before it's too late."

We take off our shoes at the edge of the sand and walk to the shore.

"So how've you been?" he asks.

"Really good. A lot of new developments. Good ones."

"Can't wait to hear."

"No, you first."

He sighs and looks out to the water. "It's nice to be back here, at the ocean. It does me good." We take a few steps in silence. The wind is chilly, and I take my scarf from my purse. "I know you probably wondered where I went."

"You could say that," I say, coldly.

"First, I was just so busy...with the New Year's gig, catching up on work since you left. I got that car commercial gig. They wanted a lot of changes. I wanted to write to you when I had more time, but then too much happened, and I wasn't sure what to write anymore, so I just let it go."

"Not a great excuse."

"I know. That's why I won't ask for an apology right now." I move toward the wet sand so that my feet get moist. "Oh, man. Where do I even start?"

"Wherever you want," I say over the rowdy waves.

"Well, after you left, I didn't know where to go with us. On the one hand, I thought, how cool it would be if you moved to Berlin. But we didn't know each other enough. And I knew how different we were. What if you came, and it didn't work out? It was too much pressure. I couldn't be responsible for you moving to another country."

"That's legitimate," I say. "We already discussed that."

"I know." He pauses again, obviously unsure how to bring up more uncomfortable issues.

"Just be honest," I say. "Say whatever you want to say. I don't know how I'll react, but just speak freely. We need more of that in the world." *We need to drop a lot of bombs—thought-bombs.* "Is it something about the Holocaust? Politics? Religion?"

He laughs. "How did you know?"

I smirk. "I can read your mind."

"You know, I never really thought about the Holocaust. At least, I didn't really want to. I mean, we learned about it in high school. It was always so dry and technical, except for a school trip to the Sachsenhausen concentration camp, which was pretty awful. But it was always those 'Germans' who did this and those 'Nazis' who did that. Those freaks of nature. Never my family. Never people I knew. Certainly not my grandparents. And if they fought or became Nazis, it was because they had no choice. But being around you made me think about it more. About my family's involvement, I mean.

"On the Dresden tour, when the guide said every industry was used for the war effort, I wondered more about where my grandfather worked, if he was really just another cog in the Nazi wheel. I didn't want to get into it while you were with me. And not with my mother. Maybe I was afraid of the answer.

"But then, when Ismael was over for Christmas, he asked her about the war with my translating help. It's funny. He had a lot more courage than me to ask her about it. She liked Ismael a lot. He was super charming and sweet and warm. I think she also liked the feeling that she's helping the underprivileged, not that he's so underprivileged. I mean, he lives pretty well. She told him the usual story, how her father worked in a lens-making factory.

"Then my mother said something I didn't know. She said that the factory once belonged to a Jew. I don't know why she said it at that moment. I asked her the name of the factory because I forgot it, so I looked it up on the internet, but nothing came up. So many documents were destroyed in the war, during the bombing. But I read about how Jewish businesses all over Germany were 'Aryanized.' I hardly learned about that. We learned more about the camps.

"So I made a trip to the Saxon state archives to see what I could find out about the factory, and I discovered that it was indeed sold to an 'Aryan' in 1937. I don't know what happened to the owner, if he left Germany or was deported—and murdered.

"And I learned something else. My grandfather must have become a member of the Nazi party that same year. I saw letters he wrote to the bank that he signed with 'Heil Hitler.' Letters back addressed him as a party member. So maybe he didn't know about Nazis murdering Jews, but he must've known the owner lost his business. Or worse: Maybe he benefited from it. He took shares in the company in 1940 when it was classified as 'central to the war effort.' My grandfather was producing lenses for guns." There's anger in his voice. "Who knows what was on the other side of those guns.

"I talked about it with my mother, and she kept apologizing for him, saying, 'How could he have known Hitler would be so bad? How could he have refused to work for the Nazi regime? He would have been jailed or executed!' Maybe last year I would have bought into that, not anymore." He pauses. "Not after meeting you."

I let his revelation sink into the sudden lowering of the tide.

"And then I talked to my mom about you. She said you were a very nice— and pretty—girl, but she didn't want me to marry a girl from Israel. She said Jews need a place to live, but that they got so much money from Germany while she and her family were struggling in East Germany. And what did Israel use the money for? Wars. I realized she's really ignorant about Israel. I don't know if you know this, but East Germany was very anti-Zionist. And I had to explain some things you explained to me—that Israel never wanted any wars. Now I know what you feel like, always on the defense."

"Not that it's so easy to defend Germany, either," I say. "I'd often have to if I were to be with a German, especially to my mother."

We're more alike than I thought.

"Your mother's not a fan?"

"To put it mildly," I say, but this is not about her or me. "And what about Ismael? Did you have to defend me to him, too?"

"No. That's what's funny. He cared the least. He had no problem with me dating you. He said his sister even applied to Ariel University and that Ariel's a good settlement that doesn't cause problems, not like the extremist ones. Actually, in Berlin, all he wanted to do was party. We went out to bars, and he kept looking for women. Even had sex with a German girl—not sure he wants you to know that. He said in Israel he doesn't do any of this. He's expected to marry a Muslim girl and work in the family business. At the end of the day, I don't think he really cares about Israel or Palestine. He just wants to live a good life.

"I invited him to my guitar class with the refugees because I found out one of them is a Palestinian from Syria. I guess he was the grandson of refugees from the War of Independence, or whatever, but Ismael didn't seem to care to meet him or hear about his plight. You know, I never really knew Palestinians lived in Syria and that they were never given Syrian citizenship or the same rights as Syrians, but the news doesn't talk about that."

"No Jews, no news," I quip. He nods in apparent agreement.

"This was right after the Christmas attack," he continues. "Through Ismael, I asked the refugees what they thought of the attack, and they said it was really bad, that they're against violence, and that they hate that it makes all the refugees look bad. They said they're worried people will start going after Muslims when these attacks have nothing to do with Islam. Then this one guy from Lebanon said the Mossad did it to make Germany like Israel more. He was really into this conspiracy theory.

"Then, for the first time since I started teaching them, I asked them straight out what they thought of Israel, and most of them said Israel was bad. That it steals land and murders Palestinian children. They said this plainly, as if I would automatically believe them or sympathize. Only one Syrian refugee said he doesn't care about Israel after what Assad did to his family. I didn't argue or fight back—neither did Ismael—even though I know it's not true. Israel's not perfect—heck, neither is Germany—but it's overall a good country, a free country, stuck in a bad neighborhood. I don't know if you know this about Germans, but we don't like confrontations. Fuck, I don't think we like confronting ourselves. We're not the most emotional people."

"You think?" *A rhetorical question.*

"Especially in Dresden. We grew up being taught that everyone in the world was bad. The Americans. The British. The West Germans. The Nazis. Then the communists. So I think so many of us grew up afraid just to have an opinion. That's why you were refreshing in some way. A woman with something to say. Maybe that's also why I was attracted to Israel-Palestine. It's not that Germans care so much about Israel's identity issues, it's just that we're confused about our own."

I'm so engrossed in his story that I don't even realize we're already off the sand, walking on a cement lot, barefoot, toward an entertainment complex housing Clara, a popular summer beachside resto-bar built on the site of the once world-famous Tel Aviv nightclub, Atlantis, which suffered a brutal suicide bombing in 2006. I point out the commemoration plaque.

"We've been dealing with jihad for much longer than you," I say.

"Yeah, you're more experienced with this shit."

We put on our shoes and throw away our beer bottles.

"Let's go sit down on one of those benches," I say, feeling a need to be still and steady with him.

We walk along the promenade where families are ambling about in costume, adding to the carnival atmosphere, one that suits this surreal moment. We sit down, and the ocean serves as a wide canvas for our thoughts to come out freely, colorfully, with full expression.

"Why didn't you ever tell me this?" I ask. "Why didn't you write to me and let me know what you were going through?"

"It was too much for me to juggle, with work, too. My schedule, my emotions, my thoughts—it was all a mess. And I had to deal with this on my own. I didn't want to be judged or preached to by anyone—not you, not my mom, not Bernd. So I did something people don't really do in Germany, except maybe in Berlin. I decided to see a therapist. Eduard. Turns out he's Jewish—which makes sense since Germans aren't the best at introspection.

"I realized I had a lot of family shit to deal with, and not just with my grandparents, but my father, too. I never really discussed him with anyone. He was just bad. And I blocked myself from his side of the family, especially because he hurt my mom. But as bad as he was to my mom, he's still my father. And if not for him, like you said, I probably wouldn't be a musician. Eduard said I couldn't live my life holding a grudge, always reacting to it, even subconsciously. So I called my father and asked to meet with him. This was right before I left to Israel."

"That's very brave of you."

"Yeah. It was. I was shaking when I called him. I haven't seen him for ten years. He has two children now with the woman he left my mother for. He's been sober for a while, working as the manager of an audio speaker company near Hannover. He always loved music, so I guess that's his way of sharing it."

"So you met?"

"Yes. At a café halfway between Berlin and Hannover. It was intense. I mean, I didn't even know how to have small talk with him, so I didn't. I told him off the bat he should have never treated my mom that way, hitting her, leaving her. It felt very good to tell him off.

"Then he caught me off guard and said he never hated my mom but East Germany. My mother never talked about that. He wanted to make more money, start a business, but he was stuck, miserable, working for the national electric company. That's why he drank so much. He took out his frustration on my mom. She was a member of the communist party; Meissen porcelain was nationalized, so she kept her job. After the war, he tried to start a business in Dresden, but it didn't work. So he moved west with the woman he now lives with; she helped him get back on his feet. He seems to regret the way he did it now, but he wanted to leave the past behind and start fresh.

"He told me something else that surprised me. He said he pushed me into music because he didn't want me to struggle like him. Music was valued in the GDR. Musicians could leave and perform in other countries. It was a way out. I never made that connection. So he did want a better life for me, somehow."

I remember thinking how unfair it was that Germany didn't have to keep fighting wars after World War II while Jews kept dying, defending themselves in Israel. But Germany suffered, too. Half the country was practically subjugated.

"My father never really had a role model," Sebastian continues. "His father came back from the war and didn't talk about it. He became a drinker. Like father, like son, I guess. He couldn't tell me much about Opa—that's my grandfather—just that he served in the Wehrmacht and was discharged early due to an injury. He's going through dementia and probably won't live much longer. Maybe when he dies, I'll go to my uncle's attic and see if I can find letters and stuff from the war years."

"Funny how both our grandparents are basically on their death bed," I say, interrupting. "My grandmother's in the hospital. It's such a shame we can't ask them all the questions we want to ask."

"Oh, no. Is she okay?"

"As okay as she can be for a ninety-six-year-old woman, I guess."

"*Gute Besserung*," he says.

"*Danke*. Yours, too." I'm surprised I wished "Opa" a good recovery; he might have been a Nazi. But in this moment, he's simply a human being who produced a man like Sebastian...a good man.

"But there's this organization in Germany that kept records of German soldiers," he continues. "I'm going to fill out a form about my grandfather to see what they could tell me. I also wrote to Yad Vashem to see if they know the fate of the Jewish owner of the Dresden factory."

His thoughts are floating on the water in stark contrasts of light and dark. Goosebumps ripple over my arms.

"You're cold," Sebastian remarks. "Maybe we could go inside somewhere?"

"We could go to The Station, sit at Vicky Christina," I suggest.

Vicky Christina is a bar named after the movie Vicky Christina Barcelona by Woody Allen about two women on vacation in Barcelona: Vicky, the engaged, prude, prim character who falls for a Spaniard, and Christina, the wild, emotional artist who indulges in her passions and becomes that Spaniard's lover. The bar is "bipolar." The "Vicky" section is designed in geometric shapes and equipped with square tables that suit quiet, reasoned conversation; "Christina" is situated under a wild fichus tree equipped with windy, tiled bars that suit drunken, loose conversation.

We sit at "Vicky" and order two hot chocolates, perfunctorily. We're not really here to drink.

"So what I'm about to tell you might hurt you," he begins.

"There's another woman?" *It's obvious.*

"Something like that. But don't worry, I got my punishment. I got sick."

"What? Are you okay?"

"Yes. I am now. It's not that kind of sick. It's an embarrassing sick."

"Alcohol poisoning?"

"No, but I blame alcohol." He looks around. People are happily drinking, chattering, but this feels like a confessional. "In Switzerland, my bandmates brought some friends. Girls. One of them, Laura, always liked me. We were never an item, but we slept with each other a few times in the past. When I got there, I was very confused about my mom, the terrorist attack, everything that happened. I thought maybe I needed to go out with a German girl, a girl who speaks my language, who understands my culture, who doesn't make me ask all these questions." I sympathize, considering I also wondered if I should stick with Israeli men. "Laura kept coming on to me. I don't know if you know that's how it works in Germany. Guys are shy, so they usually wait for the girls."

Actually, I know this by now.

"But you weren't shy with me," I say.

"Maybe it's because I was in a foreign country, I felt freer. And because you were so pretty and exotic."

The compliment does little to assuage me. My body tenses up. He's about to tell me he slept with this Laura girl.

"I don't think I have to tell you what happened," he says to my nodding. "Stupid me had sex with her. Unprotected."

"That's really stupid," I say, not knowing what's more stupid—him sleeping with her or him sleeping with her unprotected. I reason I shouldn't be upset. Fortunately, by now, I also "got under" someone else. We never pledged exclusivity.

"I got an infection," he continues. "Oh, yes. The foreskin. I won't go into it, but I couldn't have sex for a few weeks. I took some medication, and it went away by the time I got to Thailand. I was so embarrassed, I only talked about it with Eduard."

"Okay, so now you understand why circumcision is not such a bad idea," I say, feeling strangely satisfied.

"Let's just say, I'm a bit more convinced."

"You're not with this girl, Laura?" I ask.

"No, no. I took a break from sex after that. Had no choice, really."

I gloat inside, feeling ready to move onto to a lighter subject. "How was Thailand?"

"Amazing! I loafed by the beach a lot and took a diving class, which was awesome. One of the guys in my class was an Israeli guy—a gay guy. We became friends. He's the guy I went out with last night and who told me about Purim. He thinks a lot like you. Talking with him made me see your perspective more, and it was easier to hear it from him because I had no romantic interest in him."

"I'm sure he had a crush on you," I say as a compliment.

"Could be. Maybe that's why he was so generous with his time. He told me all about his family, how his grandfather was a German Jew who fled Germany in 1933 when the Nazis came to power. He had to give up his textile business in Berlin but rebuilt it in Israel. I told him about my grandfather, and you know what? He never made me feel bad for being German. This is something I noticed about Israelis. I'm always waiting for a nasty comment, and it never comes. Maybe you're all too forgiving. You see past it."

"Well, not all the time," I say. "And not everyone, like my mother. She knows nothing about you."

"See? Another obstacle for us," he says. I nod in regret. "Well, I'm talking about the Israelis I met. The younger generation, I guess. And with Noam—that's my gay friend—I could talk about politics and the Holocaust and not get too emotional about it."

"Did you tell him about me?"

He smirks. "Of course."

I blush and don't pry further.

"Then Ismael arranged this teaching gig," he continues. "At first, I wasn't sure if I wanted to go. I had a lot of work, and I knew this time the trip wouldn't be about a fun, new adventure. Then there was you. Should I call you? See you? Especially after I disappeared like that. I didn't have the guts to say 'hello' when I didn't have the guts to say 'goodbye.' But Noam said I couldn't leave you hanging like that. I had to have courage. Finally, he stuck it to me and told me to have the courage my people didn't have to do what's right. So here I am saying...'hello.'" He looks at the hot chocolate rim then back at me. "And sorry."

He stands to get something from his jacket pocket. He takes out a little box imprinted with the Meissen logo of two swords. *A ring?*

"You're supposed to give gifts on Purim, right? So here. A token of my apology." I open it; it's that heart pendant I liked from the Meissen shop.

I hold it in my palm; it feels very heavy. I'm tempted to drop it to see if it will break into pieces the way my heart did, the way the windows of the Dresden synagogue did.

"Did you find out more about the company? What it did during the war?" I ask, as if further admission of Meissen's Nazi connection will bear witness to his remorse over the *Kristallnacht* of my heart.

"I'd have to do more research, but I know it was involved in the war somehow. So many companies were. I know they printed horrible Nazi propaganda on their plates and made stupid Hitler figurines. I don't know how much they've owned up to it or made amends, but if that were a criterion, I wonder what I could buy in Germany. I just remembered that you liked it."

Looking at the pendant, despite its lavender-painted butterfly, I sense it will be a chain over my neck, a weight over my healing heart. My eyes water.

My next words come out heavily, with difficulty, but I manage to say them. "I'm sorry, but I can't take this." I hand it back to him. "I'm proud of your process, and I accept your apology, but you hurt me. I admit it. And telling me all of this, well, it can't just erase the pain. It's very sweet, but if I wear it, I'll just think about your country and its horrible past. I'll just think about you when I'm finally over you.

"I've started to get on with my life here, to go out on my own as an architect. I'm building a home in the Judean Hills. It's so cool." My voice is unapologetic, prouder. "Although you'll probably think I'm a criminal, building in an 'illegal settlement.' But I like it. I like going against the grain. And I'm happy. Finally. It took a while, but your coming here, giving me this— well, it will just complicate my life now."

"Okay, I'll take it back," he says in disappointment. I'm not sure if he's upset I refused the gift or if he ultimately doesn't want to give it to a "criminal." "Even though I'm a musician, sometimes I have bad timing. I was hoping we could spend time together. I'm here for a week. But I'll understand if you don't want to. As for the settlements—fuck. I don't care."

"Really? I thought maybe one reason why you were so standoffish is because you didn't like my architecture activism."

"No. That has nothing to do with it. You said something once to me, and it stuck: It's not my issue. It's not a German issue as much as we like to think it is. We have our own problems. And I've never even been to a settlement, so how could I really judge?"

Wow. A real breakthrough.

I wonder if he's hinting at me to take him to one.

"So what are your plans for the week?" I ask, despite myself.

"Working, taking some meetings, and basically hanging out. Tomorrow I'm going to Yad Vashem. I'll say 'hi' to the researcher I was in touch with, and then I'd like to see the museum. I didn't go there the last time. Would you like to come with me?"

I fight my urge to offer to take him to a settlement and to Yad Vashem—a double whammy—but I can't risk another pogrom against my heart. Let him redeem himself on his own.

"I think it's better you go alone," I say, then lie. "I have a very hectic week."

"Maybe," he says. "I'm glad I at least got to see you today."

I take out money to pay for my drink, but he insists on paying. We take a cab back to our meeting spot.

"Happy Purim," he says after we awkwardly hug goodbye.

"Happy Purim."

On the way back home, I immediately call Dana and tell her what happened.

"That is perfection at the highest levels," she says.

"No, it's not!" I protest. "It's more torture. Why is he doing this to me? Just when I get over him, he sucks me right back in. It's just mean. I don't want to give in. I want to be strong. I want to have dignity, something we Jews never really had with Germans."

"Nilly, you can't act out our Jewish history on a man. You just can't do that."

"That's why it's all so complicated with him."

Dana's voice is earnest, even coming out of the Bluetooth speakers. "Nilly, what do you want to do—deep in your heart? Deep, deep, deep in your heart?"

"I don't know," I say, those pesky tears finding release as I'm driving aimlessly around Tel Aviv. "My heart has been out of whack for so long."

"Do you want to be with him?"

"It's impossible."

"Do you want to hang out with him?"

"Yes," I admit. "But I'm scared."

"Why don't you just go with him to Yad Vashem? You don't have a full-time job now. You have time. I mean, he came all the way here. Be with him for that. Seems like he needs you for it. Maybe then you could get all this Holocaust stuff out of the way and start fresh."

"Or it'll just get messier."

"Maybe, but you know what—you're doing the work for a lot of us. I mean, we have a lot of shit to deal with involving the Germans. But maybe—somehow—you're like our prophet! Your being with him is a turning point for our nations. Not of forgetting—I mean, even I'll say we can't forget. Hell, I don't even think we can forgive—the Nazis, I mean, ever. But Sebastian, well, he's not a Nazi. He's trying. He has to heal, too. Maybe this is part of the healing. Nilly, it's never easy to grow."

I pull over just so I can cry. My tears are blurring my vision. "You're right, Dana. Thanks for being such a good friend. I couldn't have done this without you. What did I do to deserve you?"

"You're just you. And any time."

I text Sebastian in the morning. "I'll join you at Yad Vashem if the invitation still stands."

"*Natürlich!*"

I go to bed and do something I haven't done in an entire month. I fantasize about the time he conquered me as "Occupied Territory." Not only is my heart reassembling for him, so is my body.

But he's no longer a "product of Germany," a fetish, a curiosity. He's a man, and I am a woman. Not objects. Not commodities. Not utilities. If our two nations could also see each other not as objects, commodities, or utilities—but as independent countries with their own personalities, scars, fears, hopes, and dreams—we might grow together even more than if we always discussed the Holocaust.

CHAPTER SIX

I meet Sebastian on the deck of Jerusalem stone leading into Yad Vashem. We give each other a sturdier hug than yesterday's, all that's appropriate here. How strange being here with him, this man who could have served as an "Aryan" poster boy, and me, this darkish Jewish girl with chestnut-colored eyes.

The weather is warm today, and I wear a beige linen dress. He, too, has dressed in light tones: a white cotton shirt and khakis. While Purim is celebrated today in Jerusalem and in all walled cities, it feels more like Yom Kippur when Jews are supposed to wear white.

The last time I visited Yad Vashem was when I was twenty-years old, in the army. Yad Vashem was and continues to be a traditional stop for IDF soldiers, a source of inspiration in the fight to defend our homeland, to defend our Jewish lives when, once, no one did, not even ourselves.

I remember the pride I felt back then, feeling part of a fighting force that would prevent another Holocaust. *Oh, how far we've come!* We are free in our land, holding guns, riding tanks, and gathering intelligence to make sure no one messes with Jewish lives again, even if we fail sometimes, like last month, when that sadist rammed over IDF soldiers, unafraid of any consequence. Still, today, we stand a real, fighting chance.

In the lobby, Sebastian meets with that archivist for an in-person introduction. I can tell this middle-aged woman is impressed by him. She must be going out of her way to help him just because he's so goddamn cute. So far, she tells us, she hasn't found out anything about the fate of the Jewish owner, but she'll keep trying. She shakes my hand goodbye, jealousy dripping from her eyes.

We retrieve audio guides—whether to expand our knowledge or to shield us from interaction—I'm not sure.

At the entrance of the Holocaust History Museum, a video montage portrays the vibrant, cheerful Jewish life in Europe that once was. Then we step into a dark, boding, eerie triangular hall that feels like a gas chamber, inducing a solemn march toward the exhibition on the Third Reich.

"The impact of Jewry will never pass, and the poisoning of the people will not end, as long as the causal agent, the Jew, is not removed from our midst," Hitler spews from a screen in a language I now know from casual conversation, rock music—and lovemaking. I remember why I resisted Sebastian for speaking it.

Hitler's was the cry of every evil dictator: Murder all Jews—men, women, and children. To all those tyrants, this tiny nation within nations, a minuscule fraction of their empires, represented a monstrous threat to their rule, for as Haman warned King Ahasuerus in the *Book of Esther*, "Their laws are different from the laws of other people."

And maybe those laws *are* different, but to their credit. The Jewish God commands his subjects to live by moral absolutes—like "Thou shalt not murder" and "Thou shalt not steal"—while dictators seek to be deities by claiming absolute power over the lives and property of their subjects. Hitler wasn't simply a racist; in a demented way, he was wise. He must have sensed the Jewish ethical mission to bow only to one God representing right from wrong. Jews faithful to their tradition would have scoffed at Hitler's demand to "heil" him.

Across from Hitler's "loudspeaker" is a large photograph of a Nazi rally where thousands of Germans are bowing to their god. Who knows if and how many of Sebastian's relatives submitted to this dictator.

He looks at me with those blue eyes that are now filled with so much curiosity, so much agony, so much soul. Had I come here in the last year or so, I would've seen these murderous Nazis in a man like him. Now, I look at his strong arm and don't imagine a swastika band but a strong bicep that will protect me.

They are not he, and he is not they.

We pass an antisemitic Nazi propaganda poster featuring the blonde "Aryan" standing tall, muscular, connected to nature, versus the big-nosed, hairy, balding, greedy Jew with a finance newspaper hanging from his pocket, plotting to take over the world. Above it, a Nazi sign reads: "The Jews are our misfortune."

Funny how I too have been a victim of these stereotypes, seeing in Sebastian the athletic, proud, good-looking German compared to the homely, practical Jew.

I watch soldiers enter the exhibition hall: the "new Jews" holding guns, looking nothing like that "greedy Jew," but the stereotypes persist, with contemporary Jew-haters painting the "new Jews" as greedy "colonialists" stealing Palestinian land and oppressing the simple Arab "natives."

We walk further, hardly interacting, until we come across a placard explaining the Nuremberg Laws of 1935 prohibiting Germans from marrying or having sexual relations with "racially inferior" Jews.

Sebastian brushes my waist with his hand, his first romantic touch since his landing. It comforts me as much as those soldiers' presence.

We pass by hundreds of images that by now have become cliché: Jews being hanged in public squares, Jews being humiliated in the streets, Jews being deported on trucks. And then stories of Jews writing poetry in the ghetto instead of fighting—making theater instead of fighting—baking Passover *matzah* instead of fighting—teaching Torah instead of fighting. Jews were keeping up all those great Jewish traditions in captivity, except the greatest one: fighting spiritually, intellectually, politically, and, when necessary, physically, for their life and their right to it.

Sebastian looks at the images, shaking his head in disgust. I wonder how I would feel as a German, witnessing such acts of horror, knowing my ancestors must have participated, somehow. Does he feel like he is observing the crimes of another nation, another people?

We pass through more destruction. Romania, Croatia, Latvia, Poland. Finally, we reach Palestine—the land of Israel. Young Zionist couriers living in British-mandate Palestine came to Europe, calling upon the Jews to find refuge in the place that had formed the focal point of their prayers for 2,000 years— but those prayers, like their traditions, became ends unto themselves.

To think the land of Israel was there all along, for millennia, and, yet, Jews didn't go back *en masse*. Only a small fraction of European Jews joined their brothers and sisters already in Palestine.

The soldiers stop next to us, clearly moved. But I don't want Yad Vashem to give them inspiration. Let not the fear of death inspire them, but the love of life. We shouldn't have had to wait for six million to die to learn to live as free people in our own land. We should have been motivated by adherence to the basic idea that one should never be a victim from the start, because our values, our dreams, our lives are sacred.

Next is a section that asks: "Why wasn't Auschwitz bombed?"

I don't like that question. It implies Jewish salvation is dependent on other nations. I have a more pressing, unpleasant, unpopular question: What more could the Jews have done to save their own lives?

I can understand not "blaming the victim" in the face of 100,000 murdered. 200,000, maybe. But six million. Six million?! At that point, we must also search within.

Jews today seem to take for granted that the Holocaust generation couldn't have stopped the Nazis. They never imagined Hitler would launch a systematic scheme of mass murder, but wasn't the dispossession of their homes, their businesses, their belongings horrific enough to justify fighting back? They should've rebelled the minute they were forced into slavery, for that is our tradition.

Moses challenged Pharaoh's rule, first when he smote the Egyptian beating a Hebrew slave to death, then when he engaged in terror warfare in the form of natural disasters known as the Ten Plagues. Hundreds of years later, Mordecai took to the streets, maneuvering the strings of the halls of the Persian court, until he reached the queen, his cousin and mentee, to hatch a plan to annul the decree of genocide.

We read the story of Moses on Passover and of Mordecai and Esther on Purim every single year, but Jews either abandoned those traditions or became more concerned with preserving them ritually rather than living out their call: to rise up against slavery in the quest for liberty, first for themselves, then for their neighbors, and ultimately, for all humanity.

Even without an army, Jews could have found ways to protest and fight, as some did. Surely, they risked bloody retaliation, but at least they would have left this world with dignity, instilling fear in their haters. Unlike the Palestinians, they would have had a moral claim to become "suicide bombers." But—is it possible? Do Palestinians have more self-respect than the Jews? While Palestinians are not fighting for liberty or even for their physical lives but for the "right" to live under an oppressive, antisemitic Islamic state, they at least seem to be fighting for an identity, even though it's one now being used as a weapon against the Jewish people.

The term "Palestinian" once referred to all people—Jews, Muslims, and Christians alike—living in the region of Palestine, but now the "Palestinians" have cast themselves as a "nation" oppressed by Israelis—i.e., Jews who deserve to be terrorized. Terrorism has worked for the Palestinians. Israel, after all, left

Gaza. Maybe, had the Nazis feared Jews would've gone berserk with an ax or a vehicle if they came for their property, lives, and honor, the Jews could've pushed them back.

Ironically, Jews fought for a tradition that sanctified life to the extent that they wouldn't risk those lives even when a knife was at their throat.

And maybe Hitler was God's greatest rebuke to the Jewish people—because we abandoned the higher principles of the Torah. For had the millions of Jews who observed Passover or Purim throughout the centuries internalized the real meaning of freedom, would the world have come to a Holocaust?

Yad Vashem is more like a memorial to the Jew failing to live out the biblical call to liberty.

As we get to the exhibit on liberation, I realize the Americans ultimately upheld the Bible's highest virtue. They liberated Buchenwald, giving my grandparents the opportunity to start new lives in the Promised Land. In that sense, the Americans were more "Jewish" than the Jews and certainly more than the Russians, who suppressed Jews under communism, and the British, who prevented Jews from migrating to mandate-Palestine.

Toward the end of the museum, we reach The Hall of the Righteous dedicated to non-Jews who risked their lives to hide or smuggle Jews to safety—those brave souls who recognized evil and fought against it. At the end of the day, these people shouldn't be so exceptional. They should be normal.

Here, I take Sebastian's hand. I want to believe that based on who he is now, he would have stood up to Hitler.

We return our audio guides and enter a door that offers an inspirational ending to this horrific saga: a view of the picturesque forests of Jerusalem. The City of Gold.

We have come home, finally. Eventually, Jews fought for their lives—and won.

We step onto the terrace and lean our hands over the glass balcony. I inhale the mountain air and exhale this intense experience. We look at each other uneasily. How do we begin to discuss all that we saw?

"Thanks so much for coming with me," he says.

"You're welcome."

"I always knew it was bad," he says, "but this reminded me just how bad. These industrial death machines, this humiliation, this evil, evil, evil. So evil." His brow crinkles, and a strand of hair falls over his watering blue eyes. "I'm so sorry."

"You don't have to be sorry. You didn't do it."

"But I'll say it anyway. At least I want to say sorry for my grandparents. I know it's not my sorry to say, but I'm still their grandson. And I can only correct their mistakes by understanding their actions and trying to do better. I can't be afraid to say my grandparents made awful choices. I can find excuses for them, but I won't. That's too easy. There had to have been a different way."

I can't control my tears, and he embraces me very tightly. My trembling and tears abate in his arms; I feel comforted and protected. He lets me wipe my tears on his sleeves.

"I didn't realize how much I needed to hear that," I say, now facing him. "Thank you."

His smile is gentle. "You're welcome."

I gain my composure as we turn to face the pine.

"We have so many Holocaust memorials in Germany," he says, "but the real memorials are inside our families, inside our hearts, asking those difficult questions. I don't know if I'll get them answered in my lifetime, but I could start. I could try. I could set an example. And I can be different today by not being afraid to defend Israel against all the lies that threaten your property and lives here." If the ocean made him open and earnest, the Jerusalem pine made him brave. "I wonder, if I lived at that time, what I would've done."

I put my hand on his. "You wouldn't have been a Nazi," I say. In this moment, I believe it.

"Maybe I wouldn't have been a Nazi, but I wonder if I would've been among the Righteous. I'm not sure. Because I like my comforts. I like my apartment and my job. And I realized something about Germans: We're very practical. We like to feel secure. The stereotype of greedy Jews? Hah!

"Here's a theory: I don't think the majority of Germans hated Jews; they just didn't want to risk their jobs, their comforts. Morality was up for sale, like a commodity. Betray Jews, and you could get promoted. That's what's happening with Israel. Israel has become a controversial issue—why, I don't know. It's the only democracy in the Middle East.

"Maybe people have some sort of a financial stake in the conflict. Otherwise, I'm not sure how the NGO could put me up in such a nice hotel. So who wants to take up a controversial issue? Who wants to stick their necks out? Who wants to suffer the dirty looks if they say they like and support

Israel? Who wants to risk their jobs? I don't think the weapons we have to fear are guns and bombs and trucks, but this amorphous beast that somehow makes people afraid to say what they truly think—even when they're right. But nothing good could ever come out of lies and injustice. In the end, the Germans lost everything."

"You know, I have a similar question," I say. "Would I have been a victim like that? Would I have seen it coming and escaped? Would I have tried to warn people? Would I have tried to save others with me? Would I have tried to fight back, somehow? Or would I have been too comfortable to really—as you say—stick my neck out, for myself, my people? I mean, there were heroes. Partisans. Underground fighters. The Warsaw Ghetto Uprising. But they were few and far between. Jews waited for it to pass until they also lost everything in the most inhumane way—I mean, they were cremated, which is against Jewish law. I like to think I would've come here, to build 'Palestine.' I wish we never needed those Righteous Among the Nations."

"I'm sure you would've been a heroine. You're one of the most courageous women I know." He takes my hand and squeezes it.

"You're one of the most courageous men I know."

I hold that strong arm and lean on it. I let another tear fall as I gaze at the leaves.

"Let's take a picture here," I say, after wiping my tear. *I'd like to remember this moment.*

"Sure."

We ask a couple coming out of the exhibition to take a picture of us against the pine of eternal Jerusalem.

We hold hands as we walk a path of Jerusalem stone toward the exit. Strangely, I don't want to leave these peaceful grounds. I could roam these hills with him for the rest of the day.

"You know what else I was thinking?" I ask, feeling for the first time, that no filter exists between us. I hold his hand tighter, allowing myself to enjoy his touch. "We must learn from what happened. We must learn from our mistakes. But we can't always live in the shadow of the Holocaust. I kind of want to be reborn, to act simply from what's true and what's right."

"I would agree with you, but I can't say that. You've probably dealt with the Holocaust more than I have, than we Germans have, on a personal, emotional level, no matter how many memorials we have. For us, it's abstract.

I mean, I look at you and other Israelis I've met. You're so much more in touch with your emotions. You say what's on your mind. You've spoken about what the Germans—well, my people—did to you. You've felt it. We've thought about the Holocaust, talked about it, but I don't think we've *felt* it. The way I'm feeling it right now.

"That's why you can make Holocaust jokes, and we can't. Maybe it'll be a good sign when Germans can make Holocaust jokes. It'll mean we've really confronted it. That it's really, really removed from who we are. But deep down, I think we're afraid—of being Nazis again."

"And Jews are afraid of being Holocaust Jews again."

"Let's not live in that fear," he concludes as we reach the exit. "Because that's not our essence."

For the first time since we met, I feel as if we are of one mind, and now, I very much want him to kiss me. This time, our kiss wouldn't be the result of mere physical attraction, but spiritual understanding. I just wonder if Yad Vashem is the right place for that kiss.

We walk through a memorial forest of pine planted in deference to the idea that life grows, and always will.

"What would it take for me to plant a tree here?" Sebastian asks.

"I don't know. Maybe ask your contact here."

"Good idea."

Through soil that glitters to me, we slope down a terraced section until I notice what looks like a cabin.

"This is strange. What is it?" I ask.

"Have no idea."

We peek in. What appears to be a furnace is situated in the back. Cobwebs cling to the walls of wooden planks, flies buzzing around. We speculate: A cabin for park rangers? A replica of wooden barracks? Homage to shelters built by Jewish partisans in the forests?

He takes my hands as we step in further.

"Wow, it's so eerie here," I say. "It feels like we're back in time."

"Spooky," he says.

We're inside, and the door creaks shut.

"But at least I can kiss you here in private," he says. "Will you let me? Is it appropriate here?"

"Yes," I say, this time happy he asked for permission. We're far enough from the museum grounds.

Finally, after three months, I feel his lips cautiously touch mine for just a second, and I quiver. He looks at me tenderly, moves my hair from my face, cups my cheeks in his hands, and kisses me again, gently.

"It feels so weird to kiss you here," he says.

"Don't go having Jewish guilt on me."

"I mean, this is holy ground, no?"

I think for a few seconds. "Actually, no. This is not holy ground. This is desecrated ground. What happened in there, all that death, all that murder—that was a desecration. This, right here—this is what's holy."

To let him know I mean it, I place his hands on my waist and kiss him harder than before. As we kiss, I lower his hands and accept his pleasurable squeeze, knowing and understanding that this is an affirmation of life. Maybe our greatest sins throughout the ages have been not honoring our authentic lives: what we truly want, feel, and think deep inside.

This will be the world we'll create: a world of pleasure, not shallow pleasure, but very deep pleasure that comes from deep self-understanding and the understanding of another, expressed between us now through the physical.

I feel no guilt or shame as he lifts up my dress and his hand slips underneath my panties first over my behind then toward the front. He inserts his other hand inside my top and then bra, taking hold of my nipple. I murmur as he smudges the moisture dripping on my thigh.

But when I attempt to return the pleasure, he grips my hand, forcefully.

"No," he says firmly. "This is about you now."

He slips off my panties completely and turns me around so that I'm holding onto the edge of the furnace, not caring that I'm tearing apart the cobwebs strewn across it. After rubbing me from behind to ensure a wet playing field, he slips his finger inside me and starts driving it in and out, intensely. I try to keep my groans low in case people are walking around in the nearby brush. The pace of his finger increases, and I feel dizzy.

"Oh, my God. Oh, my God!" I say. "What are you doing to me?"

He keeps tugging without getting weary. I writhe, but he doesn't let me release him. I'm not sure if there's a name for this new, otherworldly sensation

I'm feeling, something between agony and ecstasy, physical and mental.

Suddenly, I feel liquid spill on my sandals, as if a water balloon popped from below. My right leg is drenched. Six ounces must have left my body.

"What the fuck just happened?" I ask. My head rush slowly settles.

"I think you squirted."

"Oh, my God. Did I just squirt in Yad Vashem?"

"Yes, you did my dear."

"Oh, my God. Wow."

I turn around. I put my arms around his waist and rest my head on his shoulder. I breathe in the musky air, trying to calm my body from the intensity of this new experience. But a few minutes later, his finger is at it again.

"What are you doing?"

"Just relax." He turns me around again and resumes the rubbing only to insert his finger again, diligently. I didn't think such deep, tortured pleasure could be repeated, let alone even more intensely.

"What the hell?" I cry out.

He doesn't relent, reaching manually for what must be my G-spot. Completely shaken, I release another few ounces of liquid, surprised I still have moisture to expend.

I'm too spent with pleasure to think rationally about what just happened— if it was right or wrong. This pleasure defies moral discussion. He holds me from behind, and I lean my head back. I can barely talk, but I manage to say, "I think it's safe to say you don't have to plant a tree here anymore."

CHAPTER SEVEN

The NGO indeed put him up in one of Jerusalem's finest hotels, the American Colony Hotel, an attraction in its own right, the preferred hotel among diplomats and celebrities, located on the seam of west and east Jerusalem. How fitting. We're special kinds of German and Israeli diplomats today.

The lush garden courtyard terrace leads to a room of luxury where our diplomacy accelerates on a king-sized bed fit for royalty, and we negotiate each other's continued pleasure with care and dedication. In the process, we allow ourselves to become Holocaust deniers. It doesn't exist anymore. It's over. It's no longer a cloud in our relationship.

Finally, I'm completely oblivious to his foreskin. After all, it's just a piece of skin. Wouldn't judging someone over a piece of skin make me racist? I will look past it to see his underskin—who he is, deep inside. But to find him there, we had to get under each other's skin.

In the morning, he invites me to meet him for dinner with Ismael's family in Jabel Mukaber.

"Is it safe?" I ask before he leaves for his songwriting workshop at Ismael's school. Even the name "Jabel Mukaber" suggests a "macabre" neighborhood. "The driver of that truck that rammed into soldiers in Jerusalem came from there."

"Yes. I told you, they're very against all that. Ismael knows about you, and his family wants to meet you."

I spend the day visiting some of my favorite Jerusalem haunts—the Mahane Yehuda souk, the Ben Yehuda outdoor mall, and, of course, the Western Wall, where I say a prayer that Sebastian and I discover and achieve the truth of our relationship. It's not about what he and I want, but what is best for the full actualization of who we are and our purpose on this earth.

I drive us to dinner through Jabel Mukaber. How strange that Israeli rightists criticize Europe for allowing Muslim refugees onto their soil, but Israel has created its own Muslim "no-go zones." If I ignore the Hebrew signage, this could very well be a neighborhood in an Arab country. I'm not sure if any visibly Jewish person, or for that matter, any Western woman, would feel truly safe walking these streets.

But I feel very safe driving with Sebastian in the passenger seat. The Palestinians wouldn't dare cause this beautiful German any harm.

The house of Jerusalem stone is situated on a hill, designed in what appears to be a fusion of Ottoman and Roman themes with its Doric columns, a dome-like roof, and flowery reliefs on the stone window panes.

We settle in the living room whose walls are lined with antique-looking velvety sofas surrounding a wooden, ornate coffee table in the middle. A glass door leads to a balcony through which I can see the tip of the Dome of the Rock. Sebastian and I sit within a few inches of each other as we're served soft drinks and nuts. Hanin, the matriarch, pours me some Fanta orange soda without asking.

"Please," Hanin says and pushes a bowl of roasted cashews my way.

Sebastian reintroduces me to Nabil, Ismael, and his sister Amira; they remember me from the "Battle of the Bands." Ismael's older brother, Muhammad, and his two-year-old son and pretty wife, Yasmin, have joined us for dinner.

"Thank you for having me," I tell the family. "This is a beautiful house."

"Thank you. It goes in the family back many generations."

"That's nice," I say, knowing such a statement begs the opinion that Israelis came as intruders occupying this land, which he's polite enough not to say outright.

"You live in Tel Aviv?" the father asks in a very friendly tone, in Hebrew.

"Yes, but originally from Ariel." I feel more comfortable telling an Arab from East Jerusalem than a German that I'm originally from Ariel. In Ariel, Jews have probably interacted more with West Bank Palestinians than most Europeans have, or than most Jews in Tel Aviv, for that matter.

"So you're an architect?" Ismael asks.

"Yes. I'm just starting to go out on my own." Although I won't say where my new project is.

"You liked Berlin?" Ismael asks.

"Loved it. And I hear you did, too." Although I won't say how I know exactly why he loved it.

"Yes, very much," Ismael says. "If I were younger, I'd go there and study."

Amira sits in the corner of the sofa, staring at me, in a dark blue hijab and a long-sleeve teal tunic reaching right above her knees. Should I talk to her? She's not necessarily inviting conversation.

"And you all work in the family pharmacy?" I ask.

"The brothers do," Ismael says.

"A family business," Nabil says. We continue in Hebrew, and I translate for Sebastian, although he must have already heard the story. Nabil's grandfather started the business in 1932 under the British occupation, and it has expanded over time to include three pharmacies in east Jerusalem and one in Wadi Ara (another virtual "no-go zone") in northern Israel.

"I hope you're hungry," Nabil says once Hanin announces that food is ready.

"She's an excellent cook," Sebastian says. I wish he could take my hand, but I doubt that would be appropriate here. I wonder what the family thinks of this German man and, for all intents and purposes, his Jewish girlfriend. So far, they are nothing but hospitable and sweet.

In the kitchen, we sit around a table for eight. Hanin brings out *maqluba*, an Arabic dish of rice and chicken, a lettuce salad decorated with pistachios, a plate of rice topped with toasted almonds and saffron, and a tray of lamb kabob. Amira brings out more sugary soft drinks and some water. *What a feast!*

Hanin insists on serving us, and she scoops onto my plate at least two portions, despite my protests. I don't think I could manage to eat even a quarter. I feel bad. *What a waste of food.*

I raise my brow at Sebastian; he sympathizes. Apparently, he's already experienced this overly generous, almost intrusive hospitality. Funny how so many Germans pride themselves on being feminists, egalitarians, and environmentally friendly, but when it comes to Israel, they seem to side with patriarchal societies.

We speak English over the meal, and Sebastian tells us about his workshop and the challenges of implementing Arabic half tones alongside Western scales. Ismael praises Sebastian for introducing his class to some of the great German composers, like Bach, Beethoven, and Wagner. Ismael offers to demonstrate a song he recently wrote, with Sebastian's help.

We go back to the living room for Ismael's mini-concert. Hanin, Yasmin, and Amira bring out the dessert of a meal that never seems to end.

I force down some tasty *malabi*, a creamy dessert spiced with rose water, as Ismael plays his guitar and sings a song in Arabic that I can't understand, but the sound is pleasant and his voice, smooth. I can understand why Sebastian took him under his wing. Everyone applauds, except for Amira who sits there looking sad.

"You should try out for *Kochav Nolad*," I tell him, referring to Israel's national televised singing contest.

"Yeah, but I don't really sing in Hebrew," he says.

"Is there an 'Arab Idol?'" I ask.

"Yes, in Jordan. I could apply, but I just don't have time. Between teaching and working at the pharmacy."

For the next half hour, we engage in small talk, and I feel like I'm back in Dresden, only here the atmosphere isn't as cold as porcelain, but as warm as the *maqluba*. Who wants to ruin this friendliness with pressing questions: Do you accept Israel's existence? Would you rather live under the Palestinian Authority? What do you think of the Jerusalem truck attack?

We are like enemies with a wall between us—Sebastian.

The Mansours speak Arabic amongst themselves, and I'm not sure how we'll announce our departure. Arabs seem to possess different social codes for meeting, greeting, and parting.

Ismael offers to show us around the neighborhood. Amira, quiet until now, surprisingly asks to come along.

As we step out into the calm night, Ismael shows us the community mosque and some "coffee shops" where Muslim men smoke hookahs and play backgammon over hot drinks since alcohol is forbidden. My pesky "fear of persecution" gene acts up. I have an unnerving feeling this is a trap.

Ismael and Sebastian talk about music while Amira and I stay behind. I'm not sure what to say to her, but I would like to find out more about her.

"I heard you applied to Ariel University."

"Yes. To the nursing school. I also thought about architecture."

"Really? So why not architecture?"

"Too hard. My father has a lot of connections in the medical world. In the end, I studied nursing here, and he helped me get a job at the local clinic next to the pharmacy."

"You like it here?" I ask in Hebrew.

"It's ok," she says. "I would like to live abroad."

"Why?"

"The situation."

"The 'Occupation?'" I use the language of the Palestinian narrative, an act of peace and reconciliation.

"Yes."

"Is it that bad?" I would like to hear her opinion of the conflict, not the Palestinian opinion filtered through media commentators or activists.

She pauses. "Which 'occupation?'"

"What do you mean?"

Her tone turns angry. "Everyone occupies me."

"What?" I did not expect this answer.

She hangs back so that our distance between Ismael and Sebastian grows. "Could we walk alone?"

"Yes, of course."

"I'll show Nilly around, okay?" she calls out to her brother.

She leads me further down a poorly lit, haphazardly paved street. We peek inside courtyard apartment buildings owned by clans since Arab families tend to stick together, with children raising their own families in the immediate vicinity of the parents.

I wonder if this is what she means by everyone occupying her. How can a young woman have any privacy here?

She cuts into a secluded alleyway. The "fear of persecution" gene is working overtime. *Is this a setup? I must get out of here. I will be stabbed or run over!*

Amira looks around. I keep my hand on my purse. I'm ready to take out my keys and scratch her eyes out.

"I want to know," she says. "I need to know: Are you with Sebastian?"

"What do you mean 'with him?'" I ask, suspicious.

"Is he your boyfriend?"

"I don't know," I say, the truth. "We're just dating for now."

"I need to tell you. I need to tell someone. I like him so much. He is so nice. So handsome. I never met a man like him. He is so gentle.

"I want to be in Germany. I want to be with a German man. I want to get out of here. I can't ask him if he has any friends for me. I met them. They are nice like him. I can't tell Ismael how I feel. I can't tell anyone. The situation here is so hard. All the time they want to set me up with a Muslim man, from here or Nablus or Ramallah.

"But I don't want any of them, and I'm alone. So alone. And I'm nothing here without being married at my age."

"How old are you?"

"Almost twenty-nine."

She has it worse than me.

"I'm trapped and don't know what to do," she says. "I wish I didn't have to wear this thing."

She points to her hijab and searches for an even more secluded spot further down. She eyes a construction site and leads me there. "Come!"

We're surrounded by construction equipment, sacks of cement, and concrete tiles. She pulls down her hijab.

"I have pretty hair," she says. Indeed, she does. It's dark, thick, and shiny, even here in the dim light. "I want people to see it. I want men to see it. But I don't want to fight with my parents. If I don't keep this on, if I don't marry an Arab Muslim man, they'll make it hard for me."

"Will they disown you?"

"I don't know what they'll do. But it will be a fight. I might get hurt, and I don't have the strength. Why fight when I don't even want to be here? I'm so lost. Can you help me?"

My fear has turned into empathy. I can't believe I entertained so much suspicion. Her eyes are so earnest, this must be the truth. "Of course. What can I do?"

"I want to get to Germany. I want to be free. But I need to get a visa, and it's not easy. I don't have an Israeli passport, not like Ismael. Maybe you and Sebastian could talk to the German authorities. I want to go and never come back. Maybe I could live there like a refugee. Maybe they need my skills there, as a nurse, speaking Arabic."

"Good question. I wonder if you could claim political asylum. But from which country?"

"From Palestine."

"Palestine?"

"You think Israel occupies us? No! It's Palestine. We have to live for 'Palestine' all the time. Why do you think I have to stay here? So that 'Palestine' is strong. So that I have Palestinian children. To fight the 'Occupation.' To defend 'Arab honor.' But I'm sick of all of this. I don't want to live for Palestine. I want to live for myself, in Germany, maybe even somewhere else in Europe.

So can you help me?"

"That's a big step, Amira. I don't live in Germany. I'll talk with Sebastian, okay?"

"Please." She puts her hijab back on. "But promise me—promise me!—you won't tell anyone about this. This never happened. Only Sebastian. Sweet Sebastian."

"Promise."

We get back to the hotel, and in our plush bed, I tell Sebastian about my conversation with Amira. He is as shocked as I am.

"I realized something crazy," I say to him. "We're both, in some ways, not living for ourselves but for the greater good. She must live for the sake of Palestine. I must live for the sake of Israel. I don't know if I'm really pro-Israel when Israel refers to the government or state institutions. I'm pro-people. I'm 'pro' the Israeli people, just like I'm 'pro' the Palestinian people who want to live peacefully, not as a weapon against Israelis.

"I see it with my job, in the buildings I built—these cookie-cutter, mass-produced buildings that take forever to get approved, all for the sake of the country, the state—not for the sake of the people who want to live there. At first, the Israeli government encouraged Jews to build homes in Gaza for the sake of the state, then it made them give it all up for the same reason, but shouldn't the state live for the sake of the people? Why should the government have so much control? I mean, I'm all for building, but why can't individuals buy a plot of land and build as they please? Instead, my clients are renegades for building their dream home on land no one ever claimed. Ironically, it's the Jewish state that prevents them from living the full Jewish lives they seek."

Sebastian nods in understanding. Normally, I'd refrain from criticizing Israel to a German, but he's no ordinary German. Nor do I want to feel muzzled from criticizing Israel for its faults. The Holocaust and Jewish persecution shouldn't implicitly deny us the freedom to speak out against injustices enacted by Jews against Jews.

"But Amira, she has it worse," I continue. "She might suffer more than dirty looks and insults if she goes against her society's norms. She can't say what she wants to say, date who she wants to date. I mean, I'd have to fight for you, too, but my parents wouldn't disown me. Her life is a constant 'fuck you' to Israel. Well, I don't want my life to be a constant 'fuck you' to anyone. Not to 'Palestine.' Not to Hitler. I want my life to be the best life it can be—for its own sake.

"So, you see, in Israel I guess there's a kind of 'national socialism' in a weird way, but nothing like Nazism. Actually, I don't think Hitler was a nationalist even though his party had that word in it. He exploited nationalism for plain evil. If he were a true nationalist, he would have honored his Jewish citizens, some of the biggest German patriots."

"This is why we're alike," Sebastian says. "We also have a weird kind of 'national socialism,' not Nazism, of course. We're like inverse nationalists, which is also a type of nationalism. Our lives are also like this constant 'fuck you' to Hitler. So we fight any form of nationalism until we have no national identity, until we don't believe we deserve to fight for ourselves or for our country. I mean, I don't think Germany accepted the refugees because they really felt compassion for these people. It's for the sake of our 'national consciousness,' or to spite it, so that we could shed our Nazi image and past. But after the Christmas attack, I realized we did it the wrong way, too fast, too uncontrolled. But we had to take them in, or we'd be dickheads again. In the end, we were dickheads to ourselves.

"A lot of Germans believe Israel exists mostly because of the Holocaust, so they have a special duty to make sure it's a super moral country, and for Germans, that means not to be so nationalistic. But then they promote the worst kind of nationalism: Palestinian nationalism. I saw it tonight. It felt different this time. Not as exotic and cool. I saw the pain in Amira's face. 'Palestine'—or the dream of it—limits her far more than Israel does."

"So is there anything we can do to help her? Could she get to Germany? She is like a political prisoner." As I ask these questions, I feel an unexpected jealousy that she may get to go.

"I don't know," Sebastian says. "I mean, she can't even talk to Ismael about it."

"We exchanged numbers. Should I invite her to Tel Aviv so we can talk about it together while you're still here?"

"Good idea."

I text Amira: "Amira. I'm so happy we spoke. Would you like to meet me and Sebastian in Tel Aviv this week so we can talk more?"

Sebastian leans over my shoulder as I type. "You're so sweet," he says and kisses my shoulder. "And not so silly, Nilly."

I turn to face him. "What's the power you have over us women? You changed me. You changed her." I take the bed sheet and put it over my head, mimicking a hijab. "Will you free me?"

As he does, I'm jealous of myself.

By the next morning, Amira writes back: "Thank you and Sebastian! No, it's okay. Please forget what I told you. I was just having a bad day. I will stay here. It will be okay. Please don't say anything to my family or Ismael. Regards to Sebastian."

Sebastian and I know she is not okay. I feel so much compassion that I would even consider lending Sebastian to her for one night to truly free her.

"Okay," I write back. "If you change your mind, call me. We're here for you."

CHAPTER EIGHT

I feel proud bringing this gorgeous German to the site of my new house in Sde Boaz—his first trip inside a Jewish settlement. Settlers are not used to Europeans, except for Christian Zionists, visiting them.

After we pass through the tunnel road leading into Gush Etsion, he can already tell which towns are Jewish and which are Arab.

The Jews build with distinct urban planning to maximize the use of land while ensuring a respectable modicum of trees and parks. Terracotta rooftops serve as the homes' uniforms. Arabs build organically, usually without regulation, in the valleys, hardly cutting up the natural landscape but not necessarily preserving its green spaces, unless for agriculture. Many buildings appear incomplete since they are often built haphazardly with no deadline for occupancy. Arabs seem to have a lot more building rights than Jews.

I explain how Jews lived in this region before 1948, under the British and Ottomans, but also long ago during the Temple period, when the Maccabees fought the Hellenists. After the Arab legions killed or pushed out the Jewish residents during the War of Independence, the Jordanians occupied the land, an occupation recognized only by Britain and Pakistan. Jordan relinquished its claims to the West Bank in 1988, paving the way for the PLO to lay claim to it for the establishment of a Palestinian state.

I point to the Judean Hills in the distance, in the direction of Tekoa, an established settlement.

"You see the tip of Herod's desert palace?" I ask. "It was turned into a public museum a few years ago. I wonder what would happen to all the archeology here, the architecture, the historical sites, if Jews were forced to leave. I'm sure the synagogues would be torched, like they were in Gaza. That reminds me. Remember what Stefanie said about the burning of the Old Synagogue in Dresden? How the guy was quoted saying the fire will return upon Dresden?"

"Yes."

"Well, I guess that's what happened in Gaza, and that's probably what would happen here. We fought three mini-wars in Gaza since the pullout and suffered many rocket attacks. So the fire returned not only upon Gaza but also upon Israel because it was Israel who forced the Jews to leave the land."

"Interesting," he says. *We're back to safe words.* "You know what's funny?"

"What?"

"I just realized now that Germany's also a country that's rebuilding itself; actually, it started around the same time as Israel, in the late 1940s and 50s. Dresden and other East German cities hardly developed under the Soviets. Only when Germany reunited did Dresden begin to flourish. The German government invested in it and brought back August's playground."

"And they did a wonderful job."

"It's the same with you guys. The Soviets had no stake in Dresden, no historical connection. Maybe only people who truly own the land can rebuild it in its full glory. Don't you think that would make a good argument?"

"Would you like to work in Israel advocacy?"

"Maybe I will," he says in a teasing voice.

At Sde Boaz, I say hello to some of the residents and introduce them to Sebastian as I take him to my plot; we expect the foundation to go up in about a month.

I share with him my ideas for the house, which should be any hippie's dream. It will be built as ecologically as possible. The roof will keep heat in during the winter and coolness during the summer. The sewage system will filter clean water for the garden. A natural flow of air and light will minimize energy use.

Keren invites us to her caravan for coffee and shares with us the history of Sde Boaz and why they decided to live under such conditions, which actually sound luxurious. They wake up to fresh air, stunning landscapes, and a loving, value-oriented community. The village, as she likes to call it, was started by a few anti-establishment renegades who wanted to live free from the dictates of the Israeli government. But over time, the residents learned to cooperate and compromise with the regional council; only then did they thrive. While on paper Sde Boaz is "unauthorized," the government has allowed it to grow quietly, in part for its elevated, strategic location near an army outpost.

When we say goodbye, Keren, to my surprise, hugs Sebastian.

"I hope you stay safe in Germany," she says. "You're unfortunately going through what we go through. I never thought I would say this, but we're fighting for you, too, just by living here. We don't want an Islamic dictatorship to take over this land, and we want Germany to remain the free country it is today. Maybe you won't see it. I doubt you will. But stay safe. And don't be afraid to fight. For once, we're on the same side."

"*Todah*," Sebastian says, clearly moved. "*Vielen Dank.* Thank you very much."

CHAPTER NINE

"How are you?" my mother asks me over the phone at around 7:30 the next morning, her voice cautious, Sebastian sleeping next to me. We simply let our last fight go, and she didn't ask me again about Berlin, but something must be wrong if she's calling me this early.

"Good," I say softly as I pet Sebastian's hair, not explaining why I'm good. Maybe she found out somehow that he's here, not that I care. I'll stand up for him now.

"I'm very sorry to tell you..." In this split moment, I fear she's about to disavow me for learning about Sebastian. "Safta is not with us anymore."

"*Baruch Dayan Emet*," I say, instinctively, the phrase Jews traditionally recite upon hearing of someone's death. *Blessed is the True Judge.*

"The doctor just called me. She died in her sleep. The death of the righteous."

She informs me that the funeral will take place later this afternoon followed by the *shiva*, the traditional seven-day mourning period.

"Do you want me to help set up?" I ask, sad that it took Safta's death to bring me and my mother together.

"Yes."

I get up and get dressed, no longer in the mood to lie nude with Sebastian. I can't be happy now. I sit on the edge of the bed and cry.

"What's wrong?" he asks, waking up to my tears.

"My grandmother died," I whisper.

"I'm so sorry," he says and pushes himself up to stroke my hair.

"Thanks," I say. "I'll be okay."

He puts on his shirt, sensing this moment requires modesty, and we spend the next half hour on the bed as he listens generously while I recall my fond memories with Safta: How I'd sometimes sleep at her house on Friday nights after she hosted Shabbat dinner, and in the morning she'd make me eggs and hot chocolate for breakfast while I watched TV. How I'd visit her after school, sometimes with a friend, and she'd always greet me with a delicious meal. How she'd take me on day trips to Caesarea, the Sea of Galilee, and other local sites when I was in my early twenties for quality time together. How, after all she went through, her main mission in life was to give to her children and grandchildren.

"Is there anything I can do?" Sebastian asks.

"No. You should enjoy your day. Knock 'em dead at the interview."

Today he's meeting with the CEO of an Israeli start-up who might open up a Berlin office. He's looking for Berlin-based consultants to help develop a music production app and was introduced to Sebastian through the Music for Peace program.

"When are you going to Ariel?" he asks.

"In a few hours. Jews are supposed to be buried in the ground without delay, part of the biblical saying that we're made from earth, and to earth we must return. And then we have something called a '*shiva*.'"

I explain how "*shiva*" comes from the word "*sheva*," meaning seven, for the seven days of ritual mourning observed by the immediate family members of the deceased: spouses, children, and siblings. As a sign of sorrow, the mourners sit on low stools or on the ground, their shirts torn. Mirrors are covered to avoid vanity. Family, friends, and neighbors visit during the *shiva*, but, out of respect, they must let the mourners initiate conversation. "Most of the time, we just reminisce. This gives us some structure because who really knows how to behave when someone dies?"

"That sounds beautiful," Sebastian says. "We don't really have anything like that." He pauses to think and asks: "Should I come?"

"My mother just lost her mother. She doesn't need to have a heart attack."

"You're probably right. Too bad it has to be that way. I would want to pay my respects."

"It really is too bad. Sucks," I say. "But your coming to the *shiva* would make Yad Vashem feel like a walk in the park."

"All the more reason for me to be there."

He's right. The grandson of Nazis—even though I don't see him that way anymore—paying respects to a Holocaust survivor would mean more than any Holocaust memorial, any walk through a museum, any visit to a settlement.

I can't be afraid, not like Amira. I must break this taboo.

"I'd love for you to be there," I say. "I'll feel it out and call you from there."

In the late afternoon, we gather around a relatively new cemetery in

Ariel, built on a hill neighboring a *de facto* nature reserve where packs of deer run wild through rocky hills as never before. When the Jews returned, so did the indigenous, biblical animals, especially since Ariel regulated deer hunting, an Arab pastime. I hope this nature reserve won't be sacrificed for housing developments. I don't want the "Jewish" animals to be expelled, either.

I'm sure Safta would have never imagined, as she witnessed her family being harassed, expelled, their bodies burned to dust in a furnace, that her body would find its way into the earth of the land of Israel over a shining Jewish city built out of a rock. I hope she'll forever find rest here, not like the deceased of Gush Katif whose bones were exhumed from the cemeteries as their loved ones were expelled from their homes.

I stand next to Arik as the community rabbi recites *Kaddish*, the prayer for the dead. After the funeral, I turn to him.

"Arik, can I talk to you about something."

"Sure. What's up?"

I pull him to the side, away from family and friends. I'm glad to have a family confidant regarding Sebastian.

"That guy from Germany—the one I told you about—he's here in Israel."

"And?"

"I want to bring him to the *shiva*. He wants to come, as a friend. To pay his respects to Safta. He's a very special guy. He's doing genealogical research on his family to understand their role in the Holocaust. Total friend of the Jewish people. He's also never been to Ariel. He's leaving on Saturday night, so this is the only time he can come."

"Does Ima know about him?"

"She suspects something. Would it totally tear her apart?"

"Maybe. She's sad, but we all knew this day would come." He looks at Safta's grave, as if asking her for the solution. "You know what? Don't ask. Just bring him."

"Really?"

"Maybe this is the only way you can introduce him. It might actually impress her. Besides, I'd like to meet him."

After the funeral, I help my aunt set up refreshments in our dining room. As I set down the food and plasticware, my hands shake at the prospect of Sebastian's visit. The community rabbi is expected to come with a *minyan*—a quorum of ten men—to lead the evening prayer. Even the most secular Jewish families in Ariel keep some semblance of traditional mourning rituals. Ima takes a seat on the sofa whose cushions have been removed. Visitors will arrive any minute.

As I organize family albums on the coffee table, I think about how the Holocaust generation is dying out and how oral history, books, films, recorded testimonies, and photographs will soon offer our only insight into that world. Now it's up to me and my children to tell the stories of horror and heroism.

As Ima always reminded me, the sins of the fathers visit upon the third and fourth generations.

But while she quotes the biblical phrase to remind us of German guilt, I don't interpret it as a mystical aphorism. The sins of the fathers naturally visit upon the grandchildren and great grandchildren because those are the generations still connected to the sins and their influence, through personal ties and stories. By the fifth generation, all persecutors and victims will have died out, allowing for new stock that doesn't grow up with fresh, firsthand accounts, effects, and memories of the sins.

That's why Sebastian should be here. We're working to undo the "sins" and the pain and trauma, together, so that our grandchildren can live scar free, learning from the past but not feeling burdened by it. By then, young Germans and Jews will play together with innocent eyes focused firmly on the present. And future.

I think of all the courageous acts of my life—from braving Berlin, to striking out on my own as an architect, to defending Israel when it was unpopular to do so. Inviting Sebastian here may very well be the most courageous.

Sebastian pays 250 shekels for a taxi to Ariel. It drops him off at the main junction just outside the city gate. Last year, a "lone wolf" Palestinian stabbed an IDF soldier there, but no one really thinks about that anymore. When Sebastian arrives, the pavement is lined with almond trees sprouting light pink petals and with Palestinian factory workers waiting for their rides back home.

"Welcome to Ariel," I say as he gets into my car. We drive through the gate together where the security guard smiles and says, "Shalom."

"I'll show you around before we get to the house," I tell him. "They're just finishing up prayers."

We drive past the Ariel mall in construction that will hopefully improve the quality of life for the residents. On a pine-filled hill to the left, I point out the "Leap of Faith" obstacle course belonging to our outdoor adventure park for leadership training. Individuals are hoisted atop its pole via a harness, trusting comrades holding the security cables as they leap off to catch a trapeze.

I continue my own "leap of faith" on this windy Ariel road toward the Ariel Regional Center for the Performing Arts, our state-of-the-art theater that radical left-wing artists love to boycott. From its large terrace, we look south, past the nature reserve to the roofs and minarets of the Arab town of Salfit. In the dimming sunlight, the mauve streaks of sky blend with barren, thorny hills.

"That's what Ariel looked like when the first pioneers arrived in the late 1970s," I say. "The Arabs called it the 'Mountain of Death' because even their donkeys didn't want to go up the rocky terrain. But people like my father weren't deterred. They weren't religious settlers, even though the Tomb of Joshua is located down the road in the Arab town of Kifl Haris. We could go there only with an army escort. They came to secure the land mostly for security reasons. We could see the coast if we drive up some more.

"I was three-years old when construction started on our home. Our contractor was from Salfit, that town over there. His name was Faisel. Sometimes he'd bring his son and daughter Krama over, and we'd play with the rocks near our caravan because we didn't have parks with sandboxes yet. Back then Arabs used to play with rocks with us, not throw them at us. I remember shopping in Salfit for groceries and hummus because we didn't have supermarkets, either.

"But one day, we stopped going, and when I asked my father why, he just said, 'We have everything in Ariel now.' Only when I was older did I realize that wasn't the whole truth."

"The first *intifada* broke out in 1987. It was a street uprising instigated by the PLO. The Arabs would throw stones and Molotov cocktails at Israelis. One day, one of our neighbors drove into Salfit and came back with broken windows. My father called Faisel to find out what happened, and he said it's better we don't go there anymore. For our own safety. Faisal was upset about that. He didn't agree with the violence, but the tribe elders couldn't control the youth.

"So I stopped seeing Krama, but, still, we didn't have fences around Ariel. Some people hoped things would get better with the Oslo Accords. Israelis started going back to Salfit, by now under PA rule, this time for furniture bazaars the residents would hold there every Saturday. Israelis are always up for a good bargain, especially on Saturday when most everything is closed.

"But all that ended in 2000 when the second *intifada* started. By this time, the Arabs had more than just rocks and homemade bombs. Under the Oslo Accords, Israel gave guns to Palestinian terrorist-in-chief Yasser Arafat. People from Salfit would climb the hills surrounding Ariel and start shooting into our streets. That's when the government decided to build a fence around the city and create that IDF watch tower to look into Salfit." I point to it. "That was hard for us."

Sebastian rests his arms on the railing and looks at a couple walking with a toddler along the pavement, then back up to the hills, meditative.

"Too bad my program didn't speak to 'settler groups,'" Sebastian says. "It would've been good for us to hear this. The other side of the story."

"Next time," I say.

"What does 'Ariel' mean, anyway?"

"It's another name for Jerusalem," I say. "'*Ari*' means lion. '*El*' is god. The Lion of God."

"The symbol of Dresden is a lion," he says.

"Really? You see, we're connected."

We stare at the hills in thoughtful silence, but I feel like roaring.

Chatty children pass us by and break the silence. We follow them inside where about a dozen smiling girls are dancing very professionally on stage to folk music, dressed up in traditional Russian costumes. I ask a staffer what's going on. Turns out they're members of Ariel's folk dance ensemble for youngsters, rehearsing for a show.

"They're so cute!" Sebastian enthuses.

"Totally," I say. "Ariel's very cultural. That's why our mayor really wanted this theater and raised a lot of money for it. In the 1990s, the city took in a lot of Jews from the Former Soviet Union, just like Germany did, and they brought a lot of talent in music and the arts. And the sciences. That's also why Ariel University grew so quickly."

"I never knew Ariel was so big and established," Sebastian says as we walk back to my car. "I mean, I always imagined the settlements as really primitive, but it's just like a regular Israeli town." He takes a deep breath. "And the air is nice here."

"A lot of people live here for the air and a more suburban life. Most Israelis consider Ariel a normal city, one that Israel will never give up, but you never know." We reach my car. "Now for Ariel University, my *alma mater*."

I drive, heading east, past new housing developments, until we reach Israel's seventh university, which keeps expanding with new facilities: a library, a medical school, dormitories. Curving back down to my house, I point out the sports and recreation center built with private donations to give the residents a local place to unwind. I also point out Ariel's own Holocaust museum founded by Holocaust survivors—a husband and wife team—inside their own home to create a personal educational experience for the city's youth.

I'm not taking him on this tour to change his mind about Ariel and the settlements. I'm just proud of my hometown.

In fact, I also admit to criticism I reserve for the settlements. I don't like how Arab and Jewish populations centers are divided, with different laws and rules governing each. I don't like how the Civil Administration in Judea and Samaria has special jurisdiction over "settler" lives and property, sometimes treating us as second-class citizens. I don't like the religious hegemony prevailing over the settlement movement, such that a German, or even an average secular Israeli, may not feel fully welcome or comfortable in most of the settlements.

It seems to me that the best solution is for Israel to annex Judea and Samaria, with Jews and Arabs living under one just, civilized system that protects all our lives and property against unjust assaults.

"I would love to go back and shop in Ramallah," I tell him as we almost reach my parents. "I would love for Faisel to come visit us at the house he built. I would love to see how Krama's grown. I would love for Amira to be able to find refuge in Israel rather than Germany. I would love for there to be no such thing as 'settler groups.'"

I'm glad we arrive because I feel like I'm getting preachy, even though he's listening intently, sincerely.

"I'm nervous," Sebastian says when we park, putting his hand over a heart that must be pounding as wildly as mine.

"So am I," I say.

"But I want to do this," he says. "I want to meet your family and see where you grew up. What should I say to your mom?"

"Actually, you're not really supposed to say anything unless she talks to you first, but wait. There's something you're supposed to say."

I find a pen and piece of paper in the glove compartment and write the English transliteration of the traditional phrase a visitor imparts to a Jewish mourner. "*HaMakom yenechem otchem b'toch sha'arey Tziyon V'yerushalayim.*" May God comfort you with the mourners of Zion and Jerusalem.

We enter through the back door so that my mother doesn't notice our entrance, but a neighbor does.

Na'ama approaches. "Nilly, Shalom!" she says. "Rachel was such a wonderful lady."

"Thanks, Na'ama," I say. "The world lost a light." She eyes Sebastian, baiting an introduction. This is a Jewish society, after all, one that places a premium on relationships—and on asking questions about marital status. A *shiva* may actually be an ideal setting to introduce him. Sorrow will shield us from rude nosiness.

"This is my friend, Sebastian." I don't say he's German. At this point, it's irrelevant. He is a man. A good man. "Will you excuse me," I say to Na'ama. "I want to see my mom."

In the kitchen, I introduce Sebastian to Arik, who gives him a strong shake, making him feel welcome.

"Nice of you to come," Arik tells him.

"Glad I could be here," he says.

After they engage in small talk that induces Na'ama's eavesdropping, Sebastian follows me to the living room, sensitive enough not to touch me here. Ima's slumping on the sofa, her black button down torn near her heart. Aba's sitting in a chair a few feet away from her since he's not in ritual mourning.

"Who's this?" Ima asks me. I look at both Aba and Ima, knowing Aba would be more tolerant.

"His name is Sebastian," I say. She eyes him suspiciously while Aba eyes him curiously. "My friend from Germany. He wanted to come to pay his respects to Safta."

Arik was right. Ima cannot make a scene here. She purses her lips; her silence is enough of an admonition.

"You have my deepest condolences," Sebastian says sincerely. He then looks down at the paper and tries his best to say the Hebrew as practiced. The words come out so sweetly, so clumsily in his German accent that even Ima cannot be angry with him.

I'm surprised she says, however reluctantly, in her Hebrew accent, "Thank you."

I sit with Sebastian by the coffee table and show him pictures of Safta: at a DP camp in Buchenwald where her immigration was processed, in Rosh Ha'ayin presenting Saba his sixtieth birthday cake, at our housewarming party in Ariel, in the hospital room for the birth of my nephew.

"She was born in Poland, in a small town near Lodz where the Nazis set up the ghetto." Ima volunteers, her tone half accusatory, half informative. I brace myself. With Sebastian here, she'll no doubt rip into the Germans for their crimes against her family. Sebastian nods at me in understanding and sits there patiently, graciously, openly.

For the next twenty minutes, Ima vividly describes the story of Safta's upbringing and survival with details that I either forgot or never knew, like how her father owned a store for household goods; how she was raised in a very religious household; how she and her family made pancakes from coffee grounds in the ghetto when no food was available; how, by a stroke of luck, she volunteered to be transferred from Auschwitz to a work camp when most everyone in her cell bloc refused, thinking the Nazis were lying; how Saba took care of her when she got sick at the DP camp, never leaving her side. She tops the story with their determination to build a proud Jewish family in the land of Israel.

Throughout, Sebastian's facial expressions of sorrow, sympathy, and amazement match those of the family members and friends who have joined us. The fiery indictment of the Germans or an attack on Sebastian personally never comes, and I think it's Sebastian's presence that has unexpectedly inspired this impromptu tribute to Safta's life, the most beautiful eulogy I've yet heard.

"But most of all, she just wanted all of us to be free," my mother says. "Never to live in the fear that she knew. And she and my father gave that to us."

Everyone nods, impressed, but Sebastian speaks: "The spirit of life is very strong in all of you. And in your daughter. I'm sure they're both very, very proud." He pauses as the visitors stare at this "German" in surprise. Ima appears skeptical, shocked—and pleased. "And, as the grandson of a man who was a member of the Nazi party on one side, and who fought in the Wehrmacht on the other, I want to say I'm sorry to you." He becomes teary eyed, like Ima. "They're not here to say it and maybe they wouldn't, but maybe that's why I was brought here, to this beautiful home. To at least do my part in recognizing all the pain and suffering that my grandparents' generation caused you and your family, and to say, on their behalf: I'm sorry."

If Ima hadn't cried for Safta until now, the tears come out in full force. Ima motions Sebastian toward her and says, embracing him. "Thank you. Thank you."

There's not a dry eye in the house, including mine. In this moment, I fully forgive Sebastian—for everything. I even forgive...Germany.

CHAPTER TEN

Fortunately, mourning is suspended on Shabbat, a sacred day of joy and pleasure that even death can't stop.

Friday night is our last night together, for now or forever, I don't know. On Shabbat, we're supposed to live in the moment.

I take him for Shabbat dinner to Vong, one of Tel Aviv's few Vietnamese restaurants. Vietnamese is one of Sebastian's favorite cuisines, which he tells me is plentiful in Berlin, particularly in the east where a Vietnamese community developed after East Germany invited Vietnamese guest workers to help build the communist country.

Finally, I can catch up with him about his meeting with the CEO.

Over pho soup and fluffy Vietnamese bahn rolls, he tells me how the Israeli start-up is part of a German program that fosters Tel Aviv-Berlin business relationships, particularly by offering Israeli start-ups free office space in Berlin. If the company sets up a Berlin office, they might engage him as a freelancer to create sample music production tracks.

"He said German start-ups are generally well organized and managed, but that they need that Israeli *chutzpah*—that out-of-the-box, improvisational thinking, so it's a nice marriage."

"Yeah, we complement each other," I say, smiling.

"It's not racist to say you guys are smart, right?"

"I'll take it as a compliment, even though we have stupid people, too."

"We all do," he says. "But I remember your interpretation at the Holocaust Memorial. How it stood for all these creations that never saw the light of day. Lately, I've been thinking about the musicians we slaughtered, the great Jewish composers that never were. The Gershwins, the James Horners, the Hans Zimmers—who's a German Jew, by the way. I checked. It's so clear how Germany destroyed itself by expelling and murdering one of its most brilliant, creative populations. Hitler wasn't anti-Jewish. He was anti-life. Jews are not our misfortune; you guys are our fortune." He takes my hand over the table. "We're lucky to have you back."

"Thank you," I say, beaming as I take a sip of my fruity cocktail, but I don't wonder if he's hinting at me personally. Even Ima would now be open to us dating seriously, but unlike our last night in Berlin, I have faith that if we are meant to be together, we will be. I don't have to force the future with him in any particular direction. Nor do I have to know this instant because we're friends. Real friends. Any time I reach out, he'll be there, and vice versa. We can discuss our future rationally, openly, whenever we so choose. The Berlin Wall of our hearts has fallen.

I take another sip as he takes out the Meissen necklace from his pocket. "Will you accept this now?"

"Yes." I take it without hesitation and look at the royal blue logo. I'm not sure if the company has undergone Sebastian's kind of introspection, but as long as people like Sebastian exist, speaking—and singing—freely, Germany and its people can pave a new, beautiful, moral path—for its own sake. To me, these two interlocking swords represent Germany and Israel locked in a fight for the good, as true friends. Sebastian and I both come from a city of lions.

The heart pendant reaches over my joyful heart, just next to my Star of David, a symbol that, for years in Germany, became a symbol of oppression and slavery. Today, it is a symbol of Jewish might and freedom, buttressed now, in my heart, by the strength of Meissen porcelain, which can survive firestorms.

These two pieces will learn to co-exist, no matter what happens between me and this Saxon prince. Even if I never saw Sebastian again, I would feel fully fulfilled just having had the honor to get to know him in every which way, including the biblical way.

Satiated on good food and cocktails, we head to my place. It's Shabbat, so it's a *mitzvah* for couples to "know" each other. And that's what our lovemaking finally feels like. Not a kinky game or fantasy, but the connection of two bodies deepened by the knowledge of each other's minds, hearts, and souls. A taste of the world to come.

ABOUT THE AUTHOR

Orit Arfa is an author, journalist, painter, songwriter, political commentator, and media personality.

Born in Los Angeles, she moved to Berlin in 2016 after spending over a decade in Israel working primarily as a journalist covering politics, society, and lifestyle. In Berlin, her reporting has focused on German-Israel affairs. Her work has appeared in a variety of American, Israeli, and German publications.

Her debut novel, *The Settler*, follows a young woman's rebellious journey to Tel Aviv after being expelled from her home in Gush Katif, Gaza as part of the 2005 Disengagement Plan. She holds a Bachelor's and Master's degree in Jewish Studies.

Visit her website at www.oritarfa.net.

Also by Orit Arfa

- *The Settler: A Novel of Modern Israel*
- *Ayn Rand & Esther: How The Fountainhead Can Illuminate Our Understanding of Esther, Israel and the Jews*
- *Spinoza & Ayn Rand: How to Reconcile Spinoza's God with Rand's Atheism*

www.ingramcontent.com/pod-product-compliance
Lightning Source LLC
Chambersburg PA
CBHW030301200626
46816CB00002BA/720